I0561232

Sign up for our newsletter to hear
about new and upcoming releases.

www.ylva-publishing.com

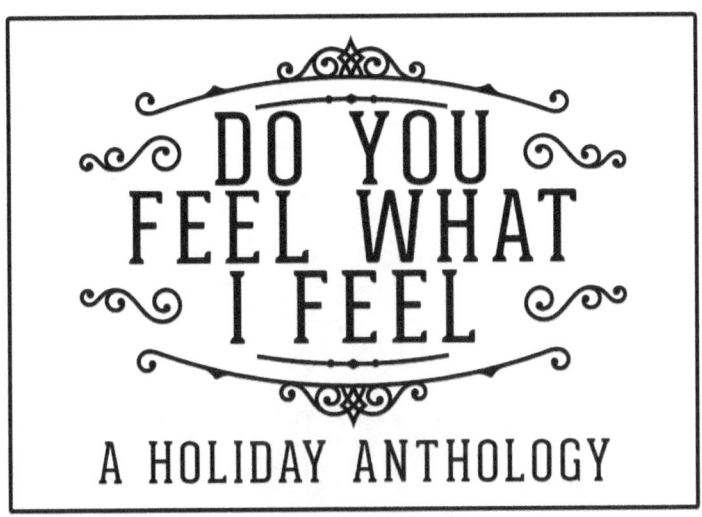

DO YOU FEEL WHAT I FEEL

A HOLIDAY ANTHOLOGY

Edited by:
Jae and
Fletcher DeLancey

TABLE OF CONTENTS

INTRODUCTION

Putting together a holiday anthology has become an annual tradition at Ylva Publishing—and one that we enjoy very much.

Holiday anthologies are like gift baskets that contain a wide variety of everything we love: There are romantic stories of established couples celebrating Christmas or Hanukkah together and stories of strangers who meet during the holidays and become so much more. We have stories written by authors from all over the world— some established writers and others newly discovered talent. There are stories set in the present, in the past, and in otherworldly realms. That versatility is what makes anthologies so special. All stories have one thing in common, though: they will leave you with a sense of love and hope.

To share some of that hope with people who are less fortunate, we decided to donate all profits from this anthology to YouthCare, a shelter for LGBT homeless youth in Seattle, and to Angalia, a group giving shelter and food to refugees in Greece.

Thank you to all the authors who submitted their stories to us and to the editors and proofreaders who supported us.

The authors and staff of Ylva Publishing wish you happy holidays and a new year filled with love, laughter, and a lot of good books.

Jae & Fletcher DeLancey

S. CLAUS

by Blythe Rippon

SELENA WAITED FOR HER FRIEND Daan's annual visit with an anticipation she hadn't felt since she was a child and her parents let her eat gingerbread cupcakes for her birthday. Standing behind a snowdrift in the waning hours of daylight, she could observe the entrance of her igloo without Daan catching her scent.

Soft hooves sounded on the powered snow, and Daan passed her igloo without giving it a second glance. Selena smiled. She trailed after him for an hour, being careful to stay downwind, until the caribou suddenly stopped and turned around. With his furry brow knit, Daan gazed left and right, then snorted. He spun around again, grumbling softly under his breath. When he sat down and studied the sky, determining the time, Selena could no longer contain her laughter. She stepped toward him and lifted the cloaking spell she had cast over herself.

He pawed the ground and snorted at her. "Think you're funny, do you?"

Relieved that he wasn't too mad for her to approach, she rubbed his nose and ears. "I wanted to know if I had enough magic to cloak my igloo so no one could discover it."

"I do so love being your guinea pig."

Over the centuries, Daan had been the unwilling object of many of Selena's magical experiments. "If you follow me home, I've got some hot elfwine with your name on it."

His ears perking up, he knelt down and invited her to climb onto his back. The return trip took significantly less time, since he had already forged a path when he overshot her igloo, and before long they were settled in her cozy kitchen, where a fire burned in the pit that occupied the center of the room. Leaning against the icy wall next to her oven, Selena sipped elfwine from a goblet, while Daan lapped it up from a bowl she typically used for baking.

As the warm liquid hit his stomach, Daan's eyes softened. "I've been meaning to ask, how is it your igloo doesn't melt when you light a fire inside?"

"I may not be as magical as my brother, but I'm not without my powers."

He studied her. "You've been practicing."

"All my life. But I've recently had a breakthrough. The magic feels easier to access, and more powerful somehow." She wasn't sure what had caused the change, but if she had to guess, it was the physical and emotional space to explore her own abilities, coupled with a lack of head-to-head competition against her overachieving brother.

Daan nodded. "Good girl. Always knew you had more power than your folks gave you credit for."

She smiled absently as she finished her elfwine. "We'll see."

"Planning something, are we?" He nosed his bowl forward, and she refilled it.

They drank in silence for a long moment before Selena turned away and paced around the kitchen. "It's about time people recognized my brother for what he really is: a two-bit hack of a wizard who takes advantage of the talents of those around him. Seriously, without the elves, and the sled-pullers, he'd just be the king of a frozen village."

Ears flickering, Daan snorted. "Sick of being known as 'Santa's sister,' are we?"

Selena slipped a bit on the ice as she passed her makeshift sink, and she gave him a dirty look. Her pacing slowed until her steps matched the measured calculations in her head. "Centuries of playing second fiddle to Santa. While he's been gathering Christian and pagan myths and forging them into a single, benevolent figure—one very forgiving of his horrid eating habits—I'm exiled from Claus Village. Some days I don't even know if I exist."

As she approached Daan on another pass around her kitchen, he reached out and nuzzled her. "It's self-exile, you know. You could return to the Village at any time."

As if she ever could. Proximity to her brother made Selena's skin crawl. "I never understood what Mother and Father must have promised Ianthe for her to commit to that overweight, pompous ass who treats her like a housekeeper." Ianthe was from one of the few magical families left, and Selena's parents had proposed the match with the Nordic girl when she and Santa were both teenagers. They seemed to think he needed a companion with a similar life span.

"I've always wondered, why didn't your parents marry you off?"

Caribou weren't known for their tact.

For this question, Selena brought the entire flask of elfwine to the table by the fire and sat down. "Oh, they were devastated when, two hundred years into Santa's marriage, it was clear that he and Ianthe would be unable to carry on the family line. Even magic has its limits. Given my paltry magical abilities, they seemed uncertain at first whether they even wanted me to reproduce. A century later, as their magic began to wane, they initiated a series of halting and awkward discussions about the importance of family and love—and when those conversations led nowhere, they tactlessly suggested I consider a well-timed one night stand." No, she wasn't at all sorry they were gone.

"Harsh," Daan said.

"Marriage is a crap institution anyway. Seems to me Santa prefers blowing smoke rings with freaky Rudolph to spending time with his wife."

"Her sister has recently taken up residence in Claus Manor," Daan said.

"She has a sister?" Ianthe had always been a bit of a mystery around the Pole, even to her sister-in-law.

"Zaida, she's called. Arrived ten months ago from whatever Nordic land Ianthe originated. Looks nothing like her, though. She's dark, like you. Tall. Slender. Nice specimen of the human form, if you're into that sort of thing."

Selena rolled her eyes and glanced at the faded photograph tacked into the ice above her sink, taken when Santa was two hundred and she was fifty. She took a moment to be grateful she looked nothing like her brother. Where he was short, ruddy, blond, and fat, she was tall, pale, raven-haired, and thin. No one understood why she looked so different from her brother, but everyone chalked it up to the unpredictability of magic. "Is Zaida a doormat like her sister?"

"No one really knows. After a rather extravagant entrance in a gilded carriage, she sort of disappeared. None of the elves, caribou, or people have seen her. Come to think if it, no one's really seen Ianthe either."

"This is rather disappointing gossip, Daan. Haven't you got anything juicier?"

"The elves are threatening to strike."

Selena nearly dropped her elfwine. "What?"

Daan polished off his second bowl while Selena shifted in her chair of hard-packed snow. "According to the elves, the human population has doubled in the last century and a half, while the elf population has shrunk. The proportion of toy makers to gift receivers is unsustainable, and the elves think Santa needs to make some changes."

"Like what, decimating all the major cities in the northern hemisphere?"

"Ah, well, the elves have been pretty vague about how they expect Santa to solve this problem. So far Santa's only proposal is to install a few private rooms with heart-shaped beds off the left wing of the toyshop. And, given the new soundtrack piping through the entire facility, he seems to think that Patsy Cline will put the elves in the mood."

"Oh, yeah, this plan sounds like a real winner. Because nothing puts lovers in the mood like doing it next door to the workbenches where the Tickle-Me Elmos are being made."

"Your brother has never been much for romance," Daan said, as if this were news.

"I don't suppose anyone has pointed out to Santa that even if he can inspire the elves to reproduce more rapidly, it will be a while before the elflings contribute to the toy shop."

"All I know is that they seem grateful for more breaks from work and, in the afternoon, most of them are too sleepy from their fraternizing to safely operate power tools."

That probably meant productivity was plummeting. It wasn't part of her plan that Santa come up short in the present department this year, but it was good to know she had backup options. "And how are the sled-pullers?" Santa might be able to bend time and space for himself, but he had never successfully conjured enough magic to move billions of presents across the globe. Magic flying caribou were the best he could do. Selena would have thought it a laughable system if she weren't about to try it out for herself.

The look of annoyance on Daan's face almost made her laugh. "Blitzen and Dasher are having an affair and it's got the whole herd in a tizzy."

"Blitzen and Dasher? But they're both—"

"I know. Kind of puts a damper on Santa's policy about the sled-pullers always being males so as to avoid entanglements that will affect the whole team."

"But they both have mates."

Daan raised a furry eyebrow. "Did. Dasher's mate left him. Blitzen then decided it would be a brilliant idea to invite Dasher into his, um, existing partnership. Both his mate and Dasher are perplexed by the idea of three reindeer joining together in such a fashion. Who knows what will happen. But Donner and Rudolph are pretty cruel about the whole thing, and Vixen seems to be vying for a piece of the action."

Having vowed years ago not to concern herself with caribou drama, Selena changed the subject. "I plan to do a little traveling over the next few weeks, Daan. Know of a caribou who might be up for an adventure?" She would have liked to take Daan, because she trusted his sense of direction and flying prowess. Unfortunately, while he might be her friend, his loyalty would always remain with the Village, and Selena didn't want to put him in an awkward position.

If he suspected anything about her plan, he gave nothing away. "Rudolph's got a granddaughter. She's much less of an ass than he is. She might be interested—what did you have in mind?"

"Oh, I just want to get away for a while. Maybe go someplace warmer for a few weeks." She knew her answer was too blasé, but it was the best she could do. Santa had always been the Claus with the ability to fool people. "What's her name?"

"Lara. She lives alone on the outskirts of the Village, just east of the House with Fifty Chimneys that Santa uses for practice. Her barn is painted purple and there's a sign outside that reads 'They used to laugh and call me names.'"

Selena liked her already. "Thanks, Daan. And thanks for being such a good sport about the cloaking spell."

Taking his cue, Daan rose and headed toward the door. "Selena Claus, I miss you. I wish you'd move back to the Village."

She waved her hand and a saddlebag filled with his favorite leaves appeared on his back. He nuzzled her cheek briefly before stomping out into the snow.

❦

Selena waited until four the next morning, when the Village was fast asleep and the moonlight was fading, to disappear from her igloo and reappear outside Lara's barn. She knocked on the door and didn't wait for an answer. Inside she found a young caribou, maybe fifty or sixty years old, with light brown fur and delicate hooves, bedded down in some hay. Waving her hands, she lit the lanterns hanging in the corners of the barn, and the sudden brightness woke Lara.

As she scrambled to her hooves and gathered her breath for what Selena expected would be a barn-rattling bellow, Selena shushed her. "I'm not here to hurt you." She turned over a bucket that had likely held oats and sat on it, taking note of the purple streak of fur in Lara's mane and the nose piercing. "I have a proposition for you."

Lara, Selena discovered, was as eager as she was to make some waves in the predictable Pole. After listening to the plan, her only question was, "When do we leave?"

"I have a couple of supplies to gather, and of course there's the business of the map. I hope to wrap up preparations tomorrow, and we can depart the following night. Does that work for you?"

Lara pawed eagerly at the wooden floorboards. "I'll be ready. You sure you don't need more caribou for this trip?"

Selena shook her head. "I won't be carrying presents for little girls and boys. Just me and the map, and supplies for a month." When Lara raised her right hoof, Selena shook it. "Two nights from now, I'll meet you here."

"See you then."

It was perhaps the first time Selena felt she'd ever met a kindred spirit.

∞⊙

It was hard to be stealthy in a toyshop.

Noise-making objects were everywhere, including scattered across the floor between the workbenches. But there was nothing for it; the hangar where Santa kept his sleigh could only be accessed through the south wing of the shop, where the electronic toys were mass-produced by the elves skilled in engineering. It had been sixty years since she last set foot in Santa's hangar, and she wasn't sure what kind of security he had these days. Her cloaking spell couldn't mute any noise she might make, nor could it mask her smell.

Her fears were for naught; she made it to the hangar without incident. Stepping through the door, she waved her hand and a small globe of light appeared in front of her, softly illuminating the space. Ahead she could just make out the silhouette of the sleigh, which was even bigger than she remembered. She was pretty sure it hadn't been accented with chrome the last time she saw it.

Her brother had long ago perfected the art of seeming open and warm while in truth ferreting away a treasure trove of secrets. His most intensely guarded possession, since he started his ridiculous Christmas Eve ritual, had been his map. While Selena may have begrudged him the innate magical power that he possessed and she lacked, she had no problem acknowledging that her brother was something of a math whiz. Even with his abilities to fold space and suspend time, it would be impossible to deliver presents to every house and every child without the map he developed. It wasn't a static object—studying wind patterns, currents, something about the position of the moon, and astronomical changes that might alter the earth's magnetic poles, Santa developed a new map every year that would ensure his success.

It was possible that Selena was the only person other than Santa who knew when he completed it, and where he hid it. Why the loser never moved out of his parents' house was beyond her, but there were some advantages to having grown up with him, she supposed.

She approached the sled, stopping every few steps to glance around and make sure the hangar was still. The left runner of the sleigh glowed ahead, and she could just see the faint lines of the panel Santa would have removed to slide his map into the metal. She had just knelt down next to it when she heard a voice above her.

"Is this what you're looking for?"

In her fright, Selena's globe of light faltered and went out. She scrambled to her feet and struggled to conjure the globe again, but she needn't have bothered. Before she could summon her magic, the entire hangar was illuminated in soft, warm light. Off balance on multiple fronts, Selena plopped down on the cement floor of the hangar and peered upward. A woman with black hair and a floor-length black cloak stood in the sleigh, gazing down at her.

Before Selena could gather her wits, the woman jumped gracefully down to the floor and leaned against the sleigh. Power radiated from her as her eyes burned, and her right hand glowed with light bright enough to cast shadows around the hangar. In her left hand she clutched Santa's map.

"You're making a mistake," she said.

"No, I'm not," Selena retorted. It was possible, she reasoned as soon as she said it, that she would be more convincing if she weren't sitting on her ass sounding like a five-year-old. Gathering what dignity she could, she stood up and brushed off her dusty pants. "You don't even know what I'm doing here."

"I know enough. I'm Zaida," she said, extending her hand. When Selena shook it, she felt warm tingles spread from her hand through her arm and into her chest. She looked up, confused, and Zaida smiled. "I thought I'd take the edge off. You're less scared now."

Selena took her hand back abruptly, and the warmth faded. "I didn't give you permission to—"

Zaida looked abashed. "No, you didn't. I apologize."

Putting more distance between them, Selena studied her face. She had deep brown eyes that seemed to devour the entire room, and her lips were parted slightly, as though she were breathing Selena in. "What are you doing here?"

"Here, as in, in the hangar? Or here, as in, in Claus Village?"

"Both. Either." Congratulating herself for such an articulate introduction to her sister-in-law's sister, Selena bit her lip before anything more mundane could come out of her mouth.

The electricity in the air lessened a bit, and as the light dimmed around her, it seemed to fade from Zaida's body, too. "My magic has become unstable. When we were younger, my sister taught me how to use it. I came hoping she could help again."

The light flickered a few times and then dimmed again. "It would appear you still have some work to do," Selena said.

"I'm not the only one. You do realize your cloaking spell faltered the minute you heard my voice."

Zaida's tone was gentler than Selena thought she deserved, particularly considering she hadn't noticed her spell dissipate, nor had it even occurred to her to wonder why Zaida could see her.

"Here, let's sit." Zaida returned to the sleigh and settled onto the seat.

Considering the sleigh was made for one overweight wizard, two slender women fit, barely. Selena was acutely aware of the feel of Zaida's thigh against hers, and warmth spread from where their shoulders touched all through her body.

Zaida pulled out a flask, unscrewed the cap, and took a swig before passing it over. "Seems a good night for brandy."

In all her years, Selena never imagined she'd be sitting in near darkness in Santa's sleigh drinking with a beautiful, slightly scary woman. Maybe she was catching up on the rebellious teenage years she had skipped. Shrugging, she took the flask and drank. After replacing the cap, she held it just out of Zaida's reach. "The flask for the map."

"Hardly a fair trade."

"I don't know, some people really value their alcohol."

Zaida laughed, a musical sound that took Selena by surprise. "I'm keeping the map. If you want to benefit from its contents, you'll have to bring me along."

"You don't even know where I'm going," Selena reasoned.

Giving her a small smile, Zaida said, "I'm the one with the map."

Damn. Selena always seemed to be one step behind. "How do you know what I'm doing, again?"

"One of the effects of my magic growing more and more unstable is that I seem to be able to, well, smell you."

Selena distinctly remembered showering that morning. It had taken her an hour to heat the ice melt and funnel it through the pipes she had conjured when she first crafted her igloo.

"Not you exactly—your anger."

Her first instinct was to clamber down the sleigh and get as far away from Zaida as possible.

Grabbing her hand, Zaida said, "Don't be afraid," and Selena was hit with another soothing pulse.

She wrenched her hand away. "You have to stop doing that. It's…invasive."

"I know. But consider it self-defense." Zaida put her hands in her lap, palms up, as though she were surrendering a weapon.

"Your resentment and anger—it was overpowering when I first arrived at the Pole. I had a migraine for the first two months and couldn't leave my room."

Selena thought about apologizing, but honestly, it wouldn't be particularly sincere. She hadn't meant to cause this stranger pain, but she wasn't about to say she was sorry for feeling things.

Zaida continued. "I tried to find you, but Ianthe wouldn't let me go. She seemed to think, for some inexplicable reason, that I might use my magic on you without your consent."

"God, wherever would she get an idea like that?" Selena muttered.

"She also hinted that you might be dangerous."

It gave Selena an odd sense of satisfaction to hear that. "I imagine two witches who don't have full control over their magic would be a bad combination."

"Perhaps. Or perhaps we could help each other." Gingerly, as though she might startle a frightened animal, Zaida moved her hand until it was just next to Selena's, their fingers almost touching. She murmured under her breath, and a soft light grew from the space between their hands and filled the hangar, noticeably brighter than it was the first time Zaida had conjured it.

Unable to tear her eyes away from their hands, Selena regretted causing Zaida pain. "Are your headaches better?"

She felt rather than saw Zaida's smile. "I feel good right now."

"So you're learning how to, I don't know, isolate yourself from other people's emotions?" Glancing at her face, she saw peace on her delicate features.

"Mm. I never had difficulties with anyone else—not since I was a child. Only you."

It occurred to Selena that she still held on to the flask. She took a long drink, and the light remained even when her hand didn't.

Zaida continued. "Evidently, Ianthe's spent the last fifty years waiting for you to try to sabotage Santa, or Christmas, or both."

"Smart woman. She deserves better than my brother."

Reaching for the flask, which Selena surrendered without a fight, Zaida sighed. "If you could separate the way your parents treated you differently from who Santa is as a person, you might find he's not that bad."

It wasn't the first time Selena wondered why she kept that photo of her and her brother in the igloo. She tried not to dwell on it. "I don't really care why you're in Claus Village, because it's none of my business." Before Zaida could protest that, if Selena was giving her headaches, maybe it *was* her business, Selena continued. "Just like it's none of your business what I want with that map. Hand it over."

"What you're planning on doing is everyone's business."

"I don't know what you think you know about me—"

"You visited a caribou named Lara last night. You're taking her around the world on some ridiculous quest to stop Santa from delivering presents. You've been practicing cloaking spells, on yourself and on the place where you live, presumably so you can cloak houses all over the world and Santa won't be able to find them."

The accuracy of her information gave Selena pause. "I thought you said you couldn't control your magic."

"I was out on a walk when I saw you leaving Lara's barn," Zaida confessed.

"It was four in the morning."

Zaida shrugged. "I couldn't sleep."

"Whatever Lara told you, this is a family affair. Stay out of it." The warmth from Zaida's shoulder against hers faded and Selena shivered.

"What you've never understood, according to my sister, is that Christmas is about more than your brother. But I can see that talking won't dissuade you. When do we leave?"

"We? I don't know you. I don't trust you. I don't want you." Something in the way Zaida looked at her made Selena shift in her seat.

"So get to know me."

Selena made a grab for the map, but Zaida slid it into a pocket inside her cloak. Beaten, Selena jumped down from the sleigh. It had been a long time since she had the potential to make a new friend—one with magical abilities and intense eyes. Since Ianthe's arrival at the Pole, in fact, and it was clear from the start that Ianthe had no patience for her sibling rivalry. "We leave tomorrow night. Find your own ride. Lara's barn at midnight."

Retreating, because there was really no other word for it, Selena made her way back to the door of the hangar and through the toyshop. She supposed if she had to bring someone along on her little scheme, Zaida wasn't that bad. At least she could keep them warm.

⃝

By the time she made it home and heated a kettle for tea, Selena's opinion had changed. Zaida seemed to have more magic than she did, and she certainly didn't want to tag along to *help*. Selena would have enough obstacles on her trip, including navigating Santa's map, selecting the perfect houses in each village to cloak, and maintaining enough magic to make it around the world before Santa started his Christmas Eve extravaganza; she didn't need to contend with someone who made her more than a little uncomfortable.

Her kettle whistled, and as she poured the hot water she made up her mind: she would just need to spend the following day stalking Zaida until she could steal the map.

Unfortunately, cloaking herself and sneaking around Santa and Ianthe's mansion produced no helpful results. She couldn't find Zaida anywhere. She did stumble upon Ianthe reading in the den, and watched her sister-in-law for a while. If things had been different, if Santa hadn't been so impossible to tolerate, maybe she could have been friends with Ianthe. But unlike children all over the world, wishing had never produced results for Selena.

At midnight, she found herself climbing onto Lara's back, having explained that they were expecting company. At twelve-thirty Selena considered leaving without the map. If she didn't make it to every village, and if she never made it back to the Pole, that would be okay. But she had Lara to worry about—the young caribou didn't deserve to lose her home because of this mission.

At one-fifteen, with no apology for her lack of punctuality, Zaida rode up on a tall, dark brown caribou.

Lara's ears flickered and she whinnied softly. "Rickard. I'm glad it's you."

Zaida's caribou trotted up to Lara and nuzzled her neck. "I heard you're off on an adventure. I couldn't risk you meeting some handsome moose along the way."

Lara nipped at his ear.

Perfect. Now she had everything she needed. Two caribou in love, an unstable sorceress, and a partridge in a pear tree.

Something about the twinkle in Zaida's eyes made Selena think she must have chosen Lara's mate intentionally.

"Where to?" Zaida asked.

"You're the one with the map, remember?"

Zaida rolled her eyes. "I mean, do you plan on following Santa's route?"

Selena nodded. "I can't manipulate time as efficiently as he can, so I'm guessing it will take us about a month to do what he can do in a single night."

"We start in western Russia, then." Zaida gave the caribou directions. They trotted to the edge of town and, with a brief straining of muscles, took flight.

The caribou flew shoulder to shoulder and Selena's left knee bumped against Zaida's right one. It had been a mistake to think that, with the wind buzzing in their ears, Zaida wouldn't try to engage her in conversation.

"You've been working tirelessly on cloaking spells, and you intend to visit every village in the world. That's a lot of energy to expend on someone you don't particularly like."

Selena used her knees to encourage Lara to fly farther away from Rickard, but her headstrong steed wasn't having it. "When Santa can't deliver presents to everyone on Christmas Eve, people will recognize that he's not this perfect benevolent figure. They'll turn on him."

All she heard for a long time was wind. She enjoyed the silence for about an hour, and then it began to grate on her. Stealing glances at Zaida gave her no indication of her flying companion's mood.

Considering that she needed to cover all of Russia and northern Europe in a single night, Selena had allowed herself fifteen minutes to breeze through western Russia and Siberia before arriving in St. Petersburg. They landed in the Kolyma region, just outside a sea town named Magadan. Encouraging Lara and Rickard forward, they approached a home on the outskirts of town and Selena dismounted. Standing at a frail fence, her palms facing the house, she concentrated on the elements of the cloaking spell. She was on the verge of exhaling and sending her magic outward when she felt a gentle touch on her arm.

"Do you want to know what the boy who lives here wants this year?" Zaida asked.

The touch on her arm was warm and tingly, which was probably why Selena didn't brush it off immediately. "Not particularly."

"A fishing rod, because his father is a fisherman. He's hoping to contribute to the family's income in a few years, if he can practice enough to become a skilled fisherman too."

Selena turned and studied the dark, gentle eyes peering at her, expecting to find judgment, or at the very least something snide lurking there. Instead, she saw an earnestness that took her aback.

"Okay, fine. We can skip this house."

The next house was a short distance away, and she walked ahead quickly, leaving Zaida and the caribou to follow. Maybe if she arrived before them she could cloak this house before Zaida opened her mouth.

No such luck. She had barely raised her hands before Zaida's voice tickled her ear.

"The girl who lives here asked for a winter coat. Her parents are shipbuilders, but the economy is so bad that no one is commissioning new vessels. They couldn't afford to buy her warm clothes to protect her from the harsh winter."

Selena spun around. "Are you going to do this at every house?"

"You need to know what you're doing."

It was easier to feel angry when Zaida wasn't touching her. "How do you even know all this?"

"You think Santa's map is just diagrams of the land and sea?"

It made sense, she supposed. She had always wondered how Santa kept straight which presents went to which house.

Things continued in much the same vein until finally Selena decided to give up on houses occupied by normal people and directed Lara to the mayor's house. Before even starting the spell—before even bothering to dismount—she turned to Zaida. "Surely you're not going to spin me some story of hardship here. The mayor's family wants for nothing."

The map glowed in Zaida's hands. "True. The mayor's a good father, and he has a policy for Christmas that his family has abided by since his daughter could walk. For every present that his daughter receives from Santa, she has to give one of her old toys to a family in need. For this house, Santa favors quantity: she gets a lot of small gifts. She's only seven, and it's unlikely that her father would convince her to give away her toys willingly if she didn't receive new ones. If you cloak this house, it will affect families all over the city."

The taste of bile in her mouth, Selena nudged Lara's neck and the caribou took off, headed for Siberia.

They made it through St. Petersburg without Selena cloaking a single house. For every residence she approached, Zaida had a story that dissuaded Selena from her plans. Any hope Selena had of pilfering the map faded when they left Moscow; she had seen Zaida stow the map in a breast pocket of her cloak, and she wasn't about to go groping around there looking for it.

Day was breaking when they arrived in Korvatunturi, the fell in Finland that purported to be Father Christmas's hometown. Yet another adorable strategy of Santa's: create places of origin all around the world to bolster civic pride and deep-seated affection for him.

As the snow around them began to glow with the soft yellow hues of morning, the caribou's hooves grew heavy. They were all exhausted, and it would take a while for everyone to adjust to the nocturnal schedule Selena had set. She begrudgingly admitted that maybe her brother's ability to cover the entire globe in a single night might perhaps be a bit impressive.

Extracting the small tent from Lara's saddlebag, Selena raised her palms and managed her first spell of the entire adventure: she imagined her igloo at home and exhaled. The tent erected itself and morphed into the architecture of her home, the snow around them gathered on top of it as a layer of insulation, and a thin plume of smoke snaked out of the chimney, beckoning them to the fire inside. She cloaked the structure and they all trudged inside.

After a quick snack of cheese and bread, the caribou snuggled up in the corner of her den. The two women stood in the only bedroom, gazing at the single bed, until Selena closed her eyes and conjured a second bed. It was a tight fit in her cozy bedroom, but they were fast asleep before either could open her mouth to complain.

ༀ

It was Cologne, Germany, before Zaida had something other than a heartwarming story to offer Selena when they stopped at a house. Her palms extended, Selena hadn't even bothered to think the words of the spell, so accustomed had she grown to interruption. When only silence filled the air around her, she lowered her hands and turned. "What, is the house abandoned?"

"No. But the kid who lives here is a real asshole."

Selena hadn't snort-laughed since, well, maybe ever. It might have been the knowledge that the world did indeed contain less-than-stellar people, but she suspected it was the profanity coming from Zaida's lips. "An asshole?"

Shrugging, Zaida folded the map and returned it to her pocket. "He bullies other kids. He's selfish and rude."

"So, what, Santa was going to bring him a lump of coal?" Obviously, cloaking a house Santa didn't really care about wasn't going to accomplish her goal.

"Actually, he was going to leave a video game called 'Animal Hospital.' You play a veterinarian, and you compete with others online to diagnose and treat wounded or ill animals in the most efficient and effective way possible. Santa was hoping to instill some empathy in the kid and, if it worked, planned to bring him a puppy next year."

"You're kidding, right? Santa plays shrink?"

"Let's just say he's never actually given someone a lump of coal."

Through central and southern Europe, and into northern Africa, Selena started guessing the story behind each house. Zaida informed her that no, the kid in the Barcelona apartment was not actually Gaudi's grandchild and the only person on Earth with the ability to finish the Sagrada Familia, if only Santa would bring him the blueprints. Nor was the teenager in Sicily the only person in the world who could cure the common cold, once Santa brought her a chemistry set. Selena found such joy in making Zaida laugh that her guesses grew more and more ridiculous and elaborate. The amusement in Zaida's eyes suffused her with warmth, and at first she thought it was magically projected happiness. But they weren't touching, and the hint of a shadow that passed over Zaida's face when she used magic never appeared.

In South Africa, she simply sat down in front of each residence and waited for Zaida to tell her a story. She wasn't sure which compelled her more: the stories themselves, or the way Zaida told them.

All her magical life, her entire universe had been the Pole, and the Pole's entire universe was Santa and his Christmas Eve extravaganza. Staring at a Zulu village, listening to Zaida give the life histories of the people inside, Selena was grateful that her world was expanding.

At the very least, listening to these stories was a hell of a lot more interesting than rereading *Lost in Santa's Toyshop: Two Elves in Love*, the only novel she had access to at the Pole.

That next morning, as they lay in her igloo-shaped tent, still cloaked in magic and now insulated with dirt, Selena studied her travel companion. Zaida looked tired, but happy. "What are you getting out of this? You've clearly already accomplished what you set out to do—why don't you just go home?"

Rolling to her side and propping her head on her hand, Zaida grinned. "This is the most fun I've had in ages. Maybe ever."

As tempting as it was to attribute Zaida's response to her company, Selena decided it probably had more to do with traveling the world and learning from Santa's map. Still, perhaps Selena was getting a Christmas present this year after all. Experiencing the entire world with Zaida at her side was more than she had bargained for, and more than she deserved.

Zaida shifted so she was on her stomach, her feet crossed in the air. Blankets weren't necessary during South Africa's summer, and Selena looked away from the small patch of skin between Zaida's silk pants and her tank top. "Does this mean you've given up trying to sabotage Christmas?"

Playing with a thread from her pillowcase, Selena sighed. "It was never about sabotaging Christmas. I wanted to ruin Santa."

"What you've never understood is that Santa has become, well, bigger than himself."

"That's saying a lot, given how much gingerbread that man eats."

But Zaida wasn't amused by her joke. "A lot of people," she said, giving Selena a pointed look, "mistake Christmas for one man, when in truth, *they* are Christmas."

"Have you always liked people this much?"

Zaida smiled. "I think it comes with the magic. I'm fascinated by the way people are motivated by pain and love." She looked at Selena. "And jealousy."

"You're going to tell me you and Ianthe were never jealous of each other?"

"Well, I certainly don't envy her life, if that's what you mean. It's cold where I come from, but it's nothing like the Pole. And besides, your brother's a nice guy, but I could never be married to him." She winked at Selena, who was pretty sure she missed the joke. "You asked why I don't just leave—do you want me to go? I'll memorize the directions back to the Pole and leave the map with you."

"What? No. I don't want you to leave." Surprise didn't even begin to cover Selena's reaction to hearing the words blurt out of her mouth. Zaida was offering what she thought she wanted, but she certainly didn't want to travel the world without her laughter, the low melody of her voice, and the way she stretched when she woke up. "We've only got North and South America left, and I want you to tell me all about the kids in Chicago and Lima, and why anyone would voluntarily live in Alaska."

"Says the woman with enough magic to fly around the world, but who has never left the North Pole before."

Selena shrugged. "We all make questionable choices."

There was that laugh she loved so much, followed by a yawn. "Let's get some sleep before we set off for Brazil tonight."

Selena nodded, and as she stared at the ceiling she listened to Zaida's breathing even out. But sleep refused to come to her.

✿

They made their way up the Americas, with Lara and Rickard taking turns making up stories about the houses they approached while Selena and Zaida laughed. Selena's favorite was Rickard's yarn about the villa in Cancun—the young girl who lived there, according to Rickard, had asked for a pet whale for Christmas and had declared that if Santa didn't bring her one, she would go find one and take up residence in its stomach—so Selena would be sentencing a young girl to a life inside a whale if she cloaked the place.

The trip home from Alaska was quiet, the women and caribou reflecting on the past month's adventure. When they arrived back at Claus Village, Selena and Zaida thanked their steeds, who trotted off together in the direction of Lara's barn.

Standing awkwardly outside Claus Manor, Selena gazed at the sky, the snow on the ground, and the door—anywhere but at Zaida. The past month had been the best of her life, and she was mourning its ending.

"Thank you for taking me along, Selena. You didn't have to—I'm sure you could have managed something on your own, map notwithstanding."

"Thanks for coming. You opened my eyes to…well, a lot."

"It's December twenty-third. I promised Ianthe I'd help her and Santa with final preparations. But I'll see you at the Feast the day after Christmas, yes?"

Selena hadn't attended the Feast since its inauguration, the year after Santa made his first trip around the world in a single night. The profuse praise lavished on her brother was more than she could take, and she had left early. "I'll think about it. How much longer will you stay in the Village?"

Zaida studied her, and Selena thought she saw something hopeful in her eyes. "Depends."

"On?"

"I'm not quite ready to say just yet."

Leaving Zaida at Claus Manor was harder than saying good-bye to the carefree attitude she had adopted during their travels. It took considerable courage for Selena to say, "Please don't leave without saying good-bye."

Taking her hands, Zaida kissed her cheek. "I wouldn't dream of it."

Her cheek burned where the contact had been, and Selena blinked back moisture from her eyes before closing them and vanishing.

♻

For decades, Selena was the only soul in Claus Village who didn't contribute to Christmas Eve, and that fact had given her pride. Now she merely felt shame. Conjuring was the one spell that came easier to her than to Santa, so the next day she whipped up enough food to feed the elves for their last push and staged it on tables in the Village Square outside the workshop. From behind a snowdrift, she observed first one elf, then a second, and then dozens stream out of the workshop, enticed by the smell of food. None of them could figure out where the banquet came from, which was fine by her; she vanished before it was half gone. Taking credit for things was her brother's job, not hers.

The following day, the Pole was a ghost town. Santa and the sled-pullers had departed, and the elves disappeared into their homes for twenty-four straight hours of sleep. Selena walked through the Square unobserved, touching the clock tower where Santa had let her win a snowball fight when she was ten. The bakery was sold out of gingerbread, but peering through the glass she could see trays of pastries lining the back wall, ready for the Feast. December twenty-sixth at the Pole was a time for celebration, food, and the occasional dance. Walking past Claus Manor, its gates of candy cane sparkling in the sunlight, Selena wondered, not for the first time, what Ianthe did while Santa was away. Closing her eyes, she pictured her childhood room, which remained empty. Moving her imagination through the house, she felt Ianthe and Zaida in the game room. The last time she was in the house, sixty years ago, there had been a pool table and shuffleboard. Wondering which sister was better at shooting combos, Selena headed home. Two months earlier, she would have appeared in her kitchen in the blink of an eye, but she felt like the magic was gone.

००/०

The feast had been going on for four hours when Selena summoned the courage to walk into the Village Square. Heat lamps strategically placed around the center fountain kept the elves' cheeks rosy while they ate at tables scattered throughout the square. In her black robe, with her black hair, she towered over the others, and while elves were too polite to stare, she knew her appearance hadn't gone unnoticed. She spotted Zaida and Ianthe at the far side of the square, playing Pin the Belly on the Santa, and was making her way over to them when she heard her brother's booming voice behind her, calling for everyone's attention.

He clambered onto the top of one of the long tables and laughed a long, full laugh. "My darling elves. My dearest caribou. My wife. My sister-in-law." His eyes lighted on her and without pausing he said warmly, "My sister. I'm proud to announce that we've put together yet another successful Christmas. I know how hard you all worked to make last night happen, and I'm so grateful that you'll all find presents—made by me, not you!—in your stockings when you return home. I love you all very much, and I hope you enjoy your month off before we're back at it again in February. For now, Good Feast!"

She didn't remember her brother being so gracious. He climbed down from the table, helped by the two tallest elves near to him, and walked straight to her. If the price for seeing Zaida again was a conversation with her brother, she supposed she could pay it.

"Selena," he said, clasping her hands. "You look beautiful. I've missed your face." He reached into his red cloak and pulled out an envelope with holly drawn on the front and the word *Selena* scrawled across the back. "You've cloaked your igloo, so I have to give you your present in person."

Inside, she discovered a map. His map.

"You're always welcome to come with me, sister, but I suspect you want to make your own journeys. I've magically connected this map with the one I'll use from now on; when I update mine, yours will change accordingly. You'll always have the most up-to-date information about geography, who lives where, and what presents they're all getting."

It was hard to hide the trembling in her hands. "Why?"

"I trust you." He kissed her cheek and walked away.

Too stunned to move, she stared at the map, wishing it also contained instructions for making amends. She had just summoned the wherewithal to look up from the parchment when a soft voice warmed her ear.

"I have something for you, too."

Spinning around, she nearly fell into Zaida's arms.

"Careful," Zaida said, steadying her. Her eyes danced in the flicker of the heat lamps, and the intensity in them was too much.

Looking away, Selena said, "I'm sorry, I don't have anything for you."

"Well, my gift is a mutual sort of thing." Zaida stepped close, and Selena's heart raced faster than Santa's team preparing for liftoff. When Zaida whispered, "Close your eyes," she obliged, grateful for a moment to regroup.

She was unprepared for the soft brush of Zaida's lips against hers. The kiss ended, leaving her mouth exposed to the frigid North Pole air, and Selena blindly reached out and pulled Zaida back in. For all she knew, they might have stood like that for a minute or a day.

After they finally separated, Selena did something she'd never done in her whole life.

She wished someone, "Merry Christmas."

THIS THING

by Jove Belle

BETH TAPS THE FOLDED ORIGAMI paper against her leg. It's cold, and the chill in the air smells like snow. Since she quit, she rarely craves a cigarette. But this morning, standing on the sidewalk and watching for Willa's little brother like a stalker, she wants one so badly her fingers curl and release in time with the craving working its way through her body.

Holden is late. Not that she's surprised by that. At fifteen, he's not a bad kid, certainly better than Beth was at that age, but he's not especially reliable. The camera crew has started to assemble in front of their store, and if Holden doesn't show up soon to let them in, one of them will call his dad. If that happens, there's no way Beth will be able to slip the angel she folded into Willa's desk.

Willa's dad is more likely to take one of his guns from the showcase and explain to Beth, slowly and carefully, why it's a bad idea for her to be *friends* with his daughter. There is a fairly high possibility that he would reinforce the message with a small sampling of gunpowder. He definitely will not nod and wink and take her present for Willa with an easy, knowing grin as Holden will. Okay, as Holden *might*. At least she's sure he won't shoot her in retaliation.

Shit. She stomps her feet and rubs her hands briskly over her arms. She should go back inside to wait, but she's afraid she'll miss Holden's arrival. Better still, she should go back inside and forget about giving the angel to Willa.

It's so risky. Starting with her ill-conceived idea that Willa will think finding a present in her desk is romantic, to the foolish declaration of love and undying devotion that she scribbled onto the paper before she quickly folded the angel into creation. She wrote the words on auto, letting the message inscribe itself without any input from her brain. Then, before she could come to her senses, she folded the whole she-bang up, quick as that.

Sure, exposing this much of herself to Willa, and anyone else who might find the note in Willa's desk, is terrifying. But she can't go even one more moment without owning her emotions in their relationship. She may well be throwing herself clumsily and without care onto the proverbial sword, but she falls on it fractionally every moment she tries to hold herself back. At least this way, she can get the bleeding over quickly instead of drawing it out.

One of the crew members complains about being outside, another about working so close to Christmas. Several agree. They all want to be home in time to open presents with their families.

Beth's lost in thought when Holden finally pulls up. She jogs across the street to meet him, and before anyone else can get to him, she stops him halfway out of his truck and thrusts the angel at his chest. "Put this in Willa's desk."

She barks it out as an order, but she doesn't feel nearly as in control as she sounds. If she doesn't fall into a morose ravine filled with tears and broken hearts, she'll call this whole thing a success.

Fuck. She's a walking cliché. She just can't *not* want Willa. And she can't not want Willa to want her. When she pushes it harder into Holden's chest, he stares at her, disbelieving.

"What the hell, Beth?"

"It's her Christmas present," she says quietly with a bit of desperate, needy dependence leaking from her like a teakettle puffing out steam. "Put it in her top drawer?"

Holden shakes his head. "My dad will kill us both. Then he'll march across the street and kill you too."

The threat of physical violence weighs heavily on Beth. Holden is trying to be a voice of reason. If Willa's dad hurts Beth, Willa won't like it at all. "Just make sure that she finds it before he does." It's a simple solution to a complex problem. Except there are so many variables and it could all go to hell with one ill-timed opening of a drawer. They both know it.

Holden chews his bottom lip, hesitating. Even though he does all the typical pain-in-the-ass little-brother stuff, Beth knows he really loves Willa. He'd do anything for her. Right now, as he frowns and his brow draws down, creating a deep crease in the middle, she can see he's struggling. "I don't know…"

"Come on, H." Beth needs the balance of his conscience to land on her side, so she looks him square in the eye and softly whispers, "Please."

Holden shakes his head and lets out a long, slow sigh. "Fine." He snatches the paper away and marches to the door without looking back.

Beth makes her way back to Bitter Ink, shaking from head to toe. She's terrified of what she's done and powerless to take it back. More so, she wouldn't even if she could.

This thing—whatever this thing between them is—can't happen. Knowing that doesn't stop Willa from staring out the window at the constant tumble of snow falling on the road between her shop and Bitter Ink. And Beth. With her short dark hair and even darker eyes. And her tattoos and ink-stained fingers. And her heavy-soled boots and blood-red nail polish. And her bright, reassuring smile that says everything will be okay even when Willa knows it won't be.

"Willa, we're almost ready for you." One of the producers, a tall, skinny guy with bad skin, touches her lightly on the arm. She forces herself not to recoil. He's nice enough even if he has been trying to get her into bed ever since he joined the crew. She might think about it if not for the blemishes. He looks like a man with all the appropriate man parts, unlike Beth, who doesn't look like a boy or a girl, but a careless blending of both. God, if that isn't the sexiest—if not the most confusing—thing ever.

"Okay." Willa stares out the window a moment longer, hoping Beth will look up. She normally doesn't. Beth is intense and passionately focused about her work in a way that makes the rest of the world disappear the moment she hears the lulling buzz of her tattoo gun. She tried to describe it to Willa once as they lay tangled together in Beth's bed, half naked and aching for more as Beth's fingers traced restless patterns over the exposed skin of her stomach. Willa can barely remember to breathe when Beth touches her like that. Listening to words and making sense of them in her pheromone-addled mind is impossible.

Willa turns away from the window, away from the view, and tries to turn away from the confusing roll of emotion and desire in her stomach. The latter stays with her the way it always does. She smiles as if everything is perfect because she never knows when the camera is focused on her. When they first started filming, she kept track of the crew. She was still in high school—too young to be on air for too many hours each week—so she paid attention to the cameras and the camera guys paid attention to her. Now, three years later, she's twenty and a student at the university. She's allowed as much airtime as possible.

She glances at the light over the confession booth. It's lit up red, which means her dad is still in there. She wanted to leave the moment it started snowing, knowing that if she doesn't get out before the drifts gets too deep, her dad will tell her it's not safe to go. It's not as if she's going to tell him—or anyone else—that all she plans to do is walk across the street and climb the stairs to Beth's apartment above Bitter Ink. Because as much as her brain knows this thing can't happen, her body insists that it can and refuses to listen to her brain.

As the light turns green, the bell over the front door tinkles, and her opportunity to duck into the booth before it gets any later is gone. She turns, hoping it's something quick like a regular customer looking for a box of ammo. They got in a shipment of .22 caliber that morning, and everybody and their mother rush to buy those when they're available.

No such luck.

"Willa! Just the girl I was looking for. Check this out." Mr. Brockney, her tenth-grade algebra teacher, holds out a gun case. An old one with leather sides and heavy metal teeth on the zipper. Sure, she wants to get out of here, but that doesn't stop the burst of excitement that settles in her chest. She's indifferent to the show, but she loves guns. How could she not? She was raised with the constant smell of gun powder in the air and spent as much time watching her dad tear down a firearm as she did learning how to read. She was the only one in her kindergarten class who could read, write, and rebuild a basic revolver without help.

"Whatcha got?" She can't help her smile as she sets the pouch carefully on the glass display case and unzips it. The camera is right up in her face, but she doesn't even care. Something awesome is about to happen. She can feel it, and so can her dad. He sidles up beside her with a smile that matches hers. She doesn't wait for Mr. Brockney to answer the question before she folds open the side and reveals a set of 1851 Colt Navy revolvers with ivory handles. Just like the pair Wild Bill Hickok had on him when he died. "Wow."

"Wow is right," her dad says, his voice hushed and reverent.

As old as the case is, the pistols look to be much older. Without documentation, there's no way to prove the provenance of any gun, but she doesn't care who the original owner was. They're beautiful and old, and she can't wait to break them down and check the production year. Except she's terrified to touch. She's good—really good considering her age—but these guns... It's better if her dad does it. Only he's not touching either.

She stuffs her hands in her pockets to keep from doing something stupid. It's not as if the 1851 Navy is *that* rare. But the grips... Well, that changes everything in terms of value— historic and financial. She steps to the side to make room for her dad.

They both know this one is his no matter how much the viewers enjoy seeing her play gunsmith. Something about her long blonde hair and manicured fingers really appeals to middle-aged, beer-drinking, would-be gun experts in the Bible

Belt. If one more guy writes to her about how she looks like the Grace Kelly of guns, she's going to shave her head and pierce something.

Or not.

Beth loves her hair even more than Willa hates those letters. She likes to lie next to her, propped up on one elbow, and kiss Willa slowly as she trails her fingers through her hair.

Willa touches the thick edge of folded paper in her pocket—an origami angel that she found in her desk drawer that morning. There's writing on the paper—Beth's writing—but it winds in and out of the form, impossible to read without unfolding Beth's creation. She scrapes her nails along the outside edge and thinks about what Beth might have written.

Sometimes, she's sweet and romantic and says things that make Willa believe in hearts and flowers and happily ever after. Other times, she's blunt and a little crude and whispers all the dirty things she dreams about doing to Willa next time she gets her alone. The effect then is sharp and powerful and leaves her throbbing and ready to beg rather than lulled into a warm sense of peace and security.

Willa doesn't know which she'd rather find tucked into the wings of her angel, so she hasn't peeled back the edges to find out what's inside. There's something else there, too. Something solid and heavy—compared to origami paper—wrapped inside along with Beth's words.

Her dad still has the same awed grin on his face. He wipes his hands against his jeans, licks his lips nervously, and reaches for the guns. Before he makes contact, someone taps her on the shoulder and reminds her that it's her turn in the confession booth.

The production crew has been watching the snow as closely as Willa. This is the last day of filming before they break for the holiday, and they all want to get home to their families before the snow traps them here.

She gives the pistol one last wistful glance, and then—just like always—she does what she's been asked to do.

Typically they ask questions about the guns that come into the shop during the week or whatever project or business deal her dad is focusing on, so she's prepared to talk about the Colt that her dad is salivating over. Instead, the producer asks her sappy questions about the holiday—what she plans to do for Christmas and what she's hoping to get? At her age, should she really be worried about what she's getting more than what she's giving?

Last year, her family collected blankets, coats, gloves, hats, and boots and delivered them to the nearest homeless shelter in Spokane. This year, they're gathering similar donations for the foster care program. She hates talking about it, though, because it makes people think she's nicer than she is. Still, she answers the questions with a smile. And when she's asked why she does charity work like this, she demurely says, "Because it's the right thing to do."

What she doesn't say is it's the only way she's found to bleed off the guilt that builds inside her every time she lets Beth kiss her. Or every time she lets her slide her hand high enough up her thigh to make Willa gasp. Or every time she lies back with a quiet moan as Beth works the buttons of her blouse free. She can't stop herself from saying yes, but she can't stop the relentless wash of remorse that follows either.

Good girls don't. That's what her parents taught her. They don't flirt with other girls. They don't flood their panties with arousal when given a roguish, careless grin. They don't sneak out after dark to meet the girl they've been forbidden to see.

They don't lie and promise that they're being good even as they're still coming down from that luscious, indescribable high from being teased over the edge by an insistent tongue. Good girls don't do any of the things Willa does.

Willa's spent too much time deep inside Beth to think their relationship goes against the will of God. Beth is…everything good and perfect, and she makes Willa feel right in a way she can't even explain. God has real things to worry about in this sad, limping, angry world. Why would He care if she finds peace in the arms of someone who loves her? Surely God isn't that petty.

But even if God isn't, her parents seem to be. They're very concerned about "Christian family values," and that doesn't leave any room for those "dirty, sinful homosexuals." And so, right or wrong, guilt seeps into her for hiding something so fundamental from her parents.

Willa rests her head against the back of her chair and lets out a deep sigh. Her fingers move to the folded angel in her pocket. She's worried over it so much that the edges are getting that rounded, soft texture that comes from wear. She pulls it from her pocket and stares at it for a long moment. Whatever is in this note isn't something she should experience inside the confession booth with the camera less than two feet away.

But the light is off, and that means the camera isn't recording. She loosens the tucked-in corner of one wing, and the whole angel flutters open in her hands. In the center of the page is a brass-colored house key, and Beth's strong, flowing cursive fills the page.

> *When I think of home, I think of you. And when I*
> *think of you, my breath stops in my chest and it's all*
> *I can do to keep from running to you right then. I*

don't care where you are, who you're with, or how far away you are.

All I want in that moment—and every other moment—is to be as close to you as possible. I want to hold you in my arms and protect you from all the things in life that weigh you down. I want to kiss you and promise to keep you safe from those who want you to believe you're less because of us, because of what I feel for you and you for me.

I want to hold you close and cherish you for as long as you'll let me—for the rest of my life if I get my way.

For now, though, I'll settle for telling you I love you. This key is yours to use, or not, whenever you want. My apartment only becomes a home when you're there too.

Willa swallows back a gasp and closes her eyes. Beth... She's unlike anyone Willa's ever met. She unravels her with a look, a touch, a few words on paper. And makes her forget about every promise she made to herself and her family, the promise that she'll try harder, be stronger...that she'll be *good*.

Logically, she knows the words Beth wrote aren't shocking or new. Beth tells her she loves her in little ways, ways that make Willa's chest ache with something so bittersweet she can't quite define it. Still, seeing Beth's thoughts about her, about them, and about their future together written down in bold, precise words, words no one can misinterpret, brings her to a quiet, but definite pause in the fabric of her life. Something indescribable, yet irrevocable, has shifted inside her until all she's left with is a clear, simple truth.

She loves Beth. She hasn't told her yet, hasn't been brave enough to give her emotions a place in the world, but it's been building for what seems like forever. Now she's reached a point where, if she continues to remain silent, to deny the most pure thing she's ever known, she'll drown right along with the tender affection she's refused to nurture. Until now.

She draws in a deep, steadying breath, tucks the letter into her pocket, and runs her fingers along the lower edge of her eyes to catch the tears that have started to gather there. She knows what she wants to do, what she *needs* to do... Now all that's left is to do it.

She leaves the confession booth and crosses the sales floor without even a glance at the 1851 Navys. After this, her dad may not ever let her touch it—or any other gun—again, and she can live with that. What she can't do is live without Beth as a solid presence in her life. She heads straight for the swinging glass door that leads to the street and says over her shoulder, "I'm leaving for the day, Dad."

"What...? Willa..."

He's still speaking when the door shuts behind her, but she doesn't turn around. Rather than going to her truck as she normally would, she walks across the street, bold as that in the middle of the day for the whole town to see. She's shaking; it might be from the cold, but more likely from nerves.

Suddenly, everything is so clear, and she doesn't know how she didn't see it before.

She steps inside Bitter Ink with a smile. Beth pauses and looks up from the rose she's tattooing on a woman's upper arm. Beth's wearing a ridiculous bright-pink, sequin-covered Santa hat that makes Willa think Beth lost some sort of bet with her boss. They do silly things like that with each other all the time. Last time Beth lost a bet, she ended up with a small tattoo of a dancing piece of toast on her forearm. Willa still doesn't understand how *that* happened.

Willa doesn't recognize the woman Beth is tattooing, but the woman probably recognizes her. She stopped being anonymous the second her parents signed the contract for that reality show.

Beth smiles, one of her rare full smiles that lights up her entire face, rather than lazy half smile she favors the rest of the time. "Hey, what's up?"

Willa bends close and kisses Beth on the mouth. The woman gasps, and Ava, Beth's boss, chuckles somewhere off to her left. Beth smiles against her lips and lets Willa set the pace. Willa curls her hand around the back of Beth's neck, teasing her fingers over the short hair she finds there. She squeezes gently as she kisses her again.

Willa ends the kiss before she's actually ready to face the fallout. But things will blow up enough over just this moment. There's no reason to stay here and make out with Beth any longer.

"I missed you." She glides her fingers over the faded scar above Beth's eye and down along the line of her jaw.

Beth arches one eyebrow, and her smile gives way to a smirk. "Missed you too." She looks pointedly past Willa and out the window behind her. "Something you want to tell me?"

Willa sighs. "Is he watching?"

"Mmm-hmm." Beth nods and focuses her attention solely on Willa.

The way she looks at her makes Willa feel cherished, as though she'll never find a more right place to be than with Beth.

Her insides turn to mushy, messy, melty goo that threatens to seep out of her pores, and it's all she can do to stay upright.

Yes, her dad is probably pissed. But his anger is worth so little when she compares it to the joy she feels in this moment. She feels liberated. Free. Fearless.

"He looks pretty pissed off, hon," the woman getting tattooed says with a full measure of sympathy. Their shared kiss may have surprised her, but nothing about her reaction says it's a bad thing.

Willa relaxes a little. "I bet." She dips her head to kiss Beth once more, then whispers in Beth's ear. "I got your present. I'm going to head upstairs. Join me after you finish up?"

Beth nods; that damn cocky glint sparks in her eyes, and Willa's breath catches in her chest. She doesn't know exactly what Beth has planned, but she's sure she's going to enjoy it.

"I'll be a few hours. I have one more appointment after I finish with Rosie, here."

Willa doesn't respond. She's said everything she needs to say, both with words and actions. She heads toward the back room and greets Ava on the way. "Okay if I head back there?"

Yes, she's going to Beth's apartment, but to get there, she has to go through Ava's office area. It's only polite to ask.

"Sure thing. You left work a little early today?" Ava smiles as if she knows exactly what it means for Willa to be here so early, and Willa's face flushes with heat.

She nods tightly as she passes through the swinging saloon-style doors that separate the front of the house from the back. She takes the stairs one at a time, moving her feet in steady, determined steps. She doesn't stop until she reaches the top. As she pulls her new key from her pocket, she pauses. Beth never locks her front door since she works right downstairs, but she gave Willa a key, and Willa is going to use it. After this, she may never again. What good's a key to an already unlocked door?

Tonight, however, the action means something. She slides the key into the lock, and the symbolism of the moment makes her smile. The door opens easily, and Willa steps inside.

⚬◌

Beth stares after Willa as she walks away. She's helpless to do anything else as long as Willa is there, her hips swaying as she moves gracefully across the room.

Rosie clears her throat, drawing Beth back to what she's supposed to be doing. Ava laughs outright at that. Beth smiles because she can't *not* smile. Yeah, she's totally cocky, but who wouldn't be? Willa is...perfection in high heels.

"You got it bad, kid." Rosie chuckles.

"Mm." Beth hums and takes the opportunity to change her gloves. It gives her a chance to settle herself into the moment and the work in front of her. As always, Willa chased all thought from Beth's mind until all she can think about is the press of Willa's lips against hers. It is overwhelming and intoxicating and completely terrifying.

When she first met Willa, when she first started flirting with her, it was a point of Lothario pride. Her friend dared her to introduce herself, to try to take her home. And so she made her way through the throng of college kids to angle her body between Willa and an oversized jock wearing a football jersey. They made sense together, the quarterback and the cheerleader. And she might have held back if Willa hadn't looked as if she were about to chew off her own arm to get away from him.

She smiled easily, confident that whatever this beautiful girl's answer would be, it wouldn't stop Beth from having fun

45

for the rest of the night. The dude rambled on, apparently unaware that Willa was no longer looking at him with a thin veil of disinterest. Instead, her gaze was focused solidly on Beth, her eyes bright and curious, and a small grin teasing across her mouth.

"Hi." Beth leaned in close, lips to Willa's ear, and spoke in a low whisper. She rested her hand on Willa's waist, curling her fingers lightly against the exposed skin at her midriff between her top and her skirt.

Willa drew in a sharp breath at her touch. "Hi." Her voice was low and sultry and so breathy it barely counted as a word.

"Come with me." Beth curled the words up just a tad at the end. She didn't want it to sound like a question, but she wasn't the sort to pressure another girl. She wanted to get Willa away from the crowd, sure, but Willa had to want it too.

She pulled back slightly, reluctant to move out of the soft cocoon of Willa's long blonde hair. She inhaled deeply, and the sweet fragrance intoxicated her more than the few beers she'd already consumed that night.

Willa nodded at her, just one stilted movement of her head. Her eyes opened wide, and her smile transformed to something closer to surprise than the easy flirtation of a moment ago. Beth threaded their fingers together loosely and led Willa through the house and out into the cool night air on the back porch.

That memory, along with every other one they created together in the months since, rolls through Beth. Rosie is right. She has it bad. She nods and tries to focus on the music filling the room and the hum of Ava's tattoo gun, rather than the feint smell of Willa's perfume that lingers in the air. She dips her liner into the black ink and says, "Let's finish this, huh?"

She loses herself in the flow of ink into flesh, and the rose comes into focus. For her first tattoo, Rosie chose her namesake flower, but instead of small and delicate, she asked for dramatic and bright. It surprised Beth when Ava let her take the appointment. Sure, she's done a lot of flowers, but this one was by far the largest and most intricate in terms of shading. It takes her two hours. Ava would have easily finished in one, but it looks good when Beth's done, and Rosie is happy enough to give her a tip.

There's a picture on the wall above her workstation—a snapshot from last winter of Beth making a snowman with her daughter. She doesn't even know who took it, but it captures the quintessential childhood moment. Gemini, barely five at the time, is stretched up on her tiptoes, pushing a carrot into place for a nose. She's beautiful in an otherworldly kind of way, and Beth can't believe that she created this amazing, perfect little creature.

Maybe Willa wants to make a snowman with them this year. It's snowed enough today, and Willa hasn't spent much time with Gem yet. Beth has been moving slow, slower than she's ever moved before. The last time she fell this hard and this fast for someone, she ended up a single, teenage mom. As much as she wants Willa, she's trying to not lose her head completely. Not to mention, the whole idea of being with another woman is new enough to make Willa skittish. She could bolt at any moment.

Well, maybe not now, not after that kiss. The touch of Willa's lips to hers was sweet and gentle, but the location—in full view of her father and whoever else might be looking—was a declaration of war. Up until today, Willa insisted on discretion. She doesn't trust her dad not to kick her out and disown her on national television. Beth hopes it doesn't come to that; Willa deserves better.

Beth sighs and tucks the twenty she got as a tip into the back of the picture frame. She's not the best parent, but the envelope labeled *college* is fat with bills. Gem deserves options. And Beth has no problem making little changes—like drinking drip coffee from her own kitchen and not smoking—to give her daughter those options. It's not Gemini's fault Beth got pregnant when she was fifteen.

She hangs the picture back up on the wall and then breaks down her station. She cleans everything and sets up for the next appointment. This one is little, just a bit of flash from the wall, and she should finish it quickly. She'll get the shop minimum, and this guy will get his ink-cherry popped.

"Are you dying to get out of here?" Ava asks with a teasing grin.

That woman is so in love with her own wife, yet she still gets off on giving Beth crap for being so ridiculously smitten. Beth doesn't blame her. If anyone else acted the way she does over Willa, it would make her teeth hurt.

"Almost done. Just a quick anchor and that's it." She shows Ava the American Traditional style tattoo that the customer chose. He just joined the navy and ships out in a few weeks. She likes working with this style of art. It's bold and illustrates the beauty and history of tattooing in the US. She likes other styles, too, and is focusing hard to improve her portrait work, but the legacy of the iconic technique makes her happy in a way she can't quite explain.

Ava checks her sketch. Sure, it's flash, but she still took the time to sketch it out and personalize it a little. She drew one version with an American flag billowing in the wind behind the anchor, and she hopes he'll pick that design. Ava nods slowly and points at the detail on the anchor. "This is nice. How long will it take, do you think?"

Beth shrugs and tries to look casual. "Maybe forty-five minutes?" She actually thinks it'll take thirty because it's relatively small and doesn't require a lot of intricate shading, but she knows Ava is sizing her up. She'll be judged by how close she comes to her mark. She'd rather come in under than over. And really, when it comes down to it, she's not so worried about how long it will take compared to how good it looks when she finishes.

Ava hands the sketch back. "What's your day like tomorrow?"

Beth glances outside at the relentless fall of snow. People in this town are hardcore and will drive in anything, but Christmas is in a few days. The few jobs she has set up might want to spend the time shopping instead. "Four, but we'll see how many cancel."

"If you have time, maybe you could do one for me?" Ava says it super casual, but Beth gasps in a sharp intake of air. More than anything else Ava's said about her tattooing, this is...huge. It's as if she's saying Beth has graduated. She knows that's not really the case, but her heart still races with the possibility.

She nods and tries not to grin like an idiot. She fails and decides she doesn't care. "Yeah? Sure."

The front door swings open, and her customer comes in. Ava turns back to her paperwork, and Beth settles into her last tattoo. She works carefully and methodically, but all she can think about it Willa and how much she wants to run up the stairs and join her.

When she finally finishes, Ava laughs at how fast she cleans up her station, but doesn't stop her when she heads for the back. "I'll be upstairs if you need me, yeah?"

"Go see your girlfriend. I've got this."

She checks the clock as she takes the stairs two at a time. Her mom is supposed to drop Gem off at nine tonight. That gives her a couple of hours to figure out what's going on with Willa and if she's staying over. It'd be a first, and Beth has a weird knot of uncertainty churning in her belly over what it might mean.

The door to her apartment is locked, and Beth bounces off of it when it doesn't swing open. She never locks her door. Ever. She's not even sure where her keys are at the moment. She slaps her pockets, hoping to find the set in one of the deep cargo pockets of her khakis. No luck. She knocks softly on the door. "Will?"

"She locked you out?" Ava isn't outright laughing at her this time, but Beth can hear it in her tone. "You give her a key of her own, and this is how she responds?"

"Don't just stand there." Beth isn't irritated, not really. But she can't hear any noise coming from the other side of the door, not even the low music that Willa favors, and the quiet is causing her to panic slightly. "Help me."

Ava grabs her own keys from the desk. "Here." She tosses them up to Beth.

"Thanks." Beth unlocks the door and drops them back down to Ava. By the time she gets inside and closes the door, Ava has given up trying to hold back and is laughing loudly. Thank God she finds Beth entertaining or she would have kicked her out a long time ago.

"Willa?" She walks through the apartment, glancing at the couch and into the kitchen on her way to the bedroom. There aren't a lot of places to hide, and she rules out all but one immediately. The Christmas tree lights are on, and they cast a soft blue glow over the living room. There are only a few presents underneath it. Gem is already crazy spoiled and will get more toys than she can play with from her grandmas.

Beth spends her money on memories, like the trip she has planned for the two of them for the following summer. She wants her daughter to see the world, to know about all the possibilities that life has to offer. So far Gem has two stamps on her passport—the same as Beth. When they add the third, Beth hopes Willa will be with them.

She half expects to find the door to her bedroom locked too, but it opens easily. The room is dark except for the weak threads of light coming through the snow-flurried window. Still, it's enough light for her to make out the splash of blonde on her pillow and the distinct Willa-shaped lump beneath her blankets.

When Beth sits on the edge of the bed and lightly touches Willa's cheek, Willa sighs in her sleep and curls her body toward Beth. Most of her—all except for her head and the hand she reaches out to Beth with—is beneath the covers, but Beth's pretty sure Willa's naked. She pulls the blanket down a bit and drops an easy kiss on the exposed skin of Willa's bare shoulder.

Willa obviously had plans when she climbed in Beth's bed earlier—plans that involved stripping off her clothes—but Beth lets her sleep. Willa looks relaxed in a way she never does when she's awake. Beth kicks off her shoes, drops her hat on the bedside table, and climbs in beside her. She moves slowly, carefully as to not jostle Willa from her sleep.

As soon as she's laid properly next to her, Willa scoots closer until all Beth's senses are swamped by the proximity. She inhales deeply and surrenders. She is so deep in this, so in love with this beautiful angel of a woman; there's no way she can deny it. Until today, Willa has been reluctant to fully embrace their relationship, but from their very first kiss, she has been willing to let Beth hold her in the privacy of her room.

"I love my present," Willa murmurs sleepily; her breath washes over Beth's skin, and the words tickle against her ear.

"Yeah?" Beth barely speaks. The answer is too important, and Willa's more likely to tell the truth in this half-awake state.

"Yeah." She snuggles in deeper, throwing one leg over Beth's hips and resting her hand easily in the valley between Beth's breasts. "But you have to fix the angel."

Willa sounds nowhere close to actually waking up, so Beth concentrates on slowing her heart rate to a normal pace. It's harder than it should be, but she's human and Willa's lips are close enough to kiss her neck and her hair is soft beneath Beth's fingers.

She wants to roll Willa onto her back and slip inside her. She wants to build her up slowly and wake her as her body surrenders to orgasm. She wants to kiss her softly and bring her back down with slow, easy strokes and then build her back up with precise circles against Willa's clit.

She wants all of that, but instead she pries the key and crumpled angel from Willa's grip and kisses the top of her head. "I love you."

"Mmmm. Love you too." Willa burrows her face into the crook of Beth's shoulder, and the words come out muffled but not so much that Beth can't understand what she's saying.

Beth holds her breath and waits for the words to register with Willa. She's tried for so long to convince her this thing between them is more than just a physical reaction; Willa has consistently rebuffed her, declaring at every turn that they are fucking, not loving.

The reaction she's waiting for never comes as Willa's breathing evens out and drops further into the deep rhythm of sleep. Beth sets the present she gave Willa on the bedside table. She almost didn't give it to her, afraid that it would make things too real—and therefore too hard—for Willa. But she's glad she forced herself to breathe through the anxiety long enough to convince Holden to help her earlier.

It was a bold, dangerous move on so many levels. But this, the feel of Willa resting in her arms, her body warm and languid and soft to the touch, makes the risk seem inconsequential. And even though she wants to talk to Willa about what it means, and even though she wants to explore Willa's naked body because she never tires of doing that, she's content—happy, even—to simply hold her.

What they share is a forever kind of thing; Beth knows it. They have every day after this to talk and touch. For now, she's happy to hold Willa to her, thankful for the gift of Willa in her life.

RED SUITS AND SECOND CHANCES

by Eve Francis

THE ELEVATOR WAS BROKEN AGAIN. Gina stood in front of the yellow sign, written in Sharpie ink so fresh the pungent smell was unmistakable.

Sorry, pls take the stares! the sign read, followed by a frowny face.

Gina sighed, fighting the impulse to correct the sign's grammar. *Stairs. Not stares.* Someone from marketing had probably written the notice—definitely not one of Lederman's copy editors. Gina had spent a few summers working as a copy editor before she was promoted to a PR person who came up with the campaigns for the large Lederman company. She saw a lot of bad grammar over that time period, where smart and savvy people, with great ideas and wonderful ways to execute them, couldn't tell the difference between there, their, and they're or any of the most basic homophones.

So maybe people in the office just sucked at grammar, and their slips with Gina's pronouns were simple mistakes and not manifestations of transphobia. *Maybe.* Gina considered this for a few, lingering moments as her high-heeled shoes grew damp from the puddles of snow which had thawed inside the front foyer. The snow on her red coat melted into the fabric on her shoulders, adding to the gray puddles of sludge already formed around her feet. Winter in Toronto always came on so suddenly, she had no time this morning to take boots instead of her nice shoes, and now she was stuck with cold toes and smarting insteps.

She'd barely realized it was almost Christmas until last night when she came back from her electrolysis appointment and saw the Christmas lights in everyone's apartment windows. Angie, her electrolysis girl, always blasted punk rock during the treatments to distract her clients from the pain. But even Angie had slipped in "Oi to The World" by the Vandals between "Why Can't I Touch It?" by The Buzzcocks and "Sheena Is a Punk Rocker" by the Ramones.

One day, it's just cold. Then it's snowing. Then the next day, it's Christmas. A little rough around the edges, Gina thought, touching her chin reflexively, *but still Christmas.*

She hated Christmas now more than ever.

Gina's hand was halfway into her purse, pushing past her cell phone and compact mirror to find a pen to correct the sign when she heard familiar footsteps behind her.

"Hey, Gina!" Felicia called from the front foyer of the Lederman PR building. Her dark hair was flecked with snow, her pale skin slightly pink from the cold, but her red lips were still immaculate. She moved the strap of her briefcase higher on her shoulder and then looked Gina up and down. Not in the way everyone else in the office did—like they were trying to see her former self under the edges of her clothing, mentally cutting her hair or removing her makeup, straining to see the former version of herself she'd left behind. No, not like that at all.

Felicia was new to Lederman by most people's standards. She'd been hired out of school as a temp three years ago, then promoted to full-time staff about a year ago. But she'd been around long enough to know Gina when she'd still been hiding her identity. Even with this information, Felicia never treated Gina any differently after the inter-office e-mail from HR had gone around, asking for Gary DiMarco to now be addressed as Gina DiMarco. Felicia looked at Gina as if she was *Gina*. Not a ghost of someone she used to know, or an aberration that was wearing a different skin suit too tight.

Felicia focused on Gina's red shoes and smiled. "Man, I saw those in the store a few weeks ago! I didn't buy them—though they were on sale—because I figured the snow would ruin them."

"Oh," Gina said, looking down. Already there was rim of salt around the edge, just above the sole. She sighed. "Well, you may have made the right choice."

Felicia smiled again, making her green eyes pop. She looked past Gina, toward the elevator door, and huffed. "This elevator is *always* broken. At least someone had the decency to put up a sign before we got on and got trapped, right?"

"Yeah. That would have been a completely different start to the day I didn't need."

"Well, maybe if we were together, I don't think it would have been so bad."

Gina lifted an eyebrow, unsure if that was a compliment or not. Being trapped in an elevator with anyone was hardly a fun time, even if you were an office butterfly. When Felicia's arm moved to dig out her iPad from her briefcase, and Gina saw the familiar account e-mail for Bed & Bath Works, she sighed. *Right. Of course.* They were both working on that account, and were under a looming deadline. Even if they got stuck in the elevator, it would still be a place to work. *That and nothing more.*

"Eeek." Felicia made a face. "Okay, our client is freaking out—and so is Sam. Everyone else is already upstairs."

Felicia tucked away her iPad without waiting for a response from Gina. She walked a few paces ahead, toward the stairwell, and propped the door open with her knee as she turned back to Gina again. "You coming? Lederman's only the second floor. It'll be good for us to get some exercise."

"Right. Sure." Gina glanced down at the sign across the elevator door again, saw the wrong word, and grabbed her pen from the bottom of her bag. "Just give me two seconds. I have one last thing to do."

As Gina crossed out *stares* and wrote in *stairs,* Felicia laughed, light and throaty.

"Happy now?" Felicia asked, still holding the door open for Gina. As she passed through the doorframe, Gina hunched her body. She was only five ten, maybe five eleven with the added height from her small heels, but Felicia's five-four frame made her feel as if she towered over her. Even when Gina had presented as a man for the first thirty-four years of her life, she had always hunched. She hated being this tall, especially when she'd rather be so much closer to Felicia.

"More or less," Gina said, referring to her minor correction. "I suppose it'll do for now."

∞◯

The only gender-neutral bathroom in the Lederman building was on the fourth floor. Gina had no idea why. The fourth floor was almost always under construction, and the company stored most of its older files there until they could be stored electronically. Located between the two typically gendered stalls, and down a long and creepy corridor, was a handicap stall that had no discernible gender marker on it. It was the type of bathroom Gina coveted in public places—in airports, malls, and even the local library. She needed to use the family or the handicap stalls in order to make sure she didn't cause a fuss. And if none of those stalls were available, then Gina learned to hold it.

Maybe this was more of an issue in the first part of her transition. Gina realized, sitting at her desk now, that she mostly passed in her day-to-day life. Her dark hair was much longer, and her electrolysis, though it seemed like the never-ending story most days, was actually doing a lot of work. Her skin was hairless, if not quite smooth. She dressed, for the most part, as well as she could with her body type. And after years of practice, she finally had the hang of makeup.

That's the thing, Gina told herself in between replying to e-mails at her desk. *I've had many years of practice at this—even if I've only been out as trans for less than one.* Gina glanced at her calendar in her office and realized that her one-year anniversary of coming out as Gina was in a few weeks. The personal meeting she had had with her boss, Sam, had occurred right after the January break—and her office had been her last place on her list. For much longer, she'd been Gina at home and going to a therapist and psychiatrist in order to get hormones for much longer than that. Those hormones had done what makeup and clothing never could—they made her feel okay in her body. Gave her breasts, softer skin, and brighter eyes. They made her feel that something, for a while at least, was finally made right.

Over her last Christmas holiday, she'd changed her name officially to Gina Andrea DiMarco. And when she returned to work, she walked right into Human Resources and Accounting and got everything switched over to her proper name. She'd prepared a speech, along with a portfolio worth of references and resources. She knew she was over prepared for her meetings, but that was part of Gina's nature by now. That was why she had been hired at one of the most cutthroat PR places in Toronto. She was dedicated to her job and did it well. Even when she was going through a life-changing transition privately, she was still better than most people at her job.

No one had made her transition *that* big of a deal. There were a lot of awkward pauses and tripping up with names and pronouns, but that wasn't just because she was trans. She was sure of it. It was just hard for people to go from calling here Gary to Gina. It was just like the elevator; people who didn't know any better said stares instead of stairs. And people who didn't know better at Lederman sometime said "Hey Ga—Gina" instead of getting it right on the first try.

Then there were people like Felicia who *always* got it right. If Felicia wasn't already so pretty, Gina's crush would have been based solely on how nice she was. But no, Felicia was also pretty and smart and wonderful. And completely out of Gina's grasp. *Is Felicia even gay? Does she want to be in a relationship with another woman? Even if she is into women,* Gina reminded herself sadly, *there's the fact that you're not like most women out there.*

Deep down, she really *was* a woman, and she didn't take crap when people tried to convince her otherwise. But being confident in her identity was a lot different when she was faced with the prospect of dating. Gina could accept herself—but could other people? She wasn't so sure. Gina had to buy her clothing online to find the right sizes, and still walk up two more floors in order to use the proper bathroom. Why would Felicia—or any other woman out there—want a woman like that?

Gina glanced over her shoulder, evaluating the rest of the office space. Felicia's cubicle—a space she shared with four other online tech and social media gurus—was to the side near a big office window that looked across at a bank and a coffee place. Gina was on the other side, closer to the boss's area and the conference rooms. There was small chatter from people working on projects together, wrapping up a few Christmastime accounts, and then a sudden peel of laughter. Gina glanced over to see Felicia and Alexa, two interns who had somehow survived this long in the PR world, laughing and slapping high fives. When their touch lingered, Gina felt a sudden pang of jealousy and recognition.

Maybe Felicia does like women. But that still doesn't mean she likes me.

Gina glanced at her e-mails again. Most of her correspondences had piled up since she wasn't actually answering them, opting instead to ponder bathroom ethics in her head. She rolled her eyes at her behaviour. She really, *really* had to pee, but was still stubborn enough to not walk up another two flights of stairs.

After soothing an angry client, Gina could wait no more. She threw her purse over her shoulder and walked across the office space. Gina swore she felt eyes on her the entire time. When she was brave enough to look up, she saw Felicia staring at her carefully. She quickly looked away, and Gina nearly walked into Sam, her boss.

"DiMarco. Great. I was looking for you."

"You were?" Gina asked, gripping her purse strap. "I've been here. Just answering e-mails before closing out some accounts."

"Oh please, you're better than that. Have you hired an assistant yet? She should do your e-mails."

"I...Uh..."

"I get it. Christmas. It's hard to find people around then. Well, we will delegate some funds so you can have someone else answer your e-mails, and I can use your brilliant brain to strategize. Think of yourself as a coach, you know? The higher you get, the less work you do!" Sam smirked, and was about to pat Gina on the arm when he held back. *A minor gender infraction*, Gina noted. *You don't slap female coworkers on the arm for a good job—even if they are in the position of a coach.* Sam was learning, albeit slowly.

"Well, I'll keep the assistant idea in mind. Now if you don't mind." Gina motioned ahead of her, toward the stairwell, and Sam stepped out of the way.

"Oh, sorry! So, where are you headed, DiMarco?"

"Um. Just to the fourth floor."

"The elevator is broken."

"Yes, I know—that's why I'm headed toward the stairs. I could use the walk." Gina smiled weakly, and Sam ran a hand through his thinning gray beard.

"Well, do me a favour while you're up there? I'm pretty sure the Christmas decorations are there. And if you're already walking...then I see no need to go myself."

"Right." Gina's breath shuddered, suddenly knowing exactly what Sam wanted to talk to her about. "I can do that. Get the decorations, I mean."

"Thanks, DiMarco. You're a very important part of the team. Get back by 11 a.m., so we can have the big meeting. Then the fun can really begin."

Gina nodded, her back stiff, and headed toward the stairs again.

❦

Gina located the decorations easily. In spite of all the high tech advances in their current office space, she actually found it quite quaint that most of the Lederman staff thought it was appropriate to store all types of festive decorations in cardboard boxes with XMAS or SPOOKY written in big bold letters, as if the fourth floor was the attic in a childhood home they all shared.

Gina's former partner, Mark, used to joke with her that being a PR person was basically like being a giant party planner, so really, Gina could understand the need to preserve decorations in this manner. It allowed them to feel as if they were setting up for something much more monumental than just a holiday time around the office. There would also be a larger office party about a week from now where their clients would come and mingle among the Lederman staff, and Sam would make sure there was oh, so much alcohol as he handed out the Christmas bonuses. The large Christmas party was also where Gina usually played Santa Claus.

Gina sighed as she caught sight of the red and white Santa suit at the bottom of the box. For the past five years, this had been her legacy. She knew how to do voices quite well—from years of trying to make her own deep baritone sound soft like a woman's, on the phone—and so she was naturally a good fit for the role of Santa Claus for a night. She'd don the beard, the baggy suit, and then walk around and wish everyone a jolly night and a happy new year.

Truthfully, she never minded it. She got to pretend to be someone else for a little while—and the beard hid her face. Instead of being sucked into awkward conversations, she got to disappear.

But now she didn't want to disappear. She didn't want to pretend to be a jolly fat man because well, she wasn't a man anymore. She never was a man to begin with. To be Santa again felt strange and disingenuous. She worked so hard these past eleven months for her coworkers to see her as Gina, not Gary. To slip on the Santa suit this time would feel closer to failure than Gina wanted to admit.

She shoved the suit deep into the box and piled Christmas lights on top of it. There were two other small boxes of garlands, and a small tree for the corner of Sam's office. She could bide her time by taking those boxes downstairs first.

Maybe I can even hide the suit, Gina thought. *Just shove it into the broken elevator and never see it again. Who would know?* She pushed the thought away. Just because *she* didn't want to be Santa anymore, didn't mean that everyone should be deprived. She just hoped, as her therapist had encouraged her to do, see could speak up during the meeting and say no when Sam inevitably asked.

Until then, there was the matter of two flights of stairs and two more boxes to carry down to Lederman's office space. She found a hair tie in her purse, pulled her black hair behind her shoulders, and began the trek.

∝✺

"Is everyone here?" Sam asked. He clapped his hands together eagerly as a few more people from the finance department filed into the largest conference room for the full staff meeting. Several people in the media department, including Alexa and Felicia, tried to respond to e-mails on their phones until Sam gave them a stern look.

"What?" Alexa asked. "Clients are going nuts right now."

"I know, I know. And you're all doing a wonderful job. But focus here, okay? This meeting will be brief—but we have to decorate and plan the Christmas party."

"Will it be here?" James from finance asked.

"Yes, of course. Why not?"

"Well, that damn elevator needs to be fixed before then. Can you imagine CEOs taking the stairs when they're completely hammered? It would be a legal nightmare."

Sam placed his finger on the cleft of his chin. "You make a good point. Has someone called the repair people?"

A few people murmured and ticked, but no one answered. Gina pulled out her phone and began to compose an e-mail. "I can do it," she said, then finished her request and hit send.

"Thank you, DiMarco. I'm sure we'll have it done by the end of the week, then."

Gina nodded, keeping her phone out by her side. She was sure that, if she focused on something else, she could avoid the question of who would be Santa Claus all together. So far, it was working. While Jay, another person from finance, and Meredith from the media department bickered about the catering, no one seemed to notice Gina. When Alexa finally picked up the boxes of decorations and began to paste some of the transparent wall decorations onto the clear conference windows, Gina took this as the end of the meeting.

She rose from her seat, headed toward the back, and was almost free when she heard her last name from Sam's mouth again.

"DiMarco! Can we count on you?"

"Yes, I was just about to call the mechanic for the elevator."

"No, not about that. For—you know—the special duty?"

Gina swallowed hard and turned around. She could see the red fabric in the bottom of the box. Even Sam wasn't calling it a Santa suit anymore. *Special duty? What the hell did that even mean?*

"Um. I was actually hoping that…"

"If this doesn't fit you anymore," Sam cut in, seemingly able to see how uncomfortable Gina was, "then we can make some alterations. Right? I know some of you people sew; I see it on your Instagram accounts all the time. And don't even act like you don't go on them during work hours."

Gina couldn't listen anymore. Her phone started to ring, and she saw the mechanic's number come up. *Saved.* She clicked accept and held her phone to her ear as she walked out of the conference room.

"Hello? Jerry? Yes, this is Gina DiMarco from Lederman's."

"Really? I thought it was Sam. Anyway, never mind, we had you guys scheduled for the elevator already. We just had a few delays today because of the weather; we should be over tomorrow afternoon at the latest."

"Sounds good. Uh-huh…" Gina nodded along to Jerry, even if his tone made her unnerved. *It doesn't matter,* Gina insisted. The elevator was being fixed, and Gina was out of the room. Even when she reached the hallway and the conversation with Jerry was done, she couldn't face everyone again. She kept walking toward the stairwell and hoped the silence would calm her.

She got about halfway up the third flight of stairs before her legs trembled. So, so much walking. All this estrogen from her new hormones had completely changed what her body could do. For the better, she knew, but her testosterone-built muscle mass had disappeared, and she grew tired much easier now. She sat down on a step, after brushing it off, and sighed with her face in her hands. She was so busy trying to stay calm, she didn't even notice when Felicia joined her.

"Hey," Felicia called.

Gina jumped slightly. She took her face out of her hands and gave her a weak smile. "Hi—sorry—I didn't hear you."

"I'm quiet. You okay, though?" Felicia asked. She walked over to where Gina sat and then, lifting an eyebrow, pointed to the small space next to her. "Can I sit?"

"Sure." Gina moved to the side. Not knowing what to say—or what to do with her hands—she wrapped them across her stomach. "How's the meeting going?"

"Oh, it's a riot. Sam and Kelly are bickering over music, so I figure there will be time before they even notice I'm gone."

"Definitely. That was my plan, at least. I don't anticipate getting much other work done today."

"But that's what the holidays are for, right?" Felicia leaned back, crossing her feet at the ankle. "We're always so swamped, working double-time, and then it suddenly peters out just after Christmas. I kind of like it here for that reason."

"Really? I thought most people found it annoying."

"It's only annoying if you have a family you're missing during that time. I don't, not really, so I figure I'm enjoying what I can."

Gina was struck for a moment by the sudden confession. Felicia was usually open about most things, but that was when the topics were fashion or TV choices. Not when discussing nonexistent families.

"You?" Felicia asked suddenly.

"Me?"

"A family. Are the late work hours keeping you from them?"

"Oh. Um." Gina trailed off, wondering how much to reveal. "Yes and no, I guess. My family lives a couple hours from here in Barrie. I used to see them once a year, but in the summer. I claimed weather was too bad in the winter. And when I had my partner Mark, well, things were difficult."

Felicia nodded. "And now?"

"Well. Now I don't have Mark. But I still won't go."

"I'm sorry to hear that."

"Nah, it's not so bad." Gina tried to smile, and it was genuine. Losing Mark had been hard, but she knew that they weren't destined to be together. Mark was gay, only interested in men. Gina had *felt* gay for most of her life, but it had taken her a long, long time to realize that she felt gay because she wanted to be with women. As a woman. So she was a lesbian, with a bit of a precarious past. But then again, who didn't have a precarious past nowadays? Apparently even Felicia, perfect and charming Felicia, didn't have a family to go home to over the holidays.

"Can I ask," Gina said after some silence, "why you're alone over the holidays?"

"Pfft," Felicia said, laughing little. "I'm not alone. I have so many people. They're just not related to me by blood."

"Right. Of course. I'm sorry. I shouldn't have assumed."

"Don't be sorry. I'm fine. My family is just…a long line of drunks. I don't like to go home to that. So I don't."

Is it really so simple? Gina wondered. She looked down at her red shoes, the shoes Felicia had liked, and thought that maybe it was that simple. *If you don't like something, you just don't do it anymore. You don't be a man because you think you have to be. And if you don't want to go home and see drunks, then you don't, either.*

"I have another question for you," Gina confessed.

"I might have an answer for you. You first." Felicia smiled, and it was enough to make Gina feel confident enough to go forward.

"You never screw up pronouns. You never screw up my name or find odd ways of getting around saying Gina by addressing me by my last name."

"Oh, man. I'm glad someone else noticed Sam did that."

Gina shrugged. She had long ago made her peace with Sam's odd behaviour around her. "You always seemed to get it, though. Why?"

"Why not? It's simple."

"It's simple for *some* people—like the ones that came after I transitioned. They have no basis of comparison and are usually cool. But you saw me as Gary, and you still don't screw up."

"I may have seen you as Gary, but I didn't know you then. I don't think anyone did."

"Yeah, I guess." Gina had been quiet—even more than now—when she was Gary. Always at a desk, always doing work, and then going home to be someone else. Now that she had merged the worlds, she was happy, but there was still a small, quiet void.

"As far as I'm concerned," Felicia went on again, "we all get second chances. You're allowed to start something again if you realize the first time it didn't work. And if you can't do that on Christmas, when can you? Isn't that what Dickens was all about?"

Gina snorted. "Yeah, I suppose so. I guess that's the point of Christmas ghosts."

"Right!" She laughed. "Of past, present, and future. Well, sometimes the ghosts are different. But they're all you, you know?"

Gina nodded. She really wanted to reach out and touch Felicia; only inches separated their hands, but it was still too much. When Gina's phone rang again, it was a client, and she excused herself.

Felicia nodded, but remained on the stairs as Gina parsed a few details back and forth.

"So, where were we?" Gina asked after the call was complete.

Felicia looked out across the stairwell. "I think the ghost of the present is calling us. Sounds like they're putting up decorations in the office."

When Gina listened, she heard the random shouts from the office space. Her face dropped in disappointment. "Yeah, I guess you're right. We should head back."

Felicia stood first, then turned around to extend a hand to help Gina to her feet. She smiled as she touched Felicia's finger, then watched as Felicia's green eyes lit up and she took a step closer. For a brief moment, the space between them disappeared—and so did the sound around them. It was just them, in the stairwell, and Gina was sure that if they left right now and ran away, no one would notice.

"So," Gina said.

"So," Felicia mirrored. "You don't have to be Santa, okay?"

"Hmm?"

"You don't have to be Santa Claus," Felicia repeated. "Before I left the meeting, I told Sam he should do it."

"Really?"

"Oh, yeah. I told him he was getting chubby, and he'd do a much better job."

"And he bought it?"

"Well, only one way to find out, right?" Felicia smirked. By the time they reached the second floor, Felicia was a few steps ahead. She leaned into the hallway to catch a glimpse into their office space, before glancing back at Gina. "I think you're safe, though."

Gina followed Felicia's line of sight. Sam walked around the office, Santa hat half skewed over his head. He laughed and grabbed his small paunch, and Felicia stifled her giggles.

"Yeah, you're definitely good. I'll have to take in some of the measurements on the suit for him, but I think he'll still be into it. He's Santa now—your torch has been passed."

"Thank you," Gina said. "I really mean it."

"Not at all. Merry early Christmas," Felicia said with a nudge.

"Yes, same to you."

∞◯

A week later, Gina showed up at the office on a snowy, Friday night with a drink in her hand. She had brought a small bottle of chardonnay as some kind of holiday good will gesture, though she really just wanted to be rid of it. She had squeezed into her version of the "little black dress" most women in their thirties have. The skirt came down just above her knee and the straps were a bit skimpy. She paired it with a black cardigan and long, black boots.

"Well," she said as she gazed at herself in the mirrored surface in the front foyer. "You certainly don't look like Santa anymore."

With her black purse around her shoulder, she also didn't look very festive. She took the bow off her chardonnay and placed it over one of her dress straps instead, fixing her hair in the same reflected surface. *Not great*, she noted, *but better. At least it doesn't look like you're attending a funeral.*

Gina smiled at her reflection, gave herself one last look, and then turned to the elevator. The working elevator. She let out a huge sigh of relief as she got on, pressed the button for the second floor, and waited. When the door opened, the low din of the crowd drifted out along with the Elvis Christmas music Jay had fought for—and clearly won. It was only an hour into the party, and most of their outside clients had already shown up. Gina's plan was to show up late, talk to one or two people, drop off her gift—evidence she'd been to the party—pick up her bonus, and then go home. Maybe, if she was lucky, she could slip into PJs and watch *Pitch Perfect* on Netflix before midnight. Not because she really loved the movie, but because it was the least Christmas thing she could think of.

She nodded to herself as she entered the party. *Yes, that sounds good.*

"Ho ho ho!"

Gina turned to see Sam in the old Santa suit, without the beard since he had grown his own out. "I have a present for you, dear Gina."

"Oh? I think you may have already given me so much."

Sam made a tsk-tsk under his breath and handed her the standard envelope containing her holiday bonus. Her name *Gina DiMarco* was written in fine handwriting with a small Christmas sticker in the corner.

"Thank you, Sam. I truly appreciate it."

"Not at all! I have to say—I owe Felicia a huge thank you for fixing up the Santa suit for me. I didn't realize how much fun this would be."

"Especially with some Christmas cheer," Gina added, handing over the bottle of chardonnay. Sam made a pleased noise and tucked it into the bottom of his bag.

"For later. I'll be naughty after I'm nice."

"Sounds like a plan."

"Merry Christmas, Gina," Sam said before departing. She barely had a chance to wish him the same before he disappeared into the crowd.

Gina tucked her bonus into her purse and felt another wave of relief wash over her. She was here, wearing what she wanted, and she wasn't Santa. Maybe she didn't have to run away so soon. Maybe Christmas, with whatever new family her work staff had formed, wasn't too bad a fate after all.

She moved to the table full of sweets and ate a couple gingerbread cookies, before she felt a small tap on her back.

"Felicia," Gina greeted, smiling wide as they came face to face. Felicia wore dark, tight jeans and a large, hideous-looking sweater that made Gina gawk. "Oh my goodness—what are you wearing?"

"You like it?" Felicia asked, pulling the sweater taut so that the image—a cat dancing around a tree with some festive mice—was stretched out and more visible. "I found it when I was out looking for fabric, and I thought it was perfect. Reflects how I feel about the holiday."

Gina was about to ask exactly what that meant, when Felicia suddenly let go of her sweater and pulled out a gift from her shoulder bag. "Here," she said as she pressed it into Gina's hand.

"For me?"

"Yes. You. Open it! I want to see."

Gina furrowed her brow. The gift was light, but wide. The shape normally made her think of a box of chocolates, but it didn't have the heft of something like that. Also, Felicia looked much too eager for it to be a standard collection of cherry chocolates.

"What is it?"

"I can't tell you! Open it."

Gina undid the bow and let the ribbon fall over her wrist. It was a good look, she figured, especially since she wasn't nearly as festive as Felicia—and she suddenly wanted to be. Gina undid the red tissue paper next and revealed a white box.

"Well, open it. You're moving far too slow for me."

"Sorry," Gina said, blushing. When she opened the box, she saw red, familiar fabric. The velvet kind that belongs in a Santa suit. Her stomach dropped, but Felicia's excitement renewed her interest. Gina continued to dig through the box, finally pulling out another red Santa suit—except with a skirt. *Not a suit*, Gina corrected, *but a Santa dress*. Past the outfit at the bottom of the box was a small kerchief with white lace instead of a hat.

"What is...?"

"It's Mrs. Claus," Felicia said. She smiled, but it soon turned crooked as Gina remained silent. "No good? I figured if you ever missed being Santa, you could be the missus. I think it would fit you better, anyway."

"You...made this?"

"Yes! I went to the fabric store to make alterations on Sam's suit, saw the pattern, and realized how much better this would look on you than me. You have the legs for a skirt like that."

Gina glanced down, blushing slightly. "You have nice legs too."

"Oh? You were looking?"

"No. Um." Gina's face went as red as the suit. She placed it in the box again, and then felt Felicia's hands glide over hers.

"It's okay to look," Felicia insisted. "Especially when I just admitted the same."

"Oh?"

"Yes." Felicia winked slightly, then glanced around at the party. Most people had been sucked into their own peer groups—and Alexa, who Gina assumed Felicia came with, was clearly too busy talking to James to notice much of anything else. Sam was done handing out gifts and was drinking while talking to some clients. Felicia looked back at Gina, her smile even wider now. "You wanna get out of here?"

"Yes, definitely," Gina said.

Felicia tugged on Gina's hand and led her toward the elevator. As she pressed the button and waited, Gina glanced at Felicia's outfit, then back at the Santa dress in the box.

"Were you going to make this for yourself?"

"Yes, but like I said—you'll do it much better."

"But what if I wanted you to also be Mrs. Claus?" Gina's heart skipped a beat, surprised she was being so bold. "What if I didn't want to be alone, up at the North Pole?"

"Well, I *do* have more fabric back at my place. I have lots of ideas for clothing, really."

"Do you?" Gina's breath hitched. Felicia bit her lip as she looked up at Gina, sneaky and mysterious.

"I think right now, I'm more like an elf than anything. Good with my hands and at making things. Besides, when you wear heels, you're so, so tall."

"Oh, well." Gina was about to bend over and unzip her boots, when the elevator rushed open. Felicia grabbed Gina's hands again and pulled her inside. Gina watched in mock horror as Felicia pressed all the buttons—from the ground floor to the eighth at the top.

"What are you doing? What if it stalls again and we're stuck?"

"Well, I know *exactly* what I want to do to pass the time." Felicia took a step forward, placing a hand on Gina's waist. "Do you?"

"Yes, I think so." Gina slouched just enough for Felicia's mouth to meet her own. They kissed chastely, the height difference making it a little difficult until Gina learned to forget about it. With the elevator stopping with a ping at each floor, Gina expected to be disturbed. But each time she opened her eyes between kisses, she found an empty floor. Everyone in the Lederman building was on the second, partying away for Christmas. So Gina finally opened her mouth for Felicia, feeling her tongue slide close to hers with glee.

"How was that?" Felicia asked, pulling away from the kiss but keeping their hands connected. "Good?"

"You have...no idea."

Felicia smirked, then brought their lips together again. "Merry Christmas, Mrs. Claus."

Gina's heart skipped a beat. "Merry Christmas...my small elf?"

Felicia laughed again. "Sure, sure, I can be called that. But we'll work on some cute pet names later."

Later, Gina thought. This was going to be more than a Christmas fling. Maybe this year coming up would be a lot more memorable—for other reasons—than the last. Felicia placed her lips on Gina's once again, the height difference and their nerves no longer a problem. When they reached the top floor, Felicia parted with another sly smile.

"You ready to go down?"

"Yes...yes, I think so."

"Good. My place or yours? You know, when we reach the ground floor."

"Hmm," Gina said. "Surprise me."

With a grin, Felicia pressed all the elevator floors—but the second—and then moved back into a kiss.

A GIFT OF WORDS

by Patricia Penn

*For Summaia, who wanted to experience
Christmas for the first time.*

THE WAREHOUSE WAS SWARMING WITH Fianna. They all brimmed with adrenaline after the fight, scratched and bruised and in just as much need of a healer as the humans they'd saved. Breathing hard, Hekate surveyed the carnage around her. It appeared that she was out of a job for a moment; her partner, Tamoh, was holding his bleeding shoulder, so they wouldn't be allowed to escort the prisoners to headquarters. Some of her colleagues were securing the exits, making sure that none of the human survivors escaped before their memories were wiped— and that none of the humans living in this neighborhood had come to investigate the ruckus. Other Fianna manacled the prisoners and checked the pulses of the enemy demons on the ground. The Fianna were the peacekeeper squad of the Boston demon clans, but these days, *peacekeeping* mostly translated to *attack* and *try not to get killed.*

Hekate threw the dead body closest to her a grimly satisfied look. Across the hall, her friend Cal Iveragh gave her a thumbs-up and smirked as if to say congratulations. Hekate rolled her eyes and huffed. She hadn't missed any of her targets, no; that went without saying.

"All right." The gravelly voice of Balor, their commander, rang through the room. "Turns out two of those bastards escaped through a back door. I want four teams of two out in the streets. Search the area until you find them. Lester and Crooks, you go up to the North End…" He rattled off names, then paused when his eyes fell on Hekate's partner. Tamoh grimaced apologetically through the pain. "Lorca…" Balor addressed Hekate. "You're with Iveragh, check Downtown. After all, I hear you two are inseparable these days."

Hekate glanced sharply at Cal. But no, Balor couldn't know about the two of them. They were among the strongest telepaths in the entire demon community of Boston. It was impossible that they could have given anything away.

Cal looked straight ahead, ostensibly busy tucking her rune stone—her weapon of choice—into the neckline of her sweater.

Very well. Seemed like they'd spent the rest of the night on the job.

∽◌

It hadn't been their first raid during this clan war, not even the first one this week. An informant had tipped them off about a group of vassals of the mutinous clan Dayville setting up camp in an abandoned warehouse down on Hanover Street. They had been luring unsuspecting humans into their lair, torturing them for fun and absorbing their energies to get high. It was disgusting, despicable business, and the reason why

Hekate had sworn allegiance to Cal's clan Iveragh—so they could fight side-by-side.

That was probably what had prompted Balor's comment. Recently, too many had remarked on how much time she and Cal spent together. Hopefully nobody thought of them as anything but a young clan leader and her right-hand woman. Still, being partnered together on Fianna business wasn't exactly a hardship for either of them.

Roaming the streets of Downtown Boston, they soon became certain that the Dayvilles had to have left the area either through a portal or by taking a mundane human cab. Their muscles ached from the fight, and they grew more tired as the night progressed without Balor sending them new orders. Sadly, Cal's status as leader of Iveragh didn't excuse her from following her commander's orders like any soldier. However, for Hekate working with Cal felt like breathing. They moved in synch, and when Cal came close, Hekate could sense her presence pulsating at the edge of her awareness.

Hekate could still clearly remember what Cal had smelled like a week before, the last time they had snuck away together. She could almost feel her skin under her fingers, picture her lean muscular frame beneath her warm winter parka—so deceptively human looking, and yet so powerful. They didn't talk about what they did with each other, though. They acted as if it wouldn't happen again, as it was a mistake—because it *was* a mistake and it *could* never happen again. There were no words among demons for what they were doing with each other, for two women doing those things—not as far as Hekate knew, anyway. It scared her, not knowing what it meant.

Hekate kept her eyes trained on the buildings and side alleys for signs of her prey instead of looking at Cal.

They'd just covered Long Wharf when they paused briefly, cold hands shoved deep in their pockets. Air condensed in front of their faces with every breath as they watched the sun dawn on the horizon. It spread pastels all across the fidgety grey sea, beautiful despite the muted clouds in the sky. Still there was no sign of the Dayvilles. However, their rune stones—Cal's around her neck, Hekate's on her belt—hadn't heated up to herald new orders. Their boss had to have special plans with those Dayvilles to waste this much man power.

The streets started to fill with activity. As the patches of sky between the tall buildings transitioned further from dark to grey, more humans poured outside. At ten o'clock, Hekate noticed how many there really were. Some even bumped into her and stupidly ignored her angry frown. When Hekate was pushed against her, Cal smirked good-naturedly, amused as always when Hekate glared.

By twelve, every traffic light produced endless car lines, and they had to circle around old people with canes, women with strollers, and person after person wrapped in scarves and gloves. Hekate slowly grew suspicious. Even though this was Downtown Boston, it was a work day, and the air was so icy that there would certainly be snow soon. Yet, on their way down the broad Atlantic Street, the crowd became thicker.

They crossed the street and turned a corner, and suddenly, everything was packed with people of all ages and sizes. Cal came to an abrupt halt. Hekate had to fight an instinctual urge to reach for her rune stone when she followed suit.

Cal whistled under her breath.

"Look at that," she said appreciatively. Though her reaction was dignified, her eyes shone like a child's.

Hekate followed her gaze to find that the entire area was covered in light chains. The streets had widened to transform into a pedestrian area—they'd reached Quincy Market. Rich whites and greens and reds and blues flashed around every tree growing along the street. Every lantern, and even parts of the historical market halls farther down the road, was dazzling. The crowd pushed through a funnel of booths and shops that had spilled onto the street for the occasion. Due to her height, Hekate had an excellent vantage point. The vendors wore costumes; elves and reindeers lined up left and right. A Santa stood at the ready to pose for pictures with children, and a Nativity scene with a mix of plastic and real animals was on display not far away. Hekate realized with a start that it was December 24.

"You can't honestly tell me you've never seen this area before when it was decorated," she told Cal in her usual dry tone. "You know the humans put on the light show for about two months each year?"

"Sure," Cal said, although her gaze was still focused on the streets. Hekate didn't believe her for one second. She knew Cal well enough, including her eerie ability to give the correct reply without having heard a word. "Christmas, right? Birth of the religious man."

"You *sound* so convincing, and yet…"

"This is *amazing*," Cal said obliviously. And then, to Hekate's shock, she felt the other woman's fingers wrapping around her hand. "Come on, let's look around."

It was impossible not to follow. Hekate, after all, had always gone blindly wherever Cal led. Since she'd known her, that had been Hekate's deepest flaw and her strongest need. Her hand was cold and so was Cal's, but they immediately started to warm each other.

Hekate feebly told herself that Quincy Market was part of their perimeter, anyway.

As Cal stopped at almost every booth, it was as if the exhaustion of years of war and young leadership fell off her for a moment. Part of Hekate couldn't help but wish that the relief had been caused at least a little by holding Hekate's hand, not just by the humans' Christmas shenanigans. This was Cal as she would have been if the dark times weren't eating away at her. She certainly didn't seem to care that the event looked more like a seized business opportunity than an actual fair. Cal inspected Christmas tree balls—beautiful, delicately crafted things of glass and silver—and Hekate watched, captivated by the way her face softened. Then she asked Hekate questions about the meaning of some ornaments, about tiny wooden angel figurines and golden stars shining like jewelry, though Hekate didn't know much more about them than Cal did.

Raised a child of one of Boston's leading clans, Hekate had never had much cause to care about the humans. She didn't want them to be mistreated—because nobody should be mistreated—but humans were just there. The demons stayed away, keeping their existence hidden, and Hekate had never interacted with them much. She happily wore their clothes, listened to their music, and had recently bought her first computer—the first Intel Pentium, newly released in 1993. But she was just as likely as not to know specific things about their lifestyle.

It was impossible not to be drawn in now, though. There was a shivering girl selling red winter roses. There was a man who artfully fashioned chains out of metal scraps, another who sold used records of Christmas carols. They passed a quartet of teenage boys, who looked Hispanic like her, playing flutes. Begrudgingly Hekate dropped a ten in their hat despite the unsettling brilliant smile the youngest shot her around his mouth piece. Both Cal and the atmosphere all around relaxed Hekate against her will. Telepathic demons were trained to never loosen their psychic shielding, but it was hard to not absorb bits of their joy and holiday spirit—especially Cal's. And not just because she was still holding Hekate's hand.

"Are those supposed to be demons, you think?" asked Cal with a shoulder nudge to point out a pointy-eared band of men with big hats. *Cal*, who was usually loath to admit that there was something she didn't know about the humans she'd sworn to protect, although there were an awful lot of those things.

"Those are elves," Hekate informed her easily. She refrained from pointing out that the humans feared their kind way too much to allow their legends about them to be featured at such a joyous celebration. There was a reason why the demons hid from the humans despite looking the same, and why all the words the humans had for them were negative. To them, *demon* or *succubus* or *vampire* equaled *evil*.

Cal was drawn into a conversation with a man handing out flyers and let go of Hekate. He was wearing antler headgear for some reason, and Hekate knew without looking that his advertisements either had motorcycles or Metallica in them—Cal's human interests weren't particularly sophisticated. Hekate fell into the loose parade rest she preferred while waiting at her usual spot on her Cal's left. The loss of contact left her feeling momentarily bereft until her gaze fell idly upon two kissing women.

It was as if the world froze.

Hekate knew a little more about Christmas than Cal, because she'd visited a few holiday bazaars, and she'd watch a movie or two. She was a demon, after all, not a hermit. However, she wasn't anywhere close to an expert. That became particularly obvious now, because in the demon world, a public display of this kind would have been impossible, and she would have supposed that the same were true for the humans.

As if on cue, somebody somewhere shouted, "Get off the street so the kids don't see, goddammed dykes!" But most of the crowd pushing past seemed to ignore both him and the...the *dykes*. One of the women ignored him entirely. The other gave him the finger. In a street full of demons, all this would have been unthinkable. The sight of two women kissing, in public or not, was unthinkable. Hands would be reaching for rune stones. Challenges would be spoken, the kind that couldn't be taken back. Reputations were guarded with the same determination as the clan houses in wartime.

The women were situated behind a makeshift display table. The one who had ignored the shouting man looked Hekate's age, twenty-three or twenty-four, sporting a cheerful purple Mohawk. As practically dressed as a Fian, almost like a man, the other woman was short and heavyset. She wore her hair in a fierce buzz cut that resembled Hekate's—an uncommon style for female demons and humans alike.

With a pang, Hekate realized that she'd somehow just assumed that she and Cal were alone in the world, and that nobody else did this. She'd thought they were just individual aberrations—freaks.

The kissing women grinned at each other for a moment, then let go, and turned their attention back to their display. Hekate gave Cal a quick look, torn. But Cal was still in deep conversation with the antler man.

Hekate made a decision.

"I'll be over there," she muttered, counting on the fact that Cal wasn't really listening, even though she nodded. She'd not made the Fianna attack squad by missing opportunities.

Her heart was certainly beating as loudly against her chest as if she were in the middle of a fight.

Weaving her way through the crowd, she made her way to the women. She came to a halt in front of a big, handmade banner—*Christmas shelter for homeless LGBT! Donate now!*

The short woman with the buzz cut sauntered up to her, giving her a once-over that normally would have made Hekate even more tense. But then something in the woman's face relaxed as if she'd decided she wouldn't need any armor here. It set Hekate off balance; humans and demons both usually had the opposite reaction to her.

Dykes. That man had called them that. Hekate soaked the word up; knowing she'd never let it go. Where there were words, there was knowledge and acceptance. There was a defense. She abruptly realized how hungry she was for all that. Suddenly, there was a lifeline in sight.

"What are you offering?" she asked, knowing that she sounded clipped and demanding, but the woman didn't seem to mind.

"Not offering," she said amiably. "Collecting. And educating." She pointed meaningfully at a tin can with a slit in the lid, then at the leaflets and flyers laid out around. Although Hekate knew she was missing something here—*LGBT* didn't ring a bell at all—she could see when money was required to gain access, so she searched her pockets for change. The woman looked as if she hadn't expected any different and swiftly moved to the educating part of the transaction.

"Now," she said, "you *might* have heard of the second partner adoption win. That was huge; that was a really big step. And we've got a so-called commission for LGBT students now, also good—let's hope it'll really go somewhere. But ain't every state as safe as Massachusetts, you know? Louisiana might reinstate its sodomy law; it's disgusting. All donations this year are going to Louisiana shelters, to make a point. We're having a Q and A on that whole issue at our Charlestown place after the holiday, couple of us dykes, some guys too. We've invited this human rights lawyer and all."

The woman had pointed at a makeshift leaflet looking as if it originated from a home printer with a broken cartridge. *It's love, not sodomy. Safety is a human right!* Another printout next to it said, *Protect lesbian teens from homophobia!*

Hekate wet her lips, mentally translating. *Lesbian, lesbos, lesbios*, Old Greek, *he or she who is from Lesbos. Homophobia*, also easy for a demon used to the old languages, *fear of that which is the same*. Her face hardened. She understood that one instinctually.

"You should come," the woman said, and Hekate nodded sharply, her hand already wrapped around one of the flyers. "Bring your girlfriend along." She nodded in Cal's direction.

Hekate stiffened.

"Or not," the woman said with a curious expression.

"We're just traveling through," Hekate muttered without making eye contact. And unsure how she should feel about the way the woman's face turned understanding and soft, a change so distinct she could make it out from the corner of her eye. It was as if Hekate had said something completely different, something she didn't even have words for.

"Well, then, I hope you've got a good hotel to stay at," the woman said. And, as if she couldn't stop herself after all, she quickly added, "Listen, it's not... Most places in Boston are all right. If two women take a room together...not like you'll get beaten up or thrown out or anything. Unless you run into some really bad eggs anyway. But it's not like you want to spend the stay getting all the long looks, you know? Here." Her hand vanished in her pocket, rummaging. It reappeared holding an assortment of business cards, and she started industriously skimming through them, picking two or three that she deemed the most fitting. "Here. That's a good place, two blocks or so over, that one's run by a trans guy. And that's us; that's Anna's number right there—that's my girlfriend—and that's the address of our meeting place. Come to one of our meetups sometime. Ask for me. I'm Kerry."

Hekate swallowed dryly. "We're just traveling through," she managed to repeat with a weak voice.

As if she wasn't human at all, but a demon with a disconcerting amount of telepathic skill, Kerry seemed to look right through her. She gave her a strange motherly look that didn't fit somebody that fierce. "Of course you are, that's why I gave you the hotel information just now," she said.

Hekate cleared her throat to say... She wasn't even sure what she wanted to say. But then she suddenly sensed Cal's attention turning toward her, felt her searching the crowd. She muttered a hurried good-bye and turned fast on her heel. The business cards were clutched in her hand so hard that their edges had to be leaving lines on the skin of her palm.

"Oh hey, so there's been news," Cal said as soon as Hekate returned to her side. Hekate didn't slow down. She just kept moving, needing to put as much distance between her and Kerry as quickly as she could. Cal fell into step with her easily, obviously noticing nothing amiss. "Guess who's graced us with an update. We're allowed to go home and everything. Mission's over. We don't even have to report in."

"Right," Hekate said, unable to properly catch her breath.

Cal shrugged. "Achna's team apprehended our two bad boys. In Natick of all places. So much for searching inside the city limits."

"About damn time," Hekate managed, hopefully sounding a little more like herself on this second try. She felt as if she were on high alert, the same way she'd felt when they'd first crashed into that building at the start of tonight's battle.

"Now I say we finish looking at all this fun stuff first," Cal continued. "Sure, we could do with some sleep, but this Christmas thing will be over when we're off the next time, right? Did you know, by the way…" she added blithely as their walk slowed to a more normal pace, leaving her with opportunities to look at displays again. "…that humans give gifts to each other on the morning of the twenty-fifth? That guy just told me. Their children think that somebody throws them into the house through the chimney. So weird."

"You want me to give you a Christmas gift now; is that it?" Hekate replied, her normal dry tone making a reappearance without it being any of her conscious doing.

Cal smirked. "I'll never say no to a present."

"Well, that's a no. I couldn't properly aim it at your head through a chimney."

This time around, they came to a stop simultaneously; miraculously, nobody bumped into them from behind. The crowd was dividing in front of them to stream around a huge Christmas tree, and they paused to take in this sight as well. It wasn't quite as massive as the one at the Boston Common that Hekate had often seen when attending to clan business on Beacon Hill, but it still dwarfed the two of them, as well as all the booths and shops around. More importantly, it was breathtakingly covered in row upon row of white Christmas lights, and it glittered like a giant diamond. It was beautiful, and it tickled Hekate just to look at it.

Dykes, she thought. *Dykes, lesbians, LGBT.* She had the gut impression that those words weren't much better to most of the humans than *demons, succubi, vampires.* But the thing was, when humans thought of demons as the spawn of evil, they were *wrong.* That meant they could be wrong about the other thing as well. Kerry thought they were wrong. There appeared to be whole groups of people who agreed with her. And that meant there was room for *change.*

The humans had *words* for them.

As the clan leader of Iveragh, Cal couldn't open herself up to public disapproval. And who even knew if she would get equally excited about learning those new words, or whether they just would mean that her secret became more real and therefore scarier. And the demon world wouldn't care that there were words, either. "The humans do it," was the last argument that would tease a positive reaction out of the Council of the Twelve.

And, yet, it didn't matter. Cal had taken Hekate's hand today and pulled her along. The humans were celebrating a holiday, handing out gifts, and now, the two of them were standing in front of a tree that looked astonishing in a way that nothing built without demonic energy had any right to look. Surely anything was possible. Hekate suddenly felt exhilarated.

She turned to face Cal, not caring that she ended up a little closer to her face than would have been decent—or rather, not caring that she cared so much about how close they were. She automatically glanced at Cal's lips before looking at her eyes again.

"Let's not go home at all," she heard herself say. "Let's go to a hotel. Everybody at the clan house will think we're still on duty. They won't miss us. Let's get a room."

"What?" Cal said, clearly startled, but she didn't move away. She seemed transfixed by Hekate as well, and that felt so empowering that she physically felt it running through her veins.

"I know a place," she said. "We can get a room together, and nobody will even blink."

It was as if that was all that had been needed to open the floodgates. It was, maybe, as if all that Cal had ever needed to hear was a firm *I want*. This wasn't how things usually went between them, this acknowledgement that there *was* something and that it *would* happen. Hekate knew that she herself had forced these encounters any number of times, although she'd never have admitted it to herself. In the end, though, it always seemed accidental when they found themselves alone with each other.

Now, there was no deniability.

A myriad of emotions moved across Cal's face at her words, caution and defensiveness, fear and confusion, but they cleared away as quickly as they had appeared, leaving behind an expression of raw need. Her gaze burned into Hekate's.

"Okay," she said breathlessly, sounding as if she'd suddenly run out of words. Then she whispered, "Show me."

So Hekate did.

∂ℓᴑ

Cal was a beautiful woman in a unique way, with long brown hair and a lean frame that never fully gave away the secret of how strong she was. She moved with a startling, dangerous grace, and she brimmed with deadly demonic powers. Hekate would never tire of undressing her.

Not that it took particularly long. They were well practiced at getting each other out of their clothes in a hurry. They had never had much time, and they were always fueled by a need to be quick so that nobody would notice something amiss—not to mention the desperate need that overruled clear thought. Now, they did have time. They just chose not to take it. This was planned. It was deliberate, and the fact that they'd be able to do it *again* once they were done just made their desire more urgent.

For the first time in this war and in her life, Hekate felt fueled by a real sense of agenda, a first glimpse at what she really wanted. And it wasn't that she knew exactly what that should be yet, except that it should involve Cal—but it was such a breathtaking start. She pushed Cal onto the bed. She kissed her, deeply, then moved to her throat and collarbone. When her mouth reached Cal's breasts, and her hand finally slid between her legs, Cal moaned helplessly; she looked at Hekate with such a desperate look that said, *I'm so sorry for wanting this so much* and *I'm sorry I need you to take the lead when that should be my job.* Hekate soothed her with a kiss that said it was perfect this way.

Telepaths were taught to keep their walls up, but that was a lot to ask if all you wanted was to crawl into each other and stay there forever. When they climaxed, one quickly followed by the other, their shielding shattered. For a moment, they really were in synch. Everything became a shared *more* and *together* and *need you* and *have you*, and they both knew with certainty that everything would be all right.

༺ஐ༻

They'd been on their feet for over twenty-four hours. When they finally fell asleep huddled against each other, they didn't wake up once through all of the afternoon or the following night. Hekate finally blinked her eyes open at dawn, and she lay there for a moment wondering why such unexpectedly bright light was falling through the window. Then she noticed the soft white snowflakes tumbling down outside, the snow film on the surrounding rooftops reflecting the sun. Right. It was Christmas morning. Somewhere in the back of her mind, she remembered snow was significant to that fact. Hekate couldn't quite recall the exact reason, but it still looked beautiful. It looked peaceful.

Cal was sprawled all across her, her hair spread out over Hekate's breasts and the blanket, her face buried in the crook of Hekate's neck. She felt very warm and incredibly soft. As Hekate took in the novel sensation of waking up so close to each other, Cal started to move, stretching as much as she could without releasing Hekate. She made a contented sound.

Hekate tried not to sigh, forbidding herself to move. The war had made her cynical, after all, and she thought that probably this would be over in a second. Cal would fully wake and give her a shocked look. She would blame yesterday's sleep deprivation or the adrenaline of battle. She'd do her mightiest to act as if this had never happened and be quick to leave the hotel. It was quite possible, after all, that only Hekate felt as if the world had changed. It might still be the same world for Cal, who hadn't seen Kerry kissing her girlfriend on the street. Hekate didn't even know if she should tell her about all that.

Then Cal was moving, apparently trying to find a more comfortable position on the pillow.

Her breath tickled against Hekate's throat.

"I think I like Christmas the best of all the human holidays," she muttered lazily.

Hekate snorted a surprised laugh.

"You don't even know what it celebrates."

"No," Cal agreed, her voice muffled. "But I like the part with the gifts."

Hekate smiled.

∞◇

A bell chimed above the door when Hekate pushed it open. A slow workday lay behind her—most workdays were slow now that the clean-up of the war was finished. Still, it had been a long war, some had thought it wouldn't ever end. So many had died, and entire clans had gone down. So Hekate glowered at the human women at the closest table when they looked up, just out of principle.

The women answered by giving her a cheerful wave.

Her lips twitched after all, at that.

It was 1996. The *LGBT Coalition* took over this Charlestown pub as it did every other Tuesday, and the first couple of members had already trickled in. The guest of honor was probably here already, in the back room, preparing their handouts or whatever they'd brought for their speech. Some activist from the West Coast had been scheduled for tonight, Hekate was reasonably sure.

"Haven't seen you in a while," the bartender said as she handed Hekate a Diet Coke. Anna still sported a proud purple Mohawk, though these days it was streaked with green for flavor. Her presence probably meant that Kerry was around somewhere as well.

Hekate sank on the bar stool, accepted the proffered bottle, and gratefully took a sip.

"I'm hard to keep away," she replied.

It was good to belong.

SNOW, WITH A CHANCE OF LOVE

by B.A. Caldwell

BRITT KELLER LOOKED AROUND HER apartment, which appeared as if a hurricane had blown through it. Couch cushions askew, shelves emptied, papers and books littered the floor. The place was torn apart. Britt raked her fingers through her short brown hair and scanned the room for the hundredth time. She had searched everywhere, in every nook and cranny of her 600-square-foot apartment.

She picked up one of the couch cushions and put it back where it belonged. After plopping down on it, she huffed out a breath. How could it have just disappeared?

A whine came from the corner of her apartment, the only corner untouched by the chaos she had created. George, her dachshund-terrier-mutt, stared back at her from his cozy dog bed.

"Well, you were no help, Georgie. Just sleeping away in your bed, while I did all the heavy lifting."

He perked up his ears, jumped out of his bed, and trotted over to her.

Britt leaned down to give him the requisite scratch behind the ears—George's favorite—when she spotted it.

The missing library book.

In George's bed.

In tatters.

"George Tiberius Keller!" Britt exclaimed.

He stopped in his tracks and adopted a guilty look.

She retrieved what was left of the Multnomah County Public Library's copy of RJ Cruse's newest mystery novel. George had obviously been thorough in his attentions to the book. The cover was riddled with bite marks; one corner was completely chewed off, and many of the pages within were shredded.

Britt shook her head. "Mystery solved, I guess," she murmured.

George whined and rolled over on his back, clearly still angling for some petting.

Sighing, she scratched his belly.

"You know I can't stay mad at you, Georgie. I guess we'll call this your early Christmas present since now I'll have to pay to replace this." She shook her head. "I didn't even get to find out how it ends."

It took an hour to straighten up her apartment. This was definitely not how she had planned to spend the first Saturday of her winter break. Her plan had been to curl up with the last hundred pages of her book and a cup of tea. She deserved it. The past two weeks had been a flurry of final exams and papers and presentations. She was only one semester away from finishing her graduate degree in chemistry, and this term had been her toughest yet. She had dutifully focused on her schoolwork instead of delving back into her book, though she was dying to see how it ended. Even when she thought she would pull her hair out from the stress of studying for her organic chemistry final, she had not even touched the novel.

The ruined book sat on her kitchen counter for the rest of the day. Britt felt guilt every time she passed it. Her mind concocted reasons not to go into the library to explain about the book. She dreaded the idea of having to talk to *her*.

By midafternoon, she knew she could put it off no longer. She would have to walk the two blocks to the library branch and fess up. She would have to talk to Dream Librarian, as Britt mentally referred to her—the librarian who flustered her and made her heartbeat quicken every time she visited the library.

She would put off the trip indefinitely, but the local weather forecasters were predicting a big snowstorm. At first she thought they were probably just making a big deal out of a few possible snowflakes, but now all signs pointed to actual snowing, sometime today. Britt, like most other Portlanders, had a love/hate relationship with winter weather. While the usual forecast called for rain, rain, and more rain, the occasional snow or ice could really throw the city into a panic.

She wanted to stock up on some fun books and DVDs from the library before the snow arrived, so Britt bundled up in a knit cap, a raincoat, and a scarf and gathered the book remains and her wallet.

"I'll be back in a little bit, Georgie," she called as she exited her apartment. "If you get hungry, there's an organic chemistry textbook by the couch that I never want to see again."

∾⚬〇

It was a short walk to the library, and the predicted snowflakes were already coming down. While Portland's skies were their usual gray, the wind was crisp and cold, even for December. Britt wrapped her scarf more securely to keep out the chill and thought about how she should handle the book situation.

Option 1: Shove the ruined book into the book drop with an apology letter attached to it.

Option 2: Tell the librarian a harrowing tale about how she had lost the book while on a jungle safari. With wild, book-stealing orangutans! Or while saving some sick people in a remote and dangerous land…somewhere. Clearly, this would need more fleshing-out.

Or option 3: Don't take the book back and never explain what happened to it. Never use the library again. Move to a new city, and change name.

Britt could almost hear Grandma Evelyn tsk-tsk-ing at her. *Honesty is the best policy, Britt!*

Humiliation is the best policy in this case, thought Britt. She sighed as she reached the entrance to the library and went in.

In contrast to the cold dreariness outside, the library was warm and cheerful. Colorful displays of picture books adorned the children's section to the right of the entrance. The walls were painted a sunny yellow, and flyers on the community bulletin board advertised things such as "Computers 101 for senior citizens" and "Book Babies Storytime."

Britt decided to pick out her blizzard entertainment first. She grabbed a few more mystery novels and a couple of holiday movies on DVD. Best to be safe in case of a prolonged snowy spell. She glanced outside, where the snow was coming down significantly faster than when she had walked in. No more delaying this.

She walked up to the circulation desk and was relieved— and, truth be told, maybe a bit disappointed—that *she* wasn't there. Perhaps she wasn't working today. Perhaps Britt would be spared having to humiliate herself in front of the most beautiful woman she'd ever seen.

No. Such. Luck.

Just as Britt arrived at the desk and was reaching into her messenger bag to pull out the book, Dream Librarian came out of the staff office and headed directly toward her.

Britt froze, staring at her. "Anne M." read the nametag attached to the librarian's cardigan. Somehow this woman with the blonde curls down her back and large blue eyes made even a simple cardigan look hot.

"Hi there, how can I help you?" Anne the Dream Librarian asked.

Britt the Speechless said nothing, making Anne give her a curious look.

Option 3! Get out now! Britt's brain was yelling.

The librarian still gazed at her, cleared her throat, and tried again after an awkward pause. "It's Ms. Keller, right? What brings you in today?"

Britt forced herself to unfreeze and take a breath. *Get it together, Keller! It's not like you haven't seen beautiful women before, and specifically this beautiful woman, pretty much every time you've visited the library branch in the past few months.*

"My dog," were the words that finally emerged from Britt's mouth.

"Your...dog?" asked Anne, her brow crinkling.

"Yes, my dog." The tightness in Britt's throat eased up a little. "His name is George. After George Washington, because he swallowed a dollar bill the first day I brought him home from the humane society."

Anne nodded understandingly, as if people came into the library every day to talk to her about their dogs.

"This is a picture of him." Britt pulled out her smartphone instead of the damaged book and showed her a photo that she had snapped of George last Halloween.

The corner of Anne's mouth hitched up. "Is he wearing a Star Trek uniform?" Amusement colored the librarian's voice.

A warm glow filled Britt inside for having made her smile.

"Yes, George is a *Star Trek* fan from way back," Britt said. "Sci-fi in general, actually. Last year he dressed up as *Dr. Who*."

At that, Anne let out a soft chuckle.

"So…you have an adorable dog who loves sci-fi. I admire his taste." Anne smiled, and Britt admired the dimple that appeared. "Does that mean you're looking for books about dogs? Or the latest season of *Dr. Who*?"

Britt enjoyed making Anne smile, but it was time to come clean. "Actually, he may turn out to be more of a mystery lover than sci-fi fan. I guess they taste better." Sheepishly, she pulled the tattered copy of *A Hot Night for Murder* out of her bag. Several pages fell out, landing in front of Anne on the desk.

"Oh, I see." Anne picked up the pages full of bite marks. Her expression went from bemused to concerned.

Britt wished she could do something to bring back the grin.

"I'm so sorry, I didn't realize I left it sitting where he could get it. I'll pay for a replacement."

"I appreciate that you brought this in and for being honest," Anne said. "You would be surprised by how many people make up fantastical stories or just move away without returning items. I'll go ahead and give this to our processing department, and they'll add the fine to your account."

The relief must have been evident on Britt's face, because Anne smiled reassuringly.

"I promise this is not the first bibliocide by canine I've seen in my five years as a librarian. Just remind George that book eating is beneath an officer of Starfleet."

Britt laughed. "Thank you for being so cool about it. I thought maybe I would lose library privileges for life or something."

"Contrary to the popular stereotype, we librarians aren't just here to glare at you while saying 'shhh.'" Anne was smiling again, and Britt felt as if she could gaze at that face all day and never get tired of it.

"I'm glad." Britt knew she probably had a goofy grin on her face, but she couldn't help it. "I'll keep these on the highest shelf." She indicated her stack of books and DVDs.

"Glad to hear it," Anne replied. "You must be doing what everyone else today has been doing, getting ready for the snowpocalypse."

"Of course, gotta be prepared. You never know how long you'll be shut in, in this town." Britt handed over her stack for Anne to scan.

"Well, as a recent transplant from California, I'll have to take your word for it." Anne scanned the items and handed them back. "I've never even seen snow before today."

"You're kidding!" Britt exclaimed.

"It's true. I love Portland, and I'm glad I moved here, but it's been a lot of adjustment. First time using public transit, first time owning a bike as an adult, and now, first snow." She pressed her hand to her lips as if she had said too much, and her cheeks turned a delightful pink.

"Well, stay safe, Anne." Britt was loath to end the conversation, but she still needed to get to the grocery store before snow started shutting down everything in the city. From the looks of the flakes coming down and the fact that it appeared to be sticking, it wouldn't take long to send Portland and its residents into a full-blown panic.

"Thanks, you too, Ms. Keller," Anne said.

Britt turned back before she headed out into the cold. "It's Britt." She smiled and walked out before she could say anything foolish. *I'll keep you warm* came to mind.

It took another hour and a half for Britt to take the bus up to New Seasons Market to pick up a few snow-day provisions. The store was packed with people who had the same idea; though by the looks of it, Portlanders' idea of essential provisions included a one-to-one ratio of beer to food.

On her bus ride back to her apartment, she checked the weather forecast on her phone. Up to twelve inches of snow predicted for the night, with more tomorrow. In some places that would be considered a light dusting. In Portland, it meant roads, transit, and businesses could be shut down. The bus she was on already had its snow chains on.

When she disembarked a block from her apartment, it was dark and the library's lights were out. She started walking toward her building, but a flicker of red caught her eye.

Across the street, Anne was standing at a bus stop in a coat that was clearly not meant for snow and a thin red scarf flapping in the wind. She noticed Britt staring from across the street and she gave a small wave.

Britt waved back and then hesitated. She wanted to offer Anne a coat or warmer scarf or something but didn't want to come across as pushy or creepy, so she made herself turn toward her own building. *I'm sure her bus will be here any minute.*

When she entered her second-floor apartment, she was greeted by exactly three happy barks from George.

"Hi, Georgie." Britt absently scratched behind his ears. She walked into her small but cozy kitchen and began emptying her bag. After putting the groceries away and stacking her library items on top of the fridge, where they were safe, she peeked out the window to see if the bus had come by yet.

It hadn't. It was getting darker, the snow was still falling, and Britt could see that Anne was shivering from all the way across the street. There were hardly any cars on the road at all now, let alone buses.

Mind made up, Britt grabbed her coat, scarf, and hat, and then an extra coat and George's leash. "Come on, Sir George, let's go for a little walk."

As soon as they exited and George set a paw on the snow, he made his feelings about that weird cold stuff clear. He immediately turned around and began tugging the leash back toward the safety of their home.

Ignoring him, Britt crossed the road with reluctant dog in tow.

Anne's head came up. She looked wary for a moment before seeming to recognize her.

"Hi, Ms. Kell—um, Britt," she said, teeth chattering.

"How long have you been waiting for your bus?" Britt asked.

"Oh, about thirty minutes or so," Anne replied and sniffed.

"I brought you this coat, because yours looks like it isn't made to handle more than a slight autumn breeze." Britt held out the coat.

"Oh, I couldn't possibly take your coat—"

"How far is your commute?" Britt cut in, still holding out the coat.

"Beaverton," said Anne with a sigh.

"Beaverton? That's at least an hour ride, plus whatever you have to walk from your stop there. You're going to need this coat. Please."

"Well, if you're sure." Anne took the coat and put it on. They were about the same size, but Britt's bulky coat seemed to engulf her. "Thank you, this is much better already. I'll bring it to the library with me tomorrow if you want to come get it back."

Britt hesitated again. This whole thing was wrong. It was freezing outside, dark, and there was no bus in sight. Then she noticed Anne's feet.

"What are those?" She stared at the ballet flats. "I thought librarians were all about sensible shoes! Your feet must be frozen."

"I told you that those librarian stereotypes weren't true." Anne gave a half laugh that came out more like a gasp between shivers.

"Listen, I think you should come with me. I know you don't know me from the next guy, but I promise I'm a normal person, and I live just across the street. I can give you the phone numbers for at least twenty people who will vouch for my normalcy."

"Oh no, I couldn't do that," Anne said. "I'm sure my bus will be here any minute."

"I don't think your bus is coming. I have a feeling they've probably already stopped running. A taxi would be hours. There's no way you'll get across the river and all the way to the suburbs in this weather. Trust me." She looked at Anne imploringly.

Anne looked conflicted. Clearly very cold, but not trusting Britt.

A whine interrupted their conversation. Anne bent down and held out her hand. "This must be the famous George."

George came over and made it clear that all petting would be welcome. After a moment though, he whined again and returned to staring at their apartment across the street.

"I promise you'll be safe with me, and I promise George will be on his best behavior," Britt said. "I couldn't live with myself if you stood out here and froze to death. My apartment is small, but it's warm and has a view of this side of the street so you can see if any buses come by. Please?"

Anne nodded slowly. "Okay, if you really don't mind. I will come up and get warm for little bit. Just until the buses start running again."

"Absolutely." Britt nodded, and the three of them headed for her apartment.

∽◌

"So why did you decide to move to Portland?" Britt asked once they were both warm and dry and sitting on opposite ends of her couch, with George curled up between them, quietly snoring.

"Actually, it was my girlfriend's idea," Anne said.

Britt tried not to cough up the tea she had just been about to swallow.

"She got a job up here, and the cost of living was lower, and I impulsively said yes even though I had never been here before."

"And how do you like it?" Britt asked.

"I love it. It really suits me, and I love the library branch where I work." Anne's smile was genuine as she took a sip from her mug of Earl Gray.

"Um, do you need to, uh, call your girlfriend...?" Britt asked. She hadn't thought about the fact that there might be someone waiting at home for this lovely woman, and she could have kicked herself for making assumptions.

"No, we broke up about three months after moving here. It turns out that an ex-girlfriend of hers was more of the reason she wanted to move up here than the job."

"Ouch. That must have been awful. But you're still here, and I'm sure Portland is the better for it."

Anne was quiet for a minute, staring into her steaming mug. "I can see myself making Portland my home for quite a while. Maybe even forever." She looked into Britt's eyes. "Obviously, I need to update my wardrobe with some more appropriate winter wear." She chuckled.

Britt took in Anne, who was wearing a pair of Britt's wooly socks with her legs tucked beneath her. She didn't know the last time she had felt so comfortable just sitting with a woman. They sat in companionable silence for a bit, each drinking her tea.

"I like your Christmas decorations." Anne indicated the three glass bulbs and a strand of multicolored Christmas lights that Britt had added to one of her houseplants. There were also two stockings hanging by the TV set: one for Britt and a smaller one for George.

"You haven't even seen the full effect yet." Britt hopped up from the couch and turned on the TV. She flipped through options until she came to the streaming video she wanted. When she pressed play, a crackling log in a fireplace appeared.

Anne laughed. "So classy!" She winked at Britt.

Warmth flood Britt's body.

"I love your apartment." Anne looked at the cluttered bookcases and the family photos hanging on the wall. "It's so homey. I keep meaning to do some decorating in my apartment, but it looks pretty impersonal right now. I didn't even decorate for the holidays. My mom and I used to decorate every surface of our house with every Christmas knickknack known to man."

"Thanks," Britt replied. "I've lived here for about three years. I like it. Nice neighbors. Not too far to school and the store. Close to the library." She flashed a grin at Anne.

Anne's phone made a dinging noise, and she pulled it out of her purse.

"Oh no. Tri-Met shut down the buses. The trains are severely delayed. Crap."

"You can stay here, you know. You can stay the night. I'll sleep on the couch, and you can have the bed." At Anne's head shaking, Britt continued. "If you're worried about it, I promise that George and I will both be on our best behavior."

"I couldn't impose like that," Anne said.

"You're not imposing, and like it or not, I think you're stuck here, at least until tomorrow. Now, what do you like to eat for dinner?"

❧

Two hours later, a frozen pizza had been cooked and consumed, a salad tossed together and eaten, and a bottle of wine finished off, and all the while Anne and Britt continued to talk about their families, their favorite places in Oregon, crazy George stories, and of course, favorite books.

"Wait, you didn't even get to finish that book that George chewed up?" Anne laughed. "That's so terrible!"

"I know, and I really wanted to find out whodunit." Britt couldn't help laughing herself. "I got about seventy-five percent through the book. I was seventy-five percent invested in that story before George got his teeth on it. I guess I'll never know." She sighed dramatically.

Anne was giggling at Britt's antics now. "I wish I had read it so I could tell you how it ends."

"But now a serious question." Britt adopted her best serious interrogation face. "What is your favorite Christmas movie?"

Anne appeared to give it some very serious thought. "There is only one movie that can claim that title: *National Lampoon's Christmas Vacation*."

"We might be soul mates, because that is also mine," Britt said.

Anne gave her an odd look but also smiled.

"Shall we watch it?"

Halfway through the movie, the wine caught up with Britt, and she nodded off. When she woke, the movie credits were playing and Anne's hand was on her shoulder. Her face was also very close, and the lights from the Christmas "tree" cast a soft light against her cheeks. Was she dreaming?

"Hey," Anne said softly. "You fell asleep, so George and I had to finish the movie without you."

Britt came a little more awake. "Oops, I guess I was more tired than I thought. Let me show you where you can sleep for the night."

"I will take the couch." Anne shook her head when Britt started to protest. "I insist. You've opened your home to me, let me eat your food and drink your wine. I will be perfectly happy sleeping on the couch. Besides, you're taller than me and you'd be more uncomfortable sleeping here."

Britt decided to give in. After giving Anne some sheets and blankets, as well as an extra toothbrush, she bade her goodnight and went into her room. George, she noticed, preferred to stay in the living room with Anne. Britt wished she could too.

∾⌒◌

Britt tossed and turned that night. It was hard to relax when the woman of your dreams was sleeping separately, approximately twenty-five feet away in a different room. She had spent a good amount of time trying to convince herself to not fall head over heels for Anne, but it was clearly too late for her brain to reason with her heart.

When they had first met at the library, Britt had a feeling that she and Anne had a connection. She convinced herself that it was all in her head and both dreaded and looked forward to seeing her whenever she was in the library.

Where did they go from here? Today Anne would go back to her own place in Beaverton, and the next time they met, it would be as librarian and patron. The thought depressed Britt. She didn't want to lose the most natural and exciting connection she'd ever made with a woman before.

Pulling herself out of bed in the morning, she glanced out the window. Maybe Anne wouldn't be leaving so soon after all.

She opened the door to the living room and saw Anne was already up, reading one of Britt's books.

"Good morning," Britt said. "Have you looked out the window?"

"Good morning yourself." Anne smiled warmly. "I have. I believe the term Winter Wonderland applies here. I can hardly see the parked cars."

"I don't know if you'll have any more luck getting across town today than yesterday. I just want you to know that you are welcome to stay as long as you want. George and I love having you here."

Anne looked at her for a moment, the gaze of her blue eyes piercing Britt. "I really appreciate that. You've been very generous. As has George. He even let me have almost half of the couch."

They took turns taking showers and made egg-and-cheese scrambles for breakfast. Afterward, they worked together to clean up their meal. Anne's presence in her apartment felt natural and easy.

"What shall we do today?" Britt asked. "More Christmas movies? George could perform his full repertoire of tricks."

"Actually," Anne began, her cheeks turning pink, "I've never been in snow before last night, and I didn't really get a chance to play in it. Do you think we could do that?"

Britt grinned. "Absolutely! I would love to do that. I'll loan you some boots and a coat so you're adequately prepared for snow fun."

"It's a date," Anne said, and they both laughed.

❧

The neighborhood was full of kids taking advantage of the rare weather, and Britt and Anne joined in the fun. Drifts at least a foot deep had accumulated in front yards and on sidewalks, and no cars were on the road. It was a free for all. Britt showed Anne how to make snow angels. Anne discovered that the snow was exactly the right kind for making snowballs and managed to get a few good ones in before Britt retaliated.

When they could no longer feel their fingers, they headed back up to Britt's apartment, breathless and laughing. Anne's cheeks were rosy from the cold and her hair wet from melting snow.

Britt helped her unwrap her snow-crusted scarf. She reached up to wipe some snow from Anne's cheek, and a jolt of electricity ran through her.

Anne looked at her with intensity. Had she felt it too?

"We should probably take these wet things off," Anne said softly.

All Britt could manage was a nod.

Anne reached up and unwrapped Britt's scarf, her fingers grazing Britt's neck in the process.

Tingles went through Britt where Anne touched her skin, and she found herself wishing Anne would take off more than just her scarf.

She realized that Anne's hand was still on her neck, just below her ear, and that Anne was staring at her mouth with hungry eyes.

"Anne—"

Anne closed the space between them, and her lips were on Britt's. She cupped Britt's face with both hands as she kissed her passionately.

Joy and electricity pulsed through her entire body. She kissed Anne back with abandon. Anne's lips were soft and warm, and Britt couldn't get enough of them. She pushed the coat off of Anne's shoulders and onto the floor, and Anne followed suit by removing Britt's bulky coat. This allowed them to get even closer, in each other's arms now.

Anne nibbled and sucked at Britt's lips, and Britt felt as if she had never really kissed anyone until this moment. Sure, there had been girls she'd dated and kissed, but not like this.

Britt had her hands on Anne's hips, gripping them, pulling her closer. She slid one hand up to Anne's stomach.

Anne gave a little yelp.

"Your hands are like ice! We should probably keep taking off the snowy clothes so we don't get hypothermia."

"I suppose you're right." Britt's voice came out husky and low.

Many minutes later they finally managed to get all of their dripping outerwear off and hang it in the bathroom to dry.

More than anything, Britt wanted to continue where they had left off, but she was also cognizant of the fact that Anne did not really have the choice to leave or go home if she felt uncomfortable with how far they went. So Britt suggested watching a movie instead.

For the rest of the day, they alternated between watching movies, talking, playing cards, and cooking. And all the while, Anne would lean over and touch her back or give her hungry looks. It was enough to drive a saint mad.

By dinnertime, Britt knew they'd have to do something to keep her mind—and hands—off Anne for a while.

"We should make something," she said. "Something Christmassy."

Anne's eyes lit up. "Did I tell you that I used to fill in for the children's librarian at my library in California? So I know a whole bunch of fun crafts. Do you have any popsicle sticks?"

"Fresh out of popsicle sticks," was Britt's smart-ass reply.

"Glitter?"

"Also out."

"Pipe cleaners?"

"Nope?"

"Googly eyes?"

"I only have googly eyes for you," Britt replied.

She was rewarded with a cheeky grin and a giggle from Anne.

"Egg carton?"

"Bingo, I do have an egg carton."

"Okay," said Anne. "I can work with this."

Martha Stewart wouldn't be calling them for advice anytime soon, but they had a ball creating makeshift garlands, ornaments, and even an advent calendar that involved a shoe box and mini bottles of alcohol. By the end, Britt's apartment looked as if it had been decorated for Christmas by a couple of drunk elves, but Britt loved it.

She couldn't remember the last time she had felt quite so carefree. Anne's hesitancy and shyness seemed to have dropped away completely.

They agreed that the best thing for Anne to do would be to spend another night. Britt loaned her some pajamas and reluctantly left her on the couch again. She did her best to avoid imagining how wonderful it would be to have Anne sleep wrapped up with her in the bed. She knew it would be heavenly but refused to even consider crossing that line. She didn't want Anne to think even for a second that her invitation hinged on whether she would sleep with Britt or not.

"Good night and sweet dreams, Britt," Anne said as they parted ways for the night and embraced her.

At first startled, Britt hugged her back, enjoying the softness of her body and the scent of glue and soap and Anne.

"Good night to you, Dream Librarian," whispered Britt.

∾◌

The sound of a snowplow woke Britt the next morning. Snowplow! That meant the roads were being cleared for cars—and buses. She heard Anne moving around in the rest of the apartment. Britt left her bedroom and found Anne already dressed in her own clothes and looking out the window at the snowplow.

"The roads are clear!" The delight was evident in Anne's voice, and Britt tried to smile in return. The past two days had been almost magical, and she hated to see them end.

"Yeah, I guess you'll be wanting to head home soon once the buses start running again." Britt's word came out more formal than she meant them to.

A wrinkle of confusion formed on Anne's face.

"Of course," Anne replied. "I'm sure you'll be glad to have me out of your hair."

"I—we, that is, Georgie and me have enjoyed having you here." Britt knew the fantasy had to end, but it was still hard to let go.

"I enjoyed being here. More than I can say, Britt."

"Maybe we'll drop by the library later this week, say hi," Britt said.

"I hope you do!" Anne smiled. "But don't forget that we're closed on Wednesday and Thursday for Christmas Eve and Christmas."

Britt just nodded.

Anne looked as if she wanted to say more, but remained silent.

After a quick breakfast of oatmeal and sausage and a check of the transit website, Anne was ready to head home. Britt insisted on walking her to the bus stop and loaning her the coat again. The sun was bright, the sky clear. Snow piled up on the side of the roads from the snowplow, but it did not take long for Anne's bus to arrive.

"Thank you again," Anne said as she gave Britt a quick hug. She looked into her eyes for a moment and then stepped onto the bus.

Britt watched the bus pull away, carrying her heart with it.

The rest of the day was decidedly anticlimactic for Britt. She took George out to play in the snow (he was definitely not as good at snow angels as Anne). She cleaned up her apartment (which now felt strangely empty). She wrapped her last few gifts for her parents and sister and then tried to read one of her other library books but found herself distracted. Her thoughts kept returning to Anne and the magical thirty-six hours they'd spent together.

How could one person make such an impact on her? She had dated women in the past, but she was always happy to retreat back to her own space after going on a date with them. She didn't crave their company the way she was craving for Anne right now.

She thought Anne felt the same connection, but what if she was wrong? Maybe she had just been caught up in the moment when she had kissed Britt. Maybe it didn't mean anything to her.

Britt sighed. Her thoughts were just going in circles now, and she needed a distraction. She tried the book again. Then threw it down in disgust after about twenty minutes of reading the same page over and over.

She decided to go out for a walk. The snow had melted enough that the streets were passable, and business as usual seemed to have resumed.

While she was walking down the street, glancing in shop windows, Britt came across a gorgeous wool hat and glove set in blue and white. Exactly what a former Californian might need for an Oregon winter. She walked into the store and bought them.

The next day passed in much the same way for Britt. She felt Anne's absence and wished she had at least thought to exchange phone numbers with her. It was two days until Christmas, and her mother called in the afternoon to remind her that Britt was on cookie duty.

"What's the matter, Britt? You sound like you're feeling down or something." There was concern in her mom's voice.

"Oh nothing, Mom," Britt answered. "It's just…this girl. I'm just pining a little bit right at this moment."

"Ahhh. A girl. Is there anything your dad and I can do?"

Britt smiled. "No, but thanks for the offer. I'll see you on Christmas, cookies in hand."

"Okay, hon, you call me if you want to talk more about it, okay?"

"Thanks, Mom. I love you."

ॐ

Britt was elbow-deep in cookie dough the next day when her apartment's intercom buzzed. Every available surface of her tiny kitchen was covered in ingredients and racks of cooling cookies.

"Yikes, hold on!" she yelled, as if the person buzzing her doorbell could hear her two stories up. She finally found her kitchen towel and managed to clean one hand off enough to press the intercom button.

"Yes? Who is it?"

There was a pause. And then, "Britt? It's me, Anne."

Surprise and elation rushed through Britt as she pressed the button to unlock the front door.

"Come on up!"

In the fifteen seconds Britt had before Anne would arrive at her door, she washed the cookie dough off of her hands and dried them on a fresh towel.

A knock sounded at her apartment door.

She opened it to find Anne standing in front of her, wearing her coat, a shy smile on her face.

"Hi," Britt said simply.

"Hi," Anne replied. "I thought I would take a chance that you would be home. Ooh, what is that? It smells delicious."

"My cookies! Come in, one sec." Britt raced back into the kitchen to pull the cookies out of the oven.

"Wow, you've been busy!" Anne had followed Britt into the kitchen and was now regarding the fruits of her labors.

"I'm the designated cookie-bringer to Christmas dinner at my parents' house tomorrow," Britt said. "Would you like to try one? I have peanut butter, sugar cookies, and just plain old chocolate." Without waiting for an answer, she held up a sugar cookie to Anne.

Instead of taking it from her, Anne leaned over and took a bite of the cookie in Britt's hand. She made a soft groan, and Britt's mouth went dry, her gaze immediately drawn to Anne's full lips.

"Those are delicious," Anne said. "I had no idea you were such a talented baker."

"I'm so glad you're here," Britt blurted out.

A wide grin appeared on Anne's face.

"I missed you. I know we haven't known each other long—"

"I know what you mean," cut in Britt, nodding. "I missed you too." She found herself moving closer to Anne. They were mere inches apart, and the space between them seemed electrically charged.

Anne was gazing back at her, studying Britt's face with hungry intensity. She had moved closer too.

"I just wanted," Anne began, then stopped. "I was hoping…"

"Yes," Britt replied.

"Can I—?" Anne was gazing at Britt's lips now.

"Yes," Britt said with relief and enthusiasm. "Yes, please."

Anne closed the remaining space between them and put her hands on either side of Britt's face. "Kiss me?"

"Yes," breathed Britt before claiming Anne's lips. They were just as warm and soft as she remembered. She held Anne close as they kissed. This kiss made their first kiss seem like an innocent peck. Anne panted as the kiss intensified.

Britt let out a low groan. She captured Anne's lower lip between her teeth and gently nibbled on it. The sound of Anne's gasp shot straight through Britt's bloodstream to pulse at every nerve ending in her body.

"Britt." Anne moaned. "I love kissing you, so much." Her hands were in Britt's hair now, and the gentle tugging felt so good.

They continued kissing for what seemed like hours, their bodies as close as possible, and their hands exploring the contours of each other's bodies.

When they finally came up for air, they pressed their foreheads together. Britt was shaken, and mussed, and aroused and amazed. How could one woman cause so many feelings in her at once?

"I could do this all day," she said, "but I will be in trouble if I don't deliver on my cookie promise."

Anne smiled. "Of course! Can I help you?"

"I would love that." Britt got in one last good kiss, which turned into another five-minute-long make-out session in the kitchen.

They spent the rest of the afternoon mixing up cookie batter and kissing, and baking cookies and kissing. And decorating cookies and kissing. By evening, they were tired, more than a little stuffed from cookie tasting, and both still reveling at being close and their new-found intimacy.

"I actually came over to give you something," Anne said after they'd put the last cookie in its festive Christmas tin. She went back into the living room, where she had left her bag, and pulled out a wrapped Christmas present.

"That reminds me. I have something for you too." Britt retrieved the hat and gloves that she had inexpertly wrapped and handed them to Anne. "You go first."

"You didn't have to get me anything" Anne opened up her gift and laughed. She immediately put her new hat on her head. Just as Britt had imagined, it looked adorable and matched Anne's blue eyes.

"It's perfect," said Anne. "And now I will be somewhat more prepared for when the next snowstorm hits."

"I don't know if we'll see another one like that," Britt said.

"Well, if we do, I hope that I can spend it with you again." Anne gave her a warm smile. "Go on, open yours."

Britt took the gift that Anne handed her and ripped the festive paper open. It was a brand-new copy of the RJ Cruse novel that George had destroyed.

She laughed and gave Anne a swift embrace and kiss.

"Thank you! I'm so glad I'll finally know how the story ends."

Anne kissed her in return, this time soft and lingering.

"I have a feeling," she said quietly in Britt's ear, "that this story is going to have a happy ending."

CROSSROADS

by Ruth F. Simon

I WAS DOUBLE-CHECKING THE FORMULAS on my
spreadsheet, trying to find the error, when my cell phone rang.
I glanced at the display out of habit, but didn't plan to answer.
The greenhouse was closed, and I had vowed not to answer the
business phone.

But my brother's name and number showed on the display.
I let out a long-suffering sigh. Thanksgiving, and my disastrous
coming-out announcement at dinner, was three weeks behind
me. Since then, Stephen was the only family member to call
me. My fraternal twin was genuinely a good guy, but I wasn't
in the mood for family drama. I had enough accounting drama
already.

So, I ignored my phone, but Stephen called again. The
third call made me decide I'd better answer; he was never that
insistent without a good reason.

"Hey, Steve."

"You know I hate when you screen my calls, B." I hated
when he called me only by my first initial, and he knew that.

"Yeah, yeah. What do you need?"

"My, aren't you grumpy tonight? Someone swipe a rare potted plant?"

I leaned back and took off my glasses to rub my eyes. "No, I'm battling with numbers. My spreadsheet formulas went screwy, and I need to make a quarterly tax payment this week."

He sucked a breath through his teeth, and it made an odd whistling sound. I knew that sound. Stephen always made it before announcing earth-shattering news. I wondered if it was good or bad news this time and grabbed the edge of my desk. "Okay, Steve: spill."

"It doesn't sound like this is a good time…" Steve was an actor, with a great voice. He made extra money reading audiobooks and doing other voice work. But his childhood stutter returned whenever he was stressed, and that simple sentence gave him fits. This was really bad.

"Little bro, everything you've done and said tells me there won't ever be a good time. Just say it."

He sucked in another whistling breath. "Did you notice Dad looking… frail… at Thanksgiving?"

My mind recalled my dad standing over my chair at the Thanksgiving table, thundering that I had to leave his house immediately. That he risked losing his congregation if they learned he had a dyke for a daughter. That I was to get out and not return until my heart and mind were right with our Lord, Jesus Christ.

"No, I didn't notice him 'looking frail.' He seemed as full of fire and energy as always. He had his tent-revival voice going strong when I walked out the door."

"He wasn't full of energy after you left." Fatigue filled Stephen's voice. I could picture the way he ran a hand along the back of his head, brushing the hair the wrong way, when he was upset. "He sort of... collapsed when the door closed behind you. Mom and I caught him and got him to the couch."

"Why didn't you tell me this sooner?"

"I thought it was just stress, you know?" Steve's voice was apologetic. "Plus, I figured you were upset enough. No reason to feel guilty that he got so worked up. I guess I... thought it was his own fault for freaking out like that."

"So, what changed?" I grabbed my stress ball and gave it a squeeze. Steve telling me this now meant something else had happened, something worse.

"He... Mom said he didn't seem to regain his energy after Thanksgiving. She just thought it was... guilt and mourning. You've always been Dad's favorite, Brandy. She thought he was just..."

"Blaming himself for my being gay. For raising a tomboy who turned out lesbian." I thought about that, and I had to chuckle a bit. Dad had taken me fishing when I was a kid, and we'd played catch with a football or our baseball gloves a lot. Stephen had always preferred spending time with Mom in the kitchen; he was now an accomplished amateur chef.

Dad used to say Mom would turn Steve "funny" if she taught him to cook, but he didn't seem to share that concern about our time together. Now, Steve has a lovely wife who is expecting my first nephew. And I'm the gay family member with a degree in horticulture, managing a greenhouse. It's a weird world.

"Yeah. Well, Dad collapsed in his office three days ago while writing a sermon."

"What?" My mind couldn't grasp the idea. "That's not possible."

"The head deacon, Mr. Sanders?" Stephen's words brought the image of a smiling, grandfatherly man to mind. "He found

Dad and called for the paramedics. Dad was admitted for tests." Stephen's voice grew muffled.

I knew he was rubbing his face this time, trying to figure out how to tell me the rest. "Just spit it out, Steve." I tried to keep my voice calm, but I'm sure he heard the quaver in it; it's a twin thing.

"He... Brandy, it's cancer."

"Oh my God."

"I know." We sat in silence, and I felt a fleeting rush of relief that it had been Steve who had made this call. If Mom or our younger sister Stacy had called, I would have felt as if I had to say something comforting right now.

But it was Stephen on the line, and he wasn't expecting me to be the eldest child with all the answers and a plan to manage whatever the crisis was. He was just letting me get my head around the idea that our father was ill. Sometimes, I thought he should have been the firstborn. He had the right temperament for it.

"Do they know...? What stage is it?" I didn't want to know, but I did. The words came off my tongue more smoothly than I had expected, as if I asked this question all the time. I actually hoped he wouldn't be offended by my businesslike tone.

"Not yet. They need more tests for that." He was quiet for a long moment. "She's... Mom isn't doing well. In some ways, I think she's in denial. She acts like Dad: she fusses at him to get feeling better and get out of bed, so they can go home—as if he has the ability to leave the hospital whenever he wants."

My mom is a small-statured and meek woman, completely dependent on my father for everything. Anytime Dad gets a cold, she flutters around the house, picking up objects and studying them as though they hold some mystical knowledge she needs. Then, she sighs in frustration, puts the item down, and wanders around the house until some other item catches her eye and she repeats the process. I imagined her communing with the TV remote in Dad's hospital room and stifled a sound that was partly a sob and partly a laugh. "Christ."

"Please, Brandy. Your language. Right now isn't the time..."

"Sorry, Stevie." My brother was a devout man, and I didn't mean to upset him. "What can I do?"

"Well, you see," Stephen's stutter came on stronger, and I realized he was about to ask me to do something unpleasant. "Dad doesn't... he'd rather..."

"He doesn't want me there." My tone was flat, and the room shifted around me, as though I were on a carnival ride. No wonder I didn't get a call sooner. Even with this crisis looming, they didn't want me around. It hurt, but I tried to push the pain away.

"He and Mom talked and..." Stephen still couldn't complete a sentence through his stutter.

"No, that's fine. I wasn't coming home for Christmas anyway. Not after..." It was my turn to trail off.

"You have to come home for Christmas. Dad's sick. It might be..." The phone clattered on his end, and I heard a muttering of voices.

"Brandy?" My sister-in-law, Renee, was also an actor, and her voice always sounded like warm caramel to me. I could listen to her read a stereo manual, and right now her honeyed tones soothed me. "Listen, I know things got... ugly, but your dad—and you—need to set that aside right now. This is more important than his bigotry. Whether or not they want to admit it, Mom and Dad need you here. And we think you have a right to be here."

"We?" I knew Steve and Renee would want me there, but I wasn't so sure about Stacy. "Listen, I appreciate it but…"

"Stacy agrees with us. She… We all need you here. You're the rock we look to when Dad can't be strong."

What I wanted, more than anything, was to be my dad's right hand through all this. But his impromptu Thanksgiving sermon still rang in my ears. Could we set that aside and stand strong as a family, or was the cut too deep and new? Would my going home help him or make things worse?

I sighed. "When will we know how bad it is?"

"Friday."

I looked at the calendar on my desk. It was Wednesday, and the tax payment was due Friday. I could drive upstate to my parents' place Saturday morning if it was bad news. That gave me a couple of days to talk to the greenhouse's owner, set up the holiday schedule for my team, and review the pressing tasks with my assistant manager.

"I'm not promising anything, but I might drive up on Saturday. If I must."

Her voice quavered, making me think her eyes were filled with tears. "We all hope it won't come to that. Steve or I will give you a call on Friday once we know more."

We signed off with some "I love you's" and extracted promises to distribute hugs to family members. I set down my cell phone and stared at the numbers on my spreadsheet. None of them made sense. Saving my work and shutting down my computer, I resolved to start fresh in the morning.

The knot of fear in my belly was unavoidable, even as I leaned back in my chair and stretched my feet forward, trying to relax. Whether I was afraid of losing my dad or seeing him again, I wasn't sure—probably both.

I thought about calling Jason, my closest friend. I decided to wait until tomorrow evening. I knew he had a big project due at work the next day. He'd drop everything for me if I asked, but I wouldn't do that to him. Tomorrow evening would be soon enough to tell him.

I rolled my neck and tried to decide what to do with the evening. I'm not much of a drinker, but a glass of wine sounded really good at that moment. But both of my grandfathers were alcoholics, and since I was craving a drink, I told myself I couldn't have one. I didn't want to start down that path, not after seeing those men battling their demons.

Instead of heading to a nearby bar, I gathered my belongings and locked up for the night. I needed to eat dinner but had no appetite. Nevertheless, the ingredients for a chicken Caesar salad waited at home, and I headed in its direction.

∾⌀

The house was dark and empty, just as it had been since November first. That was the irony of my estrangement from my parents. Liz and I had lived together for three years. She had been to their house for a few small get-togethers, and they seemed to like her. My siblings figured out the situation between us the first time they met her, but either my parents were unobservant or they were willfully ignorant; they claimed to think we were just roommates.

Granted, I never told them she was more than a roommate, which caused some friction in our relationship. But she hadn't introduced me that way to her parents either, and I'd celebrated three of her birthdays with them. We didn't make any proclamations partly because we had started out as roommates.

Our romantic relationship developed later, and we still hadn't completely defined it when she moved out.

Anyway, I'd made my formal declaration at the Thanksgiving dinner table because she'd left me on Halloween, our anniversary. Dad insisted that we all state something we were grateful for after he said grace. I had nothing to say, other than I was glad she left the cat with me when she moved out.

Somehow, that simple statement turned into me tearfully listing all the things I missed about Liz. My parents couldn't pretend to misunderstand when I said I missed lazy Saturday mornings cuddling and kissing her in bed.

Dad threw me out before we even got the turkey carved.

Now he was in a hospital waiting for details about his treatment options. If I ever wanted Liz back—and I didn't, not after she left me for her boss—it would be now. I just wanted a little... sympathy while I got my head around all this.

Fortunately, Samwise, our Siamese mix, was still with me. He had always preferred my company, even though Liz claimed he was her cat because she found him.

Before I put my stuff down, he was reaching his front paws up my thighs and meowing to be held. I obliged and buried my face in his fur while he placed his front paws on my shoulder, snuggled in, and purred. We cuddled for several minutes, and then he moved away from me and leaned over my arms. That was my cue to set him down.

"Thanks, buddy. You ready for dinner?" He pranced and arched his way to the mat where I fed him. I grabbed a can of cat food from the cupboard, along with a clean bowl, and dished out his dinner.

While Samwise ate, I changed into sweats and a comfortable T-shirt. He twined himself around my ankles while I mixed the

Caesar salad dressing, washed lettuce, and grilled the chicken. I chatted at him, telling him about Stephen's call and the misbehaving spreadsheet. I imagined that his pale blue eyes showed signs of understanding and sympathy for my rotten day.

Although I hadn't thought I was hungry, I wolfed down my salad and wished I had grilled a second chicken breast. One breast was plenty, but I craved more.

To distract myself, I headed for what had once been Liz's bedroom, which was where I kept my guitar and music stand. Stephen was the real talent in the family, but Stacy and I both played instruments and sang. Growing up as preacher's kids, we were expected to participate in Sunday services. The Southern Baptists were conservative, and they loved when a pastor's family was active in the church's activities.

That was especially true of Dad's congregation. Every summer, they held a week-long tent revival. During that time, each member of our family would be forced to spend time huddled over the vaporizer and sucking on throat lozenges to baby our tired vocal cords.

I wasn't planning to play anything in particular, maybe run through a few scales. But as my memories of those tent revivals came back, I found myself playing and humming the hymns I used to perform. I hadn't played most of them in years, and I fumbled with the chords from time to time, but something about playing those old songs made me feel calmer.

When I set my guitar back on its stand, the clock said I'd been playing for over ninety minutes, and I couldn't have listed the names of all the pieces I'd played. Bemused, I decided an early bedtime was wise. I had a lot to do before driving up to my old hometown on Saturday, and something told me I'd be making that drive.

∝◇

Stephen's call on Friday put me on the road early Saturday morning. Dad had stage IV lung cancer, and the doctors thought he might need part of a lung removed. I pondered that, along with the host of treatment options Stephen had mentioned, while I drove the nearly 300 miles from my home to my parents'.

Stephen and Renee were between shows, but both expected callbacks at any moment. Stephen had auditioned for a Broadway musical before Dad's collapse, and he couldn't turn that opportunity down if offered the role. He'd been trying to get a Broadway show for the past five years. Renee's show was a short, off-off-Broadway run, but it would give her additional New York connections. As much as they both wanted to be home helping Mom and Dad, we all knew it wasn't an option for them.

Stacy was the baby and quite a bit younger than Steve and me, so she was eyeball-deep in her senior year of college. She couldn't take time off to be home with Mom and Dad, not if she didn't want to postpone enrolling in law school. She had been accepted to her top choice school, but they didn't seem willing to hold her slot. I couldn't ask her to sacrifice that.

Whether or not my parents wanted any help remained to be seen. I knew they wouldn't want me there, but none of us had many options. Mom would soon be overwhelmed by the errands and stress, and we couldn't let her do this alone. I hadn't planned on an extended leave from work, but the greenhouse's owner understood the situation.

I heard Dwayne's comforting words again as I drove: "You take all the time you need to care for your parents. I'll muddle through here, with the help of the team you've assembled. I was planning to offer you part ownership in this place after the first of the year, but we can work out those details later."

So, I was homeward bound with Heart blasting on the car's stereo and Samwise grumbling from his carrier in the backseat. And Christmas was ten days away. It really was a weird ol' world.

Samwise and I made good time, and I pulled up to the Living Inn a few blocks from my parents' house about five hours after hitting the road. I was home to help out, but Dad didn't like cats, and really, after Thanksgiving, I wouldn't presume I could stay in the family home. And this hotel allowed guests to have pets.

I didn't like the extra expense, but it couldn't be helped.

After settling my cat into the room and hanging up the Do Not Disturb sign, I drove to the parsonage where my parents lived; time for the face-off. I was relieved Stephen's car was in the drive when I pulled in.

I drummed my fingers on the steering wheel and listened to the engine ticking as it cooled, looking over the house's façade. Dad wasn't a fan of gaudy Christmas decorations, believing they detracted from the true meaning of the season, but for her part, Mom insisted on lights hung along the eaves. Given Dad's diagnosis, I hadn't been sure if she would browbeat him into hanging them this year. But her beloved lights lined the edge of the roof, waiting for evening so they could shine forth in a modest demonstration of holiday cheer.

Their presence loosened the tightness in my chest, and a smile made my cheeks ache. Maybe Dad wasn't as sick as we feared. If he was out of the hospital and felt well enough to hang the lights, that was good news.

I opened my car door and climbed out. As I closed it, Stephen came around the side of the house, carrying a ladder. My brief moment of hope faded. He had hung them.

Steve jerked a thumb over his shoulder. "How do the lights look?"

I swallowed. "Good. You just get them up?"

He nodded. "Yeah, Dad hates hanging them. But it looked weird without them. So, I decided to get them up. Just so something's normal, you know?"

I smiled, but it must have been a weak one, because he set down the ladder and pulled me into a crushing hug. We held one another, and I fought back tears.

"This looks interesting," a familiar voice said.

"Stacy?" I asked.

Before I could pull away from Steve, her weight collided against my back, and her arms reached around me to grasp his shoulders.

Someone else cleared her throat with a fake cough before saying, "You wenches shall unhand my espoused love now, else I'll snatch thy hair from thy noggins."

"Noggins?" Stephen said. "Really, Renee? All the Bard's great insults, and that's what my actress-wife cobbles together?" Laughing, I let go of Stephen and tried to turn to Stacy.

She wasn't letting go, so I finally relaxed in her arms and let my younger sister lean against me. From the way we shook, she was either laughing or crying. I assumed the latter, since she wouldn't let me see her face.

Eventually, Stacy released her death grip around my shoulders, and I could finally turn to look at her. Her eyes were red, but a huge smile made her face light up. She grabbed me for another hug.

"Good to see you, Brandy." She squeezed me hard.

I squeezed back just as hard. "You too."

We stayed that way for a few moments, and then she eased her grip. I followed her lead, and we both took a step back. She looked me up and down.

"You've lost weight since Thanksgi… since I last saw you." I fidgeted under her scrutiny. "It doesn't suit you. We should make an ice cream run."

We shared an addiction for Dairy Maid's Butter Crunch blended ice cream. It was Dad's special treat whenever one of us celebrated a good report card or needed comforting after a fight with a friend. Once I got my driver's license, we snuck out for those treats a lot, even without Dad along. We hadn't made that run since she graduated high school.

"Think we could smuggle one in for Dad?" Stephen asked.

"We can try," said Stacy.

Renee and I just exchanged glances. We both knew the nurses wouldn't let him have it. More importantly, would he throw me out again?

But Stephen and Stacy were jazzed about smuggling Dad a treat, so I went along with it. On the drive, I learned Mom was already at the hospital with Dad.

Renee called the hospital while we waited for our order, asking if Mom needed anything and letting her know I had arrived. With Dad listening in, Mom probably couldn't say much in response. Renee insisted that Mom sounded relieved to hear I was coming with them to the hospital, though.

Stephen and Renee took the backseat and held the stuff for our parents. Stacy rode shotgun and alternated between eating her ice cream and feeding me bites of mine. She'd perfected her technique about six months after I got my driver's license, and the memory of those earlier good times calmed some of my fears.

Before it seemed humanly possible, we pulled into an empty space in the hospital's parking lot. My appetite vanished when I saw its front entrance, and my half-eaten treat got tossed into the trash.

Stacy grimaced and followed my lead. A sign on the door said no outside food or drink could be brought in, but Stephen ignored it as he strode past. His left hand held Dad's blended ice cream, and a chocolate-dipped cone for Mom was in his right. He ignored the guard's expression and startled, "hey!" and marched to an elevator.

The elevator doors opened on cue as he approached, leaving the rest of us scrambling to catch up.

"Showoff," Stacy muttered, giving him a half-admiring, half-annoyed look. He always pulled crap like that off.

"It's his gift," Renee said. "He's an actor who can make people forget what they know. It's like your dad in the pulpit. He can convince a congregation of anything."

A frisson of unease ran down my spine when she said that. Dad was charismatic, but Renee's comments didn't seem to be a compliment. Instead, I took them as a warning of trouble to come. The elevator's walls closed in around me, and I had to force myself to take slow, deep breaths to fight my rising fear. Given how little oxygen that box held, I wasn't sure it would work.

When it chimed for our floor and the doors opened, I swear a blast of sweet air hit my face. I inhaled, and the stench of antiseptic and sickness made me choke.

"Panic attack?" Stephen asked.

"Yeah. I'm good, though." I wiped away tears caused by the coughing. Then, to prove I was fine, I marched off the elevator first. Realizing I didn't know where to go, I paused and let the others get ahead of me. I couldn't remember Dad's room number. Besides, I was afraid to be the first one through the door. I wanted to slip in while Dad was preoccupied with his ice cream.

Of course, I failed to account for my twin's flair for the dramatic. He handed Mom and Dad their surprises before turning to the door. "See who I found when I finished hanging the Christmas lights?"

"Brandy!" Mom gasped as though she hadn't known I was coming.

My gaze cut to Dad, who froze with his spoon in his mouth.

Mom glanced at him and rushed to hug me before he could swallow down his ice cream and throw me out. "He's been just sick with guilt," she whispered as she held me close. We rocked back and forth for a moment but broke apart when he spoke.

"I told you not to come back until your heart and mind were right with God."

I stepped away from Mom and looked him in the eye. "I remember what you said."

"So, you've repented?"

I took a deep breath. "I never had anything to repent, Dad."

His mouth twisted in disgust. "So, you're still a..."

"Dad," Stephen's voice was firm. "We aren't discussing that now." When our father tried to interrupt him, Steve raised a commanding hand. "I mean it. That topic is off-limits during this family crisis. All of us need to work together through this. You always taught us our family is strong together."

"We are." I could see Dad hated to say it, but he wouldn't contradict one of the mantras he'd taught us.

"So, Brandy is here for as long as you and Mom need a hand. Renee, Stacy, and I will help but…"

"I know you all have other demands on your time," said Mom. "I'm grateful you've been here as long as you have." She made eye contact with each of them before turning to me. "Honey, will this be a problem for you at work?"

"No, Mom. Dwayne said I can take as much time as needed. He said I'll become a part owner after New Year's."

Mom hugged me again, and my family's congratulations rang in my ears. Finally, Mom let go, and I could see Dad's face. He looked both proud and angry. It gave him an expression akin to indigestion. A nurse picked that moment to walk in. After one glance at his expression, she took his ice cream away.

After lecturing us about his diet, the nurse marched from the room. I found myself staring at the door, trying to figure out why she looked familiar. Stephen and Stacy, giggling at the embarrassment on Dad's face, interrupted my musings. He hated to be fussed at. Before he could scold them, the nurse marched back in.

"I need to see to this patient." She glared at each of us in turn, and I noticed her eyes widen when our gazes met. Something about making eye contact with her caused my pulse to race. I swallowed hard, but my mouth was dry.

Mom cleared her throat, and the connection I felt with the nurse was broken. "All right, my children. We need to let Monica do her job." She gave Dad a kiss on the cheek and gestured us toward the door. I glanced back, but Dad wouldn't look at me. I rolled my eyes, knowing another sermon awaited me.

 споро

The next day started my new routine. Early each morning, I drove Mom to the hospital, where she held Dad's hand through his chemotherapy and radiation treatments. He didn't speak to me much and seemed to prefer when I waited out of sight.

At first, I stayed behind in his room while he was taken for treatment. By the second day, I lurked in the sitting area near the nurses' station. The nurses chatted with me, and I soon knew their names.

It turned out the reason Monica looked familiar was because we did know one another. She was a freshman when I was a senior, and we had performed in our high school's chorus together.

During the long hours of Dad's treatment, Monica and I found a few minutes here and there to chat about old times. We reminisced about shows and songs from our chorus days. She caught me up on the latest news regarding old classmates, but her duties kept our conversations short. About five days into Dad's treatment, I found myself wishing Monica and I could find time to talk without interruption.

I hadn't found any woman interesting since Liz left. Nothing about Monica suggested she might be a lesbian, but she was easy to talk to. And I often struggled to make friends.

A few days later, I dug deep for some courage. "Hey Monica, when is your lunch break today?" It was Christmas Eve, and I wasn't sure how I would spend tonight or tomorrow. Dad and I hadn't fully reconciled yet. Mom ran hot and cold, depending on whether or not Dad was in the room. Perhaps eating lunch with a friendly face could help make today feel a bit more like a holiday.

She glanced up from the chart she was reviewing. "Probably around one or so. Why?"

"I was wondering, could we maybe have lunch together? In the cafeteria?"

She seemed surprised by the question, and I noticed a slight blush on her face and throat. "Um, sure." She glanced at her two colleagues, both of whom wore smirks but pretended not to be listening to us. "I'll find you," she said.

I don't think I was supposed to see her smack the other nurses before she headed down the hall to a patient's room. I pretended not to notice how they kept glancing at me and whispering after she left. Instead, I just tried to settle my roiling stomach and wondered why her answer mattered so much. And what did that blush mean?

A few hours later, we were both picking at our lunches. "What kept you in our old hometown?" She had just told me she went to college out of state, and I was surprised she'd come home.

She gave me a sad smile. "My parents. Really, my mom." She didn't say anything for a few moments, and I wasn't sure if she intended to tell me anything more. We sat in silence while I tried to find another topic to bring up.

Before I found one, she said, "My sophomore year of high school, my dad had an argument with our parish priest." Monica fingered a saint's medallion she wore on a chain. It was so worn that I couldn't tell which saint it depicted. "After that argument, Dad started trying other churches in the area. We would attend one for four or six months, and then Papa would pick another to try." She met my gaze and smiled. "We even attended your dad's church. That was the last semester of my senior year."

"Your dad tried a Protestant church?" I knew Monica's older brother slightly. The Echado family was staunchly Catholic, and Jose had been an altar boy.

"Papa tried a lot of denominations, but he either wouldn't or couldn't tell us what he was looking for."

"So, how does that get you to come home for college?" I didn't want to push, but I wasn't sure what her dad's hunt for a home church had to do with her return.

Monica sighed again. "My dad had cancer. It was diagnosed a few days after I took my licensure exam."

"I'm so sorry."

She tried to smile, but it was more of a grimace. "The irony was that I had studied to be an oncology nurse, and I wanted to work with children. When Mama called, I knew exactly how bad his condition was. I'm not sure either of them did."

My brain flashed to the fact that my dad was in another part of this hospital getting his chemo. I flinched at the idea of having her level of understanding of a loved one's condition. Something must have shown on my face, because she reached across the table for my hand and squeezed.

"He'll be fine, Brandy." Her voice held conviction, and her expression was open. Perhaps she was just really good at her job, but I decided to trust her. It was Christmas, and I couldn't risk doubts right now.

"So, your dad was ill." I prompted and squeezed her hand back.

She pulled away, and I missed the warmth of the contact. "Yeah. So I applied for work nearby. I knew I couldn't play an official role in treating him, but my mama needed me here." She took a sip of coffee. "When he got sick, Mama insisted the entire family return to our parish church—'where we belong' as she put it—for Mass. A new priest was in charge, so Papa agreed."

"I'm sure that was a comfort." I was a PK, a preacher's kid, so I knew how people returned to the familiar in times of crisis. Sometimes the faith helped, sometimes it didn't; but lots of people tried it.

She shrugged. "To them, maybe. Not to me. College made me..." She paused and thought for a moment. "I found I saw the world differently after college. I had a hard time attending Mass with them, because now I knew more about the Church's history." She took a bite of food and chewed thoughtfully, meeting my gaze. "I tried a few of the other churches, especially those I had liked back in high school. Like your dad's."

"How did that go?" I knew some pastors were welcoming to those raised Catholic, while others were hostile.

She frowned. "Most pastors turned me off with their false piety and hypocrisy. A few learned my name and upbringing and then expressed anti-Latino and anti-Catholic sentiments." She brushed hair from her eyes. "Your dad didn't do either. He said he remembered me from before and made me feel welcome. He visited Papa in the hospital and prayed with my parents. When Mama reminded him they were Catholic, he told her, 'God hears the prayers we say together, and He hears those you and your priest say. He isn't concerned about where we pray or which denomination we follow. All God wants is our love and devotion.'"

I'd heard Dad say things like that before, and it had caused a few problems with congregants who wanted to imagine that one church was superior to another. It was a bit of Dad's private dogma that wasn't strictly in line with Southern Baptist teaching, but he wouldn't change it. He truly believed that all prayers, when prayed earnestly, would be heard. "That definitely sounds like my dad."

She smiled. "I was impressed, so I attended church more often after that. I even attended one of his week-long revivals."

I winced, and she chuckled. "I'm sorry."

"So was I, but I'm glad I experienced it. I like to read books set in earlier times in America, and tent revivals are often mentioned. It gave me a sense of living in a moment that was... simpler." She shook her head. "It also made me stop attending his church."

I knew the revivals were intense experiences, but most people found a stronger connection to the church afterward, so I was a bit surprised. "What turned you off?"

Her gaze locked with mine, and I felt stripped. I knew what she would say before she said it.

"His subject that year—in all seven revival sermons—was..."

"Homosexuality." I finished her sentence.

"Right." She gave me a crisp nod but didn't break our eye contact. "I came out to my family in my senior year of college. This was about six months after that, and I didn't appreciate his... fire-and-brimstone approach to the subject."

I did some quick math, and I realized that particular revival was about three months after Mom and Dad had visited me. It was the first time they had seen me at home with Liz and six months after she and I had become lovers. "Ah, damn."

"What?" Monica raised an eyebrow at me.

"That sermon was probably my fault." Her expression said she wanted more information, so I explained about my parents' visit.

"Is that when you told them?" Realizing what she had asked, she laughed. "I guess it's time for the time-honored tradition of sharing our coming-out stories."

I laughed, but my laugh was half-hearted. She had come out to her very Catholic family at twenty-two. I didn't come out until a month ago, just after my twenty-ninth birthday. What would she think about that?

"No, I…um…" I sipped my now-cold coffee and grimaced, then stared down at my plate. "I just came out to them. This past Thanksgiving."

She gasped. "You're kidding me."

"Nope."

"What happened?"

I gave her a quick recap of the day's events and wrapped up with, "I think he's probably really perfected that fire-and-brimstone sermon now."

She laughed. "Surely they all knew before that."

"Well, Stephen, his wife, and Stacy did." I shrugged. "If my parents didn't know, it was because they didn't want to face it; I wasn't really hiding it. Liz came with me to every family function."

"But you didn't announce it until Thanksgiving, which was after she left?" She studied my face. "Why not?"

I spun my coffee cup, while considering how to answer. "I'm…I'm not really sure. I guess because Liz wasn't that important to me. I knew telling them was a risk, that he might react by throwing me out."

She nodded but didn't say anything for a bit. "No need to rock the boat for a minor fling."

"Exactly." I spun my cup some more. "That's not very courageous, I suppose. And it speaks volumes about my most recent relationship."

"Brandy, no one can push us to come out before we're ready. You weren't ready to tell them. That's your path to walk."

Her words caused a warm glow to spread over my face. "Thanks."

She glanced at the clock. "I should get back."

I also checked the time and nodded. "Mom should be ready for a break soon."

As we walked to the elevator, Monica asked, "Are you and your family doing something this evening? Perhaps a midnight Christmas Eve service?"

I nodded. "The assistant pastor at Dad's church is officiating. Dad can't attend, but Mom wants the rest of us there."

She looked disappointed. "That makes sense."

"How about you?"

She shrugged. "I won't be attending services, but I might play babysitter to the younger nieces and nephews so my siblings can go."

The elevator started to ascend, and the silence between us felt uncomfortable. "Will you still be in town for New Year's Eve?" She tried to keep her voice casual, but her words were hurried, the way a teenage boy sounds when asking a girl to the prom. It took me a moment to figure out what was going on here.

"New Year's Eve?" I said slowly. "Yeah, I'll still be here then."

"Do you have any plans?" She leaned back against the elevator wall, but something about her posture said she wasn't feeling as relaxed as the gesture suggested. I began to understand what she was really asking me.

"No, I don't." My tongue felt thick in my mouth, the way it did each time someone asked me out. Even if I wasn't attracted to the person, the flood of nervous energy always made me feel that way.

"Good," she said as the elevator chimed past another floor. "That's good." Her right hand brushed and grasped my left. I glanced down at our hands and then met her gaze. A questioning look was in her eyes.

As I entwined my fingers with hers, I said, "It is."

MORE THAN A HOLIDAY ROMANCE

by Chris Zett

"I COME BEARING GIFTS," PAMELA announced as she knocked on the frame of the open office door. She carried a small stack of mail and used it as a fan. "Hot and sexy gifts, I hope."

Carol laughed. Pamela was incorrigible. "You hope? So you pretend you haven't read my mail yet, Ms. Barker?" Pamela started to answer, but Carol stopped her with a raised hand. "What do you mean by sexy?"

Pamela grinned. "Professor Barker to you, Ms. Baker, or I won't give you this envelope marked *not safe for work,* which was in a large envelope with a note attached. I only noticed it was one of yours when I started reading it." She sat on one of the chairs, stretched her legs under Carol's desk, and sighed. "What a disappointment."

Since their last names were nearly identical, they met daily to exchange misdirected mail over lunch. A few times they had inadvertently opened letters, but nothing too private until now.

Carol took a large plastic container from her bag and set it on the table, along with two plates and glasses. "Were you hoping for indecent fan mail from your students? It's probably only a joke from my brother. And if you insist on formal titles, it's Professor Baker to you, too, or you won't get any of my chicken tikka sandwiches."

Pamela distributed the bread while Carol poured them both water. "Who's Laura?"

Carol nearly spilled her water. "Laura? The letter's from her?" She reached for the stack, but Pamela was faster.

"Oh, this must be good. You're blushing!"

Carol tried to get to the mail that Pamela hid behind her back, and they both started laughing. When she realized she wouldn't be able to reach it, she sat down again and held out her hand.

"Laura is my friend from New York. You know, my traveling buddy."

Pamela grinned and handed over the envelope and note. "You mean your fuck buddy. You've mentioned her before."

Carol's face heated even more. "Don't be crude." She hit Pamela with the mail. "But yeah, my traveling slash seasonal sex partner. I don't know what this is about; she's never sent me an actual letter before. We used to e-mail every few weeks."

She played with the folded note. What did Laura want? Should she read it in front of Pamela? Well, Pamela had already read the note, or she wouldn't be asking about Laura. Curiosity won, and she opened the heavy cream paper.

Dear Carol,

This is the beginning of an advent calendar. But instead of twenty-four pieces of chocolate to count down to Christmas, you'll get twenty-four envelopes.

When you open the first one, you'll notice the theme. I want to share some of my memories of our past with you.

The first one might not be safe to open at work, so contain your curiosity until you're home. (I just love to tease you...)

Love,
Laura

"That's just cruel. She knows I hate surprises. And now I have to wait five more hours." Carol wanted to frown, but found that she smiled instead. Laura knew her too well; whatever was in the envelope would be worth the wait.

Pamela took a bite from the sandwich and moaned. "I love Indian food. Is this another recipe you picked up on your travels? Have you been there with Laura as well?"

"Sure, we've been to over twenty countries. We spent nearly two month there and in Sri Lanka."

"How long have you been traveling together? Ten years?" Pamela asked.

"Twelve actually. Since our college graduation. The first trip was supposed to be with a large group of friends, a classical tour of Europe. We didn't know each other and ended up sharing a room as the only single girls. The others all quit in the first week or so; we endured and really started to enjoy the trip after we were left alone." Carol traced the marks the pen had left in the heavy paper and smiled. The writing looked so elegant, almost artistic. "We noticed that we're extremely compatible travelers; we share the same expectations, want to see the same sights and, most importantly, can tolerate each other's quirks." Carol bit into her own sandwich, and the fragrant smell triggered a memory of eating the spicy grilled chicken for the first time. It had not been in India, but in London, where she had huddled with Laura on a small bench in a crowded Indian fast food place.

Pamela watched her for a long moment before she spoke again. "And you've been lovers ever since?"

"After the last couple left us, we went out and shared a celebratory bottle of French wine as we sat on the bank of the Seine and watched Paris at night. It was all very romantic and intense."

"But you never tried to have a relationship after that summer?"

Carol stood and stacked the empty food containers and tucked them into her lunch bag. "No, we were both headed to different coasts. I went to graduate school here, and she was accepted to med school in New York. We talked about it and decided to concentrate on studying and being friends instead of maintaining a long-distance relationship that was doomed from the beginning. It saved us both some heartbreak." Even as she said it, she had to wonder if it really had saved them. The pain from last summer still lingered behind her breastbone. She took a breath and pushed it deeper inside where it could hide from Pamela's scrutiny. Carol turned to her desk and sorted through her mail. "Nothing for you today. So, see you tomorrow in your office?"

Pamela stood. "Mary's cooking tonight. I'll bring leftovers." She hesitated at the door as if she wanted to add something, but then she shrugged and smiled. "See you."

༄

When she was finally at home, it took all of Carol's willpower to change into comfortable clothes, make herself a tea, and sit down before examining the envelope. *Not safe for work*, written in bold letters, was the only outward marking. She carefully cut the letter at the side and took out a self-made postcard. It showed the illuminated Eiffel Tower in Paris at night, half hidden behind several dark houses. It was an unusual angle and didn't appear to be a professional picture at all. She smiled when she realized what it was. She turned it around.

Remember me taking you to the Seine at night and making you sit through my amateurish attempts to get the perfect picture? This is the best of them, but I care more for the memory it evokes. I have recently sorted all my travel memorabilia and noticed that we have made love in twenty-four countries so far.

Do you remember them all?

Carol closed her eyes and tried to list all the places they'd been together. *Had it really been twenty-four?* She couldn't concentrate as her thoughts returned to Paris. She remembered that night very well. They had shared wine, laughter, and kisses. Later at night, they had shared themselves for the first time. She had been so impressed by the earnest and focused way in which Laura had tweaked the settings of her camera. Her long slender fingers played with the zoom, and as she finally found the right angle, she'd crouched down to finish the settings and awarded Carol with a good view of Laura's tight fitting jeans. She sighed. The image of a younger Laura stirred a longing she'd better suppress.

Before she could think better of it, she picked up her phone and dialed from memory.

"Hey, stranger, thanks for the tease. You made my afternoon at work unbearable," Carol said, after Laura answered on the first ring.

"You could never resist a hint. But I knew you'd follow the rules." Laura's voice was soft and full of laughter.

"What rules? Writing *not safe for work* hardly constitutes a rule!"

"Yeah, but I knew you would believe in the warning and spend all day thinking about me. Did it work?"

Carol wasn't sure if she should be annoyed or amused. She decided to go with the latter for now. "Cocky. But what part of it wasn't safe? Your picture? Or the note with your subtle allusion?"

"Um…the sketch?" Laura seemed puzzled.

"What sketch? Was there anything else in it?" Carol took the envelope and found a thin sheet of paper stuck inside it. It looked like a page from a notepad. When she turned it around, she saw a rough pencil sketch of herself. A much younger, completely naked, and obviously sleeping self. "Ooooh. I found it. Wow, when did you make this?"

"After our first time together. I couldn't sleep, I still had this terrible jet lag a week after my first transatlantic flight and sat at the window, trying to find an artistic inspiration." Laura chuckled. "I've never told you about this. At first I was too self-conscious, and later I forgot about the sketches."

"Sketches? Plural?" Carol traced the silhouette with her finger. "I can't believe how young I was."

"Weren't we both? I made maybe a half dozen that night. And a few more over the next years. Later I grew out of the jet lag and slept more."

"You're really talented. I've only ever seen your street scenes and landscapes. So, where are the other sketches? Did you keep them? Are they as good as this one?"

"I hid them in the books I was reading." Laura chuckled. "You never touched my crime novels. Too mainstream, you called them."

Carol wondered why Laura had never shown her. Was she embarrassed because her perfectionism underestimated the quality? Or because of the content? They'd never been shy with each other, at first because they both pretended to be mature and nonchalant, later because they had nothing to hide, at least nothing about their bodies.

She decided to steer their conversation towards safer ground. "What are you reading now?"

For the next hour they skimmed from one topic to another, always staying close to the surface, never taking the conversation deeper. Carol avoided the more important subjects—like last summer—and guessed that Laura was doing the same. She toyed with the empty teacup and wondered who'd bring it up first.

"Listen, I'd like to ask you something—" *Beep, beep, beep.* An annoying alarm interrupted Laura. She didn't speak for a moment as she probably concentrated on whatever her beeper said. "Carol, I'm sorry; I'm on call and I need to go. I just wanted to let you know that I'm at a conference in San Francisco after Christmas. Would you like to meet? You don't have to decide now. I can call you back in a few days."

"Why don't you stay at my place?" Carol regretted the invitation as soon as she said it. What was she thinking? They hadn't even talked about the most important things yet.

"Okay, yeah, I'd love to. Thanks, I'll call you with the details. Sorry, I need to go. Bye." Laura talked really fast, as if she wanted to accept before Carol could take it back.

Before Carol could reply, the call was over. And she had twenty-four days left to think about how she wanted to face Laura again.

∽◌

Paris. Amsterdam. Berlin. Vienna. Day after day new postcards arrived and brought with them the memories of their first trip. Carol and Laura had visited most western European capitals, but got only small glimpses of the countries surrounding them. They dutifully went to museums and the major sights as recommended by their guidebook during the day and partied at night.

Amalfi, Italy. After three weeks of traveling nonstop, they were finally exhausted and decided to find a small room in an Italian seaside town. The postcard showed only a close-up of a large lemon, but Carol was instantly transported back. She could almost smell the warm air, laced with traces of herbs, salt, and citrus, enveloping them while they were lying on old beach chairs. The sunlight flickered through the leaves of the lemon trees as the warm wind played lazily over their bodies. Every couple of hours they'd climb down the nearly two hundred steps to the Mediterranean Sea, the old granite smooth under their bare feet. They did nothing but swim, sleep, and make love for a week, interrupted only by irregular trips to the small village for olives, bread, and wine. Carol sighed. Everything had felt so easy then—even believing they were in love.

Carol took the stack of postcards and placed it on the mantelpiece. Today was Sunday and she hadn't expected a card, but a messenger had surprised her early that morning. She smiled and touched the picture of the lemon with a finger. Laura was crazy to spend so much money and time on an advent calendar. What was she thinking? Carol snatched her hand back and turned away from the cards. Was it an apology? Was there even a reason she should apologize? Or was it just an innocent expression of their friendship? She started pacing the living room and wondered if she should just call and ask Laura exactly that.

As if on autopilot she went to the large window overlooking her small garden. Usually the view of the unruly green and old trees calmed and centered her, but traces of her anger and disappointment with Laura rose like the thick gray fog that covered most of the garden.

The ringing of her phone was a welcome distraction until she saw Laura's picture on her display. The bright smile and the laughing eyes seemed to mock her own somber mood.

"Laura. Hi." Carol's voice was harsher than intended.

"Hey, is this a good time? Are you okay?"

"Yeah, I'm okay. You just caught me..." *Staring into the garden? Feeling alone and unwarrantedly betrayed?* "...thinking too much. Why are you calling?"

"I just wanted to talk to you. Have you gotten your postcard today?"

"An hour ago."

"Oh, that's good. Did you like the lemon?"

"Yes."

"Okay, fine." Laura hesitated. "Is anything wrong? You don't sound like yourself."

"If you say so." Carol knew she was too curt, but she couldn't help herself.

For a minute that lasted an eternity, only their breathing could be heard over the phone, then they both started talking at once.

"I'll call you back," Laura said.

"I'm sorry." Carol took a deep breath. "Don't hang up. I'm just in a funk. The fog is covering the garden."

"It's okay. I know how your emotions are run by the weather. I've never understood why you moved to San Francisco in the first place." Laura's voice was soft, almost wistful.

Carol should have left it at that. "You know the reasons. My university was, and I guess still is, the best one for me. I've got tenure now. And the weather is usually great. Besides, I think I grew up in the past few years, and part of that is coping with what life throws at me. Even if it's fog."

"Yeah. But sometimes I think that's only partly true. I don't want to just settle with whatever comes my way. You have to reach out and search for what you need. Not just for the necessities, but for your dreams as well." Laura talked louder and faster; this was obviously something she was passionate about.

A year ago, Carol had thought the same. Ironic, that Laura now moved the discussion from the weather to the heart of the problem. Carol asked, "How is your girlfriend?"

"What? Who?" Laura exhaled loudly. "You mean Jenny?"

"I can't remember her name." That was a lie. "The perfect match you found just before we wanted to leave last summer. Did she enjoy Bolivia?" Carol wouldn't forget the name of the woman who had thrown herself in the path of Carol's dream.

"We didn't go. We went to a resort in the Bahamas instead. And I've no idea how she is." Laura hesitated. "We...I...we split up just as we came home. The holiday was a catastrophe. The soul mate stage didn't even last a month."

Tears welled up in her eyes, and Carol had to clear her throat before she could speak again. "I'm sorry." *I'm sorry we missed our chance to be together. I'm sorry that you couldn't talk to me sooner. I'm sorry that I'm glad you've left her.*

"Thanks. I was too embarrassed to mention it. I can't believe I was so stupidly in lust that I confused it with love. It probably didn't help that I compared her to you all the time." Laura laughed. "I'm afraid she hates you now even though you've never met."

"That's okay. I can live with a little hate from afar." Especially since Jenny obviously paled in comparison. Carol grinned. She changed the topic to lighten the conversation. "So, tell me about the conference you're going to."

While Laura was talking about new and—at least for her—exciting discoveries in the field of interventional cardiology, Carol moved from side table to mantelpiece to windowsill and lit her large collection of candles. When the weather was uncooperative, she had to help herself. With the warm glow reflected on the glass, the fog suddenly didn't seem so depressing anymore.

❧

The next week's postcards finished their tour of Europe (Barcelona, Lisbon and London) and started on the trips where they concentrated more on one country or region, exploring the countryside between the major cities. That had sometimes been a challenge, as they not only needed to navigate the unknown waters of foreign transportation and communication, but of their own growing friendship and expectations as well. While

Carol preferred to plan ahead, Laura loved spontaneous side trips. Laura was the more conservative eater and happily settled with a major chain cheeseburger, whereas Carol couldn't eat exotic enough. But both preferred a room with a double bed as opposed to two twins.

The postcard from Scotland showed an ancient stone circle on Lewis Island. They had arrived in the evening during a downpour, and the bus driver made a detour to deliver them to the only guesthouse that was still open. The owner seemed nice enough and first showed them a large double room but, after watching them settle in for a few minutes, switched them to two singles. He claimed he had forgotten another booking, but when Laura sneaked out of Carol's room in the early morning, the open door showed that the larger room was still empty. It had been the first time they had been discriminated against as lesbians traveling together.

On Sunday Laura called again, and they kept to light topics, focusing on their work and comparing highlights of their travels. Carol didn't notice the hours passing and was surprised that they still found new things to talk about.

Pamela seemed fascinated by the memories that poured out of Carol. Their usual lunch break turned into retellings of most of their holidays. After the relatively easy and secure trips through Europe, they moved on to Asia via Australia and New Zealand. Sometimes the postcards reminded Carol of funny incidents, sometimes unexpected highlights. And again and again, they focused on her relationship with Laura.

The rainy beach of Sri Lanka brought back the memory of an afternoon and night spent locked in their little room by the sea, making love until the rain finally gave way to a brilliant sunrise.

"Who's the cutie?" Pamela pointed to a close-up of a very young Chinese girl with two bouncy braids, peeking around a half-open door.

"She was in the train compartment next to ours. We were in the same train for seventy-two hours, crossing half of China to reach the Yangtze River." Carol smiled. "We were probably the first white people she'd seen in person, and she was so adorably curious. I was down with flu, and Laura tried to feed me disgusting instant chicken broth. When I mimed to her just how awful it was, the girl offered me her sweets."

Carol closed her eyes and recalled how good it had felt to be pampered. Laura had fed her, tried to cool the fever with cold, wet towels, and finally just held her. When the fever broke, Laura caressed her sweaty hair, and Carol thought she might fall out of the narrow bunk from shivering so much.

"Where did you just go?" Pamela interrupted her reverie.

"Sorry. Just remembering something." Carol opened her eyes und shrugged. "Nothing important."

"No, no. You can't get all dreamy with that sweet private smile without telling me the sexy details. You know I'm living vicariously through your lunch stories." Pamela attempted to pout, but ended up giggling like a teenager instead.

Carol rolled her eyes. "Please. I don't know much about your love life, but I can't believe you and Mary need any help. Last week at dinner, I nearly melted from all the heat of your not-so-secret gazes."

"No, no, this is not about me and my wife. Tell me, what were you thinking about?" Pamela regarded her unwaveringly, and Carol had to look away first.

"Nothing sexy happened. We shared the compartment with two business travelers, and I had a terrible cold. But Laura took care of me. It was the first time I really saw her tender side; she had this whole 'I'm a butch doctor and I'm decisive and I can't show feelings' thing going on. In the beginning, while she was in med school and her residency, it was even worse. She's mellowed quite a bit since then and is now a fully evolved human being. My fever was really high, and she later admitted that she was really afraid for my life because of all the terrible viral epidemics originated in China, like the bird flu and SARS." Carol played with the postcard and chuckled as she read the inscription.

I've finally perfected my recipe. The next chicken broth won't be instant.

The note seemed to promise more than soup, but what? Care during future travels? Or a future with domesticity? How would Laura be able to cook for her when they lived thousands of miles apart?

"What do you think Laura wants to achieve with this advent calendar? She doesn't seem like a woman who just crafts for the fun of it." Pamela voiced Carol's thoughts.

"I've wondered that myself. I don't know. And I'm afraid to ask."

"Why are you afraid? Obviously she invested a lot of time and thought into this. Not to mention the money for all the timed deliveries. That can't be bad." Pamela regarded her calmly.

Carol turned the card back around and looked at the little girl. "Maybe...I think this might be an elaborate apology. Last summer she cancelled our plans at the last minute because she had a new girlfriend, her *soul mate*, or so she thought. Turned out to be another fling. This is probably her way of saying that she still values my friendship and wants to travel again next summer." She put the card on top of a stack of exams she planned to take home later.

"And what do you want?"

"The same. I want to travel with her as friends." Even as she said it, Carol knew it wasn't true. She admitted to herself last year that she wanted more than just a traveling companion and occasional lover and had been devastated when Laura replaced her so easily. Now she was afraid of getting hurt again. She stood up and took the remains of her lunch with her. "I think I need to finish my break early. I've tons to do still before the end of the term."

Pamela exaggeratedly raised her eyebrows. "Don't think you can escape that easily. There's more at stake here than you're telling me. As your best friend, it's my duty to keep digging." She walked around the large desk and hugged Carol. "See you Monday."

∞

Sunday morning brought a postcard of Botswana. Exotic trees lined an endless and lazy river, the Okavango Delta, where they'd rowed a tiny boat to a remote island and camped in the wilderness. Carol couldn't decide if the growing unease in her stomach reminded her of the brilliant butterflies that Laura had chased for hours with her camera or the herd of elephants that had nearly followed their group back to the camp. The caller ID on her phone made her heart beat as fast and irregular as the native drums that their guides had played at night as part of the tourist entertainment.

"We're already in Africa?" she asked by way of a greeting.

"Yep. Only five countries left in our trip around the world. We need to make some more memories soon." Laura yawned. "I'm sorry. Just got done with the night shift from hell."

Carol was disappointed. She had looked forward to Laura's weekly phone call. "Okay. Don't apologize, that happens. You want to go to bed?"

Laura hummed. "Is this an invitation?" Her voice was suddenly husky.

"You wish. Phone sex? Really? You think you're up for it? I can't have you falling asleep in the middle." Carol knew it was stupid. Laura was only joking, but the flirtation brought back the butterflies and chased off the elephants.

"Okay. I'll behave." Laura's tone suggested she would quit behaving if she was encouraged.

Please don't. But Carol was afraid to go there. "So, what happened last week?" As they talked about all the little mundane details of everyday life, Carol marveled that their new routine had rekindled their friendship. Sharing more than the most important events every few month in an awkward e-mail was important to her. In the beginning they had talked as much, but different time zones and busy schedules quickly became too much for two graduate students. And, as the demands of their work had taken precedence, they'd fallen out of the habit of writing longer e-mails.

After an hour, the frequency of Laura's yawns increased, and Carol offered to hang up again.

"Before I let you go, I've got a question." Laura sounded more awake now. "What are you doing for Christmas? Are you meeting someone? Or your family?"

Carol wondered where this was going. Was this Laura's way of asking her if she had a girlfriend? And why wasn't she more direct? "I've nothing planned. I'll probably take my time to cook a healthy dinner and lounge all day in front of the TV to watch old movies. Why, you want to join me?"

"Is this an invitation?" Laura echoed her earlier question, only this time the flirtation seemed to mask a serious intent.

Carol remembered her initial unease when she invited Laura to stay at her place during the conference. But after three weeks of regular phone calls and daily recollection of happy memories, all her trepidation was gone. "Yes, why not? Would you like to come here early? Don't you have to work?"

"No, this year I won the shift lottery." Laura hesitated. "Really? That would be fantastic! A few days just for us until the conference starts. I wanted to ask if you have time to talk on the phone, but this is so much better."

Carol heard rapid clicking of a keyboard and then muffled curses. She chuckled and said, "Are you already researching flights?"

"Can you believe how much a direct flight on Christmas costs?"

Carol had to laugh. "Don't whine. You're a filthy rich cardiologist. Or you could spend some of your miles."

Laura snorted indignantly. "I'm not that rich. Or I wouldn't have to work anymore and could travel for the rest of my life. Okay. I'll hang up now and concentrate on my search. I'll let you know when I'm scheduled to arrive."

After they had hung up, Carol stayed in her window seat and stared out into the sunlit garden for a long time. She cradled her phone to her breast and wondered if she should prepare the guest room or not. Was it presumptuous to expect them to continue as they had left their friends-with-benefits relationship sixteen month ago? And would she even want to?

Her body screamed yes, and her heart whispered the same, but her mind was still undecided.

∾⦿

The last days before Christmas passed in a blur. Carol worked late on campus to finish grading exams, fielded panicked questions from her students, and suffered through the annual faculty Christmas party. The only highlights were the postcards. The messages were cute, funny, and safe to share with Pamela, as if Laura was giving her some space to absorb the prospect of sharing her house for over a week.

The red dunes of the Namib Desert, the soft hills of South African vineyards, and the Peruvian llama with a silly hat sparked more memories, and Pamela was a patient listener.

When she woke up on the twenty-fourth, Carol started to make a list of everything she needed to do—shopping, cleaning, preparing a fancy meal, deciding what to wear... Was there time for a haircut? She laughed at herself as she got ready for the day, dressing in an old sweatshirt and faded jeans for cleaning. The hoodie was one of Laura's; she loaned it to Carol at the drafty airport in London, and Carol had forgotten to return it the next year. Maybe not so much forgotten as purposefully avoided packing it. She snuggled into it and sighed. This constant thinking about Laura was unprecedented, and she was afraid to call it anything more than a crush. It was getting ridiculous. Over the course of their twelve-year relationship, she'd never spent so much time analyzing their talks and past interactions. Until last year. Before the fiasco this past summer. Determined to sweat it out of her system, she gathered her bucket full of cleaning supplies and started to work.

Three hours later, her house glistened like a Christmas ornament. As Carol looked around the living room, the absence of seasonal decoration hit her. She usually spent the holiday with family, so she didn't own any herself. This year, they decided to go to Disneyworld together, and Carol had politely declined.

Fuck! Where do I get a decent tree this late? A panicked phone call to Pamela didn't help. After Carol had explained her predicament, Pamela had laughed so hard that her wife took control of the phone.

"What's going on with you, Carol?" Mary asked. "Every day Pamela comes home from work and tells me more bits and pieces of your love story. It's like a soap opera."

"It's not a love story! Not really." Carol didn't have the patience today to be her friends' entertainment. "And don't change the topic. I desperately need help. Where can I find a last minute tree and decorations?"

Mary gave the location of a tree lot in her neighborhood and promised Carol some leftover decorations from her own tree. "And Saturday you can both come over for dinner if you want to. Just in case you're not too occupied with each other."

Carol sighed. "Oh no, don't you start again. We're just friends, and I think we'd love to come over if Laura hasn't planned anything else. I'll let you know. And thank you. See you later."

After one look at the overflowing parking lot in front of the supermarket, she detoured to a local organic grocery store. She'd rather spend more money for better quality food, and the added benefit of fewer frantic shoppers was a bonus. When she finished there, she was happy to find that the tree lot was surprisingly well stocked. The seller reassured her that she wasn't the only person to wait until Christmas Eve to buy a tree.

Half an hour later, Pamela handed her the box of decorations with a wink.

Carol rolled her eyes. "Please stop it, Pam. I'm nervous enough about tomorrow. This will be just a lovely few days with a good friend."

Pamela nodded. "I know, C. That's what you both agreed on. But I still think you'd be happier in the long run if you told her how you feel. After reading most of the postcards and listening to your stories, I really believe she is feeling more than friendship as well."

Hope surged in Carol, closely followed and smothered by a familiar mixture of fear and insecurity. "How can you know what we feel for one another? I'm not even sure of my own feelings." She turned to the car and busied herself with wedging the box on the backseat without disturbing the six-foot tree sticking out of the back of the car. "Okay, I think I might have developed a stupid crush since she started sending the postcards," she admitted.

Pamela opened the door of the other side of the car, felt her way around the tree, and pulled the box while Carol pushed. "Yes. I noticed. If you want my opinion, I think the advent calendar was more than an elaborate apology. And I'm convinced that both of you are way past a crush stage, but we'll see. Whatever you decide to do, a least you've got your friend back."

After jamming the box into the open space, they ducked out of the car. Carol went to the back of the vehicle and tried to adjust the tree, even though it fit perfectly. "I'm afraid of risking our friendship," she whispered.

Pamela joined her and took Carol's hands away from the tree. "After twelve years, I'm sure you couldn't. Go home and don't over think it. Have fun with your tree and our ornament collection."

Carol hugged Pamela. "Thank you." She wasn't talking about the decorations alone, and by the squeeze she got back, Pamela knew that.

After the Christmas tree stood tall and proud in one corner of the living room, Carol opened the box. Several strands of lights were tangled together with various ornaments stuck in between. Nothing seemed to match and the whole mess looked as if someone had swept up the remnants on the day after Christmas and put the box out on the street. She might have neither experience nor her own traditions, but Carol liked to think she had better taste than that. The lights *might* be salvageable, but the rest of the decorations were a loss. She found a ball of a golden ribbon and contemplated adding simple bows. Then her gaze returned to the stack of postcards on her mantelpiece. She grinned. It might be a bit too much, but then again, it might work.

Just as she'd attached the last piece of ribbon to a postcard and hung it in the tree, the doorbell rang. She hadn't received the last postcard yet, so she rushed to the door without a second thought. Rather than the courier she expected, Laura stood on her porch. She'd arrived one day early. In shock, Carol almost slammed the door in her face.

Laura slowly took in Carol's old jeans, bare feet, and hair—which Carol could feel sticking out in every direction. Laura's smile was as beautiful as it was genuine. "Surprised?"

When Carol didn't react, Laura's smile faltered.

"Not a good idea?" Laura asked.

Carol shook her head and couldn't help but smile back. "Surprised, yeah! What a great idea. Come in!"

Carol stepped aside to let Laura enter, and the close proximity sent heat to her cheeks. To hide the obvious signs of her embarrassment, she hugged Laura and hid her head in her hair. This wasn't helping the heat situation, but it felt right. By the way Laura was pressing her head onto Carol's shoulder she must be feeling the same.

The moments she spent in Laura's arms made her forget her surroundings. A gust of wind reminded Carol of the open door. She struggled to regain her composure and tried to switch from hopeful would-be lover to friend. All she could manage was hostess mode. She showed Laura the bungalow, made small talk about the countless restorations she had done over the past few years, and finally showed Laura the guest room so she could freshen up. Even as she said it, she could hear her mother's voice in her head. *Freshen up? Who actually says that?* Carol hastened to her own bedroom to shower and change. This superficial politeness was not the way it should feel between friends. She hoped cooking dinner together would help.

"I love what you've done to the tree," Laura said as she entered the kitchen. Her short hair—still damp from the shower—looked even darker than usual, and she had changed into comfortable clothes similar to what Carol was wearing. "What are we cooking?"

Carol smiled at Laura's choice of words. With a limited travel budget in their earlier years, they had become quite adept at cooking together in small and badly equipped kitchens in cheap hostels all over the world. "I expected you tomorrow, so nothing fancy, I'm afraid. Salad and homemade tomato soup sound okay?"

Laura chuckled as she took the cutting board from Carol and helped herself to one of the knives from a large wooden block. "Perfect. I still crave fresh vegetables after a long flight. It must be the dry air or something."

The familiar routine of chopping and cooking relaxed them both, and by the end of it, they were chatting comfortably as they had always done.

Carol opened one of the South African merlots they bought together, gave a healthy portion over the onions and garlic sizzling in her pot, and then added the thyme they had collected on a Greek island and the fresh chopped tomatoes she'd bought earlier that day. She showed the bottle to Laura. "You want a glass?"

"Really? You trust me with that?" Laura grimaced.

"Well, you had a whole bottle after running around in the heat all day in the vineyards. I bet today you don't have heatstroke." Carol poured them both a glass and took them to the comfortable breakfast nook. She wasn't ready to leave the sanctuary of the warm kitchen, and the dining room seemed too formal for their small meal. And for their reunion.

"Okay," Laura said. "Just give me some water to go with it, and I promise not to puke on you again."

Carol laughed. "Deal."

Laura followed her with the salad bowl. "I really like your place. It's cozy, feels like a real home."

Carol busied herself with seasoning the soup and dividing it into two bowls. "I had a lot of free time to work on it last summer." As soon as she said it, she regretted mentioning it.

Only a short pause of the sound of wooden spoons clicking against the salad bowl indicated that Laura heard her. Just as Carol wondered if she should press on or retreat from the topic of conversation, Laura stepped directly behind her and squeezed her shoulder.

"Not now, okay?" Laura said softly. "I promise, we'll talk."

Carol leaned back into her and nodded. She had missed their interaction, the easy way they read each other when they were close.

After dinner, Laura took their glasses and stood up. "Can we sit next to the tree?"

Carol followed her into the living room, started a fire, and lit several candles before plugging in the tree lights. The effect was very romantic, and she was suddenly reluctant. *What kind of signal is this? Do we even need signals?*

Laura held out her hand and drew her down on the sofa next to her. She played with Carol's fingers, obviously unwilling to let go as she stared at the tree. Finally, she started talking, her voice low. "I missed you this summer. That's why I split up with Jenny. I constantly compared everything about her to you. We had some major arguments about it, but I finally realized that she couldn't compete with you. None of them could, over the years."

As Carol started to answer, Laura squeezed her hand as if asking her to wait.

Laura continued, "Retrospectively, I guess I just fell for her because I was jealous of your relationship. I'm sorry it didn't work out, by the way."

"What relationship? With whom?" Carol was confused. She hadn't been on a second date for years, let alone shared something remotely close to a relationship with another woman.

Laura didn't look at her. "You never told me her name. But when you wrote about looking for another job and if it was better to sell or rent your house, I put two and two together. You wouldn't move for a fling."

Oh shit! That's what went wrong. Carol felt the blood rush from her head and explode in her heart. She took a deep breath. Slowly, the shattered pieces realigned, and she noticed Laura's hand trembling over hers. She turned her own and squeezed Laura's firmly. "I'm an idiot. We're both idiots."

That made Laura raise her head and meet Carol's gaze directly, but she didn't comment.

Carol shook her head. "I wrote about all that because I was thinking about moving closer to you. And can you imagine my disappointment when you wrote to me about a new girlfriend, your soul mate?" Carol knew she sounded bitter.

"Wait...you mean..." Laura visibly paled. "I had no idea. And I was too afraid to ask you directly about her. I didn't want to stand in your way to happiness. But..." She frowned. "Why didn't you just tell me what you wanted?"

Now Carol couldn't hold Laura's gaze. "Because I was insecure. I thought maybe you wouldn't want me near you when you didn't react to my hints. I guess I was too cryptic, I'm sorry." She tried to remove her hand, but Laura held fast.

"Oh no, C. You're right. I was an idiot. I turned away from you at the slightest sign of an obstacle rather than just talking to you. There was no one else for you, yet I ran out and found a rebound relationship. I'm sorry."

Carol shook her head. "We should stop apologizing. I went through an emotional rollercoaster last year. I'll try to be clearer when communicating what I want and need, not only to others, but to myself as well." She grimaced. "I've really done a bad job of that recently. I want you in my life, your friendship...no. *You* mean too much to me. And I'm grateful that you did all this to rekindle our connection." Carol gestured with her free hand toward the tree decorated with the postcards. "I couldn't even think of dating anyone else after Greece. Our last holiday was just too perfect, the weeks with you on the small boat made me long for more of it, but I guess I ruined it." Her heart raced, and she had to look away so that Laura wouldn't see the tears that filled her eyes.

Laura intertwined their fingers and used her other hand to lift Carol's chin. "You didn't ruin it." Her voice was soft and warm, like the light from the flickering candles. "Without the fear of losing you to someone else, I wouldn't have realized how much was at stake." She leaned forward slowly, giving Carol enough time to move away.

Carol smiled and closed the distance herself. The kiss was as sweet as she remembered. The wine and tomato couldn't mask Laura's taste. Soft reassurance led to tender re-acquaintance and finally to passionate explorations.

Gasping for breath, Carol stood up and tried to pull Laura with her, their hands still clasped firmly together. "Bedroom?"

Laura just shook her head and pulled her back down. "I want to stay close to your tree." She let go of Carol's hand to unbutton her blouse. Her fingers trailed from Carol's collarbone to the swell of her breasts. "We've made love on worse surfaces than your sofa."

Carol laughed. They really didn't need a bed.

∾❀∾

Cold morning light filtered through the fog outside the window. The candles had burned down hours ago, and only a few glowing embers remained in the fireplace. But the warmth of the tree lights and the naked body snuggled against her own, chased off any lingering doubts Carol had about her feelings.

Laura stirred and slowly opened her eyes; a content smile spread across her face.

"Merry Christmas." Carol traced the smile with her finger. "Do you want to unwrap your presents?"

Laura laughed softly and ran her hands all over Carol. "Merry Christmas! And no. Everything I wanted is unwrapped already."

They kissed, and Carol pulled the quilt snug around them.

"You know, this was not what I planned when I came here." Laura sighed and rested her head on Carol's shoulder. "After your e-mail on Thanksgiving when you mentioned that your mother was after you again for still being single, I had this idea of asking you out on a date and wooing you properly for weeks before we end up together...again...well, here on your sofa."

"Weeks?" Carol tried to turn so she could get a better look at Laura. "This would be difficult to do cross-country."

"Yeah, well, the conference I was talking about? There's more to it." Laura took a deep breath and continued very fast as if she was afraid of an interruption. "I'm meeting with an old friend from med school. He has offered me a partnership in his practice when I asked him about job opportunities here." She looked up, her eyes shifting rapidly from left to right as she tried to hold Carol's gaze at such a close distance. "Would you date me, to find out if we could have a real relationship? I think we can have more than a holiday romance."

Carol grinned. "No."

"No?" Laura's voice was much higher than usual.

"No. I won't date you. I know enough about you. I've seen you happy and sad, hungry and pissed off. I've smelled you after a week of hiking and held you when you were ill. And I know how you take care of me when I'm at my worst. We've even puked on each other. What more do you think we can learn?"

A radiant smile swept over Laura's face as she listened to Carol. "I love you, you know."

Carol couldn't stop herself from kissing Laura again. And again. And again. They had kissed a thousand times before, but now it felt unbelievably better. This was what she had hoped for last year, but even in her wildest dreams, she hadn't imagined the surge of real happiness that flowed through her. "And I love you, too. Thanks for the best Christmas ever."

WE WISH YOU A MERRY CHRISTMAS
by Lyn Thorne-Alder

"THREE DAYS IN A CABIN in the woods. At Christmas time. With all of our parents. What could possibly go wrong?" Joan folded another sweater into their suitcase and set it on top of the set of rowan stakes.

"Oh, come on. It won't be that bad." Elena tossed her cargo pants on the pile and, after a moment of contemplation, added the soft velvet pants Joan had given her. "Your parents are mellow and kind; it's only my dad and the stepmonster we have to worry about. And your mother seems to have a calming effect on everyone she encounters."

"You shouldn't call her that, especially considering." Joan checked her spare holdout pistol before she added it to a side pocket; the ammo went into another. "Your parents are perfectly nice and human."

"I don't know." Elena tossed her ugliest sweater atop the pants. "She might have fangs. The way she smiles," she demonstrated with a wide, tight grimace, lips closed, "you'd never know."

"May I remind you…" Joan picked up Elena's sweater and folded it, adding it to the side of the suitcase. "This was your idea. Don't forget the flare gun and the lighters."

"Already packed." Elena dumped her duffle bag on the bed. "Along with *Tedwithle's Compendium of Rare and Mythic Creatures,* the bottled holy water, and that weird formula you whipped up for those banshees last month."

"Just in case we encounter a banshee in the Adirondacks?" Joan smirked affectionately at her wife.

"Just in case it turns out that the stepmonster is a banshee. Look, I know it was my idea, but it was really Dad's idea, okay? He's been all moping about lately, and he wants to have Christmas as a family."

"Like, stop at their place for two hours, ooh and aah over the tree, drink eggnog, and pretend to like their presents? This didn't need to turn into an expedition, Lena." That was a lie, of course. Everything Elena did turned into an expedition. It was part of the adventure of being married to her.

Elena twitched her shoulders and looked away from Joan. "I prefer not to see her in that house."

"But it'll be fine seeing her in your mother's cabin? Elena, are you aware you're being irrational?"

"You don't know the woman. I'd rather not deal with her on her own territory. The cabin is mine—it's ours," she allowed. She nodded cautiously at Joan, the slip seeming to throw her off her rant. "I'm sorry?" She tried it out as if she wasn't sure it would fit. "I know it's a lot to ask. But it's only three days."

And that, Joan could tell, was as good as she was going to get. "It'll be fine. We can pretend to be normal for a couple days." She tidied the rest of Elena's belongings into the suitcase. "Don't forget the presents."

"It's snowing awfully heavily. I hope everyone's going to make it all right." Joan stared out the car window at the mountainside, which was already covered in a heavy blanket of white.

"Oh, they'll be fine. It's not like the airport here isn't used to snow. It's New York in December." Elena handled the little SUV as if she were driving on a dry, straight road, gunning up the winding mountain trail. "We'll probably have just enough time to get the cabin aired out and ready before everyone gets there."

Joan had heard much about "the cabin," a small mountain property that Elena's mother—and later Elena—had used as a base camp for hunting bogeys. There had always been one reason or another not to go there—weather, a hunt, an event, anything. Now they were finally going, and they were going to share the place with their parents. Joan hummed "We Wish You a Merry Christmas" to herself and tried to be upbeat. "It's lovely out here."

"It is." Elena's voice softened. "I used to love coming out here in the winter. We'd practice tracking deer and rabbits, and there'd be a roaring fire in the wood stove and a pot of soup waiting when we got back home. It was like living in another time."

Joan glanced at her wife. "It sounds beautiful."

Elena flashed a bright smile. "It was. Mom taught me to hunt up here—not just deer and rabbits. This is where I took down my first bogey, too. I thought it was so big and nasty, but it was really just a little elf-thing. I've never seen another one like it, in all the years I've been hunting. Oh, here it is." She lifted her foot off the gas and made a rather graceful fishtail.

Joan never would have seen the side road if they hadn't been driving down it. In the snow, it looked like a very small gap in the trees. It curved around a large boulder—bigger than the SUV they were driving—and headed straight up a hill.

"There are wards all over this place, but if we're lucky, I did things right, and they'll recognize you."

Joan raised her eyebrows. "From anyone else, Lena, that would be terrifying." From Elena, it brought forth immediate other questions. "Ah—your parents? My parents?"

"Your parents are fine if you are; it thinks they're part of you. My dad and the stepmonster have been attuned to the wards for years. They used to come up here when I was a kid." She made a noise as if she was spitting out the whole idea while she navigated the SUV around a hairpin turn that bent the road around a giant oak tree. "It's fine, Joan. I thought of everything."

"I know you did," Joan murmured. "And if you didn't, I did. That's why we're a team."

"You just think I'd let my stepmonster run into a kick-me ward for giggles," Elena accused. The road was surprisingly smooth, but it was also heading upwards at an angle usually reserved for walls.

"Well, am I wrong?"

"If it wasn't for Dad, I might. But if it wasn't for Dad, I wouldn't have any reason to hate her. Hold on," she added.

Joan took her seriously, grabbed two handholds, and braced her feet.

Normal cars should not be able to do the tricks Elena put theirs through in the next few moments. Then again, their sturdy SUV had more charms on it than most crystal stores.

Elena and Joan had been working on it for years, and their mechanic had done the same more than a few times. Their line of work was hard on cars. They tried not to think about that more than they had to. It was hard to be married *and* be hunters. It was hard to *have friends* and be hunters.

"There." Elena put the car in park and leaned back in her seat as if she'd just landed a head shot. The SUV was level again, but Joan pulled up the emergency brake anyway.

In front of them was the *solidest* looking cabin Joan had ever seen. No surprise; it was a hunter's hideout. It was built out of what looked to be boulders up to shoulder height, and then out of very large rocks, topped with a slate roof.

"Nobody's burning that down," Joan murmured. She approved. They'd had to flee burning buildings a couple times. It was still on her list of all-time least favorite dates.

"Or sieging it, or shooting the windows out, or quite a few other things. Grandma built this thing to last, and she did a really good job of it." Elena sounded justifiably proud. "It's a good old shack."

By Joan's estimation, the "old shack" could probably comfortably hold eight or possibly eighty people for the duration of a heavy winter storm. "Grandma built *big*, too."

"Well," Elena shrugged, "she was part giant. What?" she added, at Joan's raised eyebrows. "You knew my family was weird."

"Didn't we just hunt down a giant last month? Didn't you tell me giants were horrible, nasty creatures without a speck of human compassion in them, a relic of a bygone era that could never be tamed?"

"You never met my grandmother. That just about describes her to a T. Come on in; it's not like there are giants there now."

Joan's phone rang as they were hauling suitcases, groceries, and bags of presents into the cabin. She balanced it against her shoulder while she tried to follow Elena's gestured directions. In Elena's usual manner, giving those directions involved pointing in more directions at once than should be possible. The end result, as usual, was that Joan just went where she wanted anyway.

It seemed the New York airports weren't as sturdy as all that. Her parents' flight was cancelled, and the airports up and down the East Coast were closed.

"No, I understand," she said as she re-emerged into the living room. "Stay safe, and Lena and I will visit you sometime when the snow stops. No, we're safe. It's Lena's mother's cabin; it's very sturdy. I promise you, Mom, we're not going to be buried in an avalanche. And if we are, well, there's enough firewood here for a month or three anyway."

Truth be told, if it weren't for the tension of dealing with Elena's father and stepmother, Joan wouldn't *mind* being stuck in a giant stone cabin with her wife. The monsters probably couldn't find them up here.

"No, Mom, it's okay. I'm sure the gifts can wait."

She glanced up to find Elena on the phone as well, frowning off into the rafters while she made impatient listening noises.

"Well, I've got to get to unpacking here, Mom." She followed Elena's gaze—oh. Someone had left a yeti-spear mounted to the largest beam. That did not speak of a calm life chasing down decimal points and scolding untidy accountants—Joan's current cover story for family and other mundane acquaintances.

And, to either side of the yeti-spear, were the peculiar barbed nets they used when they chased down poltergeists.

"We'll call you on Christmas, and we can all sing carols by speakerphone."

"…if you're passing the firs, you're about ten minutes away. Yeah, we just got here. The place is just like I remember it. All right, Dad, I'm getting off the phone so we can start getting settled. We'll see you in a bit."

They hung up their phones and looked at each other. The place was dripping with weapons.

"I haven't been here in a couple years," Elena muttered. "I used it as a base a couple times, that's all. Before you and I—"

Her hand wave took in everything that was their relationship, and Joan nodded, because *when we just hunted together* was too complex to go into when they had to make the place look tidy and sedate in nine minutes. Elena's mother might have been a hunter—but her father had never been in the life, and her stepmother certainly wasn't!

"I thought your mom used to bring family here." Joan opened a cupboard in the small kitchen and cleared a space to stash the shorter and more damning things.

"Well, back in the day, yeah, and everything was a lot more tidy then. If you can get the guns on the back wall—you could probably do something with that fir garland we brought to cover the pegs—then I can get the spear and the nets. Most of this mess is my fault." She dragged a sturdy-looking chair under the beams while Joan did as suggested with a collection of antique guns with modifications that would drive a collector to tears. Someone had screwed a semi-modern scope onto the top of an antique rifle, for one.

"Mom spent a lot of time up here, the last couple years. I'd come out and we'd hunt together, and then I'd go back to—to Pittsburgh, and she'd come back here. Then she died, and I just spent months up here." Elena made a noise. "Our bags, Joan, quick. I didn't notice until now; they have pistol bulges."

"The grocery bags are safe, right? You didn't pack anything too strange in there?"

"Nah, most of that is straight from the store or the pantry. First bedroom, all the way on the right upstairs. It was—it was mine as a kid. It will be incrementally less strange, knowing the monster is sleeping in Mom's old bed than it will be to sleep there myself." She paused, a long wooden knife in one hand. "Was that your parents saying they couldn't make it?"

"The airport is entirely snowed in. From the sounds of it, the whole city is snowed in. So no Mom to buffer your stepmother. But, on the other hand, we only have to keep our stories straight for two people."

"Which reminds me." Elena pointed over Joan's shoulder. "Consecrated boar spear…So, did you get that raise you were talking about the last time your mom asked questions?"

"I did, but it came with a whole bunch of extra responsibilities. You know how the school is—never pay for something you can guilt someone into doing for free." They had long practice checking their lies against each other. "And what about that annoying co-worker that kept stepping on your toes?" Joan grabbed the spear from its place of honor on a low shelf and replaced it with a series of candles she'd packed for ambiance.

"You know what happened to Nathan. The werewolf in Santa Fe got him." Elena twisted her lips. "Okay. Oh shit, that's not a walking stick."

"Leave it; it looks close enough. What are the odds your father's going to grab it and discovered it's a viper's-head cane sword?" Joan headed up the narrow, steep stairs to the upstairs bedrooms. There were three of them, small rooms with large, plastic-covered beds. Everything smelled of lavender and cedar, mothballs and the faint aroma of church incense. "Try again with Nathan," she called down. "You can't tell your parents we last saw him inside of a werewolf's stomach."

"They're pulling in the driveway. Where did you put the incense? The normal sandalwood stuff or the scented vanilla candles or—"

"Candles are on the shelf where the boar spear was. Incense is in the lovely kitschy burner, remember, your co-worker Natalie gave it to you in the office secret Santa. Matches are in the kitchen bag."

Joan stopped in the doorway of the last bedroom on the right.

On the other side of the bed, something short and humanoid and vicious glared at her. "Elena? Does your house have—"

"Dad! Laura! Glad you could make it all the way up the mountain!" Elena's musical, fake-friendly voice drifted up the stairway.

The creature was gone—or perhaps it had never been there. In all her years of hunting, she had never seen something so very much like an evil Christmas elf.

She shook her head. All the carols were getting to her. "Oh, is that your folks?" she called down. "Hold on, I'll be right there."

She dumped the luggage on the bed. She could worry about sheets and blankets and short elves later.

❧

Elena's stepmother, it turned out, was a slender, pale, brunette woman, about as far from Elena as you could get and still be in the general field of "woman." She was also cheerful, with a pushy sort of friendliness that could be both endearing and irritating.

"Oh, I remember this place." She didn't so much talk as she sang over her shoulder as she bounced from place to place. Elena's father, who was a couple inches shorter than his daughter, followed along behind her like a balloon on a string. "Don't you, Fred? Back when we were all young and wild, and we'd come up here in the summer and go skinny-dipping in the pond back there? Oh, that was lovely. Don't you remember? And Stephania would scold, she always loved to scold."

Stephania was Elena's mother. Joan noticed Elena tensing—but over her wife's shoulder, she also noticed the trident-pointed arrows they used for hunting wendigo. The bow with them could be a decoration, maybe; the arrows were far more modern looking, and one of them had a smidge of blood dried onto it.

"Oh, I think it's going to be a bit too chill for skinny-dipping on this trip," Joan joked. She gave Elena a subtle push towards the arrows. "A winter like this, it's hungry and frozen, just as happy to eat you. Like the old song, right? 'Jack Frost comes nipping at your toes?' Only this one's down from Canada; it won't stop at your toes."

"Oh, you're poetic," Laura sighed. "I wouldn't imagine an accountant would have such a musical soul."

"She sings, too." Elena cheerfully offered Joan up to the wolves. "Sing that thing you were humming on the way up here, Joan. It was lovely."

Joan smiled brightly, because you couldn't threaten murder in front of your wife's parents. "How about over here by the hearth?" she suggested. They'd already cleaned up the hearth area. "The acoustics might be better."

She glanced back at Elena as they crossed the several miles between the entryway and the hearth; Elena was tucking arrows behind her back one at a time, like a kid sneaking sweets.

"It seems so much more open than when we were young, doesn't it, Fred?" Laura ran a finger over the mantle, where Joan had hastily arranged some fir boughs just minutes before. "Echo-y."

"We sold a lot of the furniture when Stephania died." Fred's amiable expression went cold and warning. Interesting.

Joan cleared her throat and began to sing. She had a passable voice—nothing radio worthy, but she'd sung in school choir as a child, and for a while, in church choir.

"We *wish* you a Merry—"

"Oh, not that one." Laura flapped her hands. "Anything but that one, please. It gives me the heebie-jeebies."

Maybe she really was a monster. Joan smiled, made some apologetic noises, and started in on "O Christmas Tree." She watched over Laura's shoulder while Elena cleaned up the bow and arrows, tucking them deep into a cupboard in the small kitchen area.

"Lovely," Laura murmured, when Joan finally ran out of verses. "You have a beautiful voice. And I bet this place will be beautiful again, with a little work. We brought you a few things to get you started."

"Oh, we're not—" Joan swallowed a gasp. There was another one of those awful things, a humanoid figure that came maybe up to Joan's hip, climbing up the stairs.

"Oh, honey, this is the twenty-first century." Laura set her hand on Joan's arm. "You don't really think we were going to buy that 'good friends who happen to be roommates' story, did you?"

Joan coughed and tried to catch Elena's eye. Elena, however, was glaring at her stepmother and glowering. "I don't believe we ever said anything like that."

"We might have, sweetie." Joan draped her arm around Elena's waist and tugged her close, camping it up a little bit for Elana's stepmother. "Remember? Back when we *were* good friends—that happened to be roommates?"

"Oh, yes, back when it was—" Elena trailed off.

"Seriously, girls, you don't need to pretend for our benefit." Laura shook her head. "Fred and I are very forward-thinking. Aren't we, Fred?"

Fred was looking at the mantle thoughtfully. "Mmm? Oh, forward-thinking. We were hippies, you know, Stephania and I and Laura and John. Back in the day. There's not much you can do that will shock us, and it's not like lesbianism is a new thing, you know." He smiled over his wire-rimmed glasses. "I promise, your generation did not invent spooning or whatever they call it these days."

There was another one of those creatures standing behind him! Joan coughed and hoped she looked nearly as embarrassed as she felt.

"Well, since you guys are familiar with this place," she tried gamely to change the subject, "maybe you can help Elena and I get the kitchen set up. We brought enough food for a small army, but if we want a warm meal, I might need a primer."

"Oh, remember the fondue we used to make?" Laura smiled warmly. "And then we'd feed it to each other, while we lay on our backs here on that big sheepskin rug that used to be here." She flopped on her back in the middle of the plank-wood floor. "I miss that rug."

"If you two are going to settle down here, you're really going to need more rugs. You can burn enough wood to stay warm, sure, but this heap really heats up once you've hung some tapestries." Fred looked around the building, once again narrowly missing sighting one of the elf-creatures. "Where did all of that stuff go, anyway?"

"Some of it went to Mom's friends." Elena's voice was harsh and had no room in it for discussion. Joan winced in sympathy, noting the way Fred cringed. "Some of it I have in storage, and a few pieces I sold."

Laura clucked in disapproval. "I know your mother left you this place, Ellie, but it's not as if other people don't have memories here. Your father used to come here with your mother, too."

It was exactly the wrong thing to say, *and* Joan had spotted three more of the awful creatures scurrying under the old leather couch. How did they even fit? She needed to get Elena away. Maybe they were just part of the decor. Maybe giants kept symbiotic elves.

Maybe Elena was going to kill her stepmother and then claim, the way that hunters who'd gone rouge would, that the woman was really a banshee.

"I followed my mother's instructions exactly." Elena's every word dripped ice.

"Honey," Laura tried, seemingly oblivious to the ice, "Stephania died suddenly. She can't have worked out all of this with you. And some of those pieces, well, they were important to all of us."

"My mother had an extensive will." Elena stared Laura down. "Don't you?"

"Hey, Lena, you were going to show me how this wood stove works." Joan grabbed her wife's arm. "Come on, love, we want to get something heating up for dinner. That will help make this place feel lived in again, don't you think?" She hauled on Elena's arm, hoping to move her by social pressure. Accountants didn't employ fireman's carries as far as Joan knew.

"And some cookies," Laura called. They both ignored her.

"Right." Elena let herself be dragged. "It's a bit tricky, but once you get used to it, it's a bit fun."

"I'm sure. You know how I feel about flames, Lena." She bent down next to the contraption so that her lips were near her wife's ear. "Did you see—"

At the same time, Elena hissed at her. "Remember my first bogey?"

They shared a glance. "The little elf thing?" Joan whispered. "We need the *Compendium.*"

"So it's just like any other wood-burning stove, except you have to stack a little more narrowly." Elena piled kindling into the firebox. "Things. This place is infested, but they're not like any other goblins in the book—"

"What about the tapestry that hung over the fireplace?" Fred's voice came from far too close, just a few feet behind them. If there had been anything on which to bump their heads, both Elena and Joan would be nursing concussions. As it was, Joan fumbled the box of matches in her hands.

Elena, damn her, remained calm and cool. "It's hanging in our living room—in the place Joan and I call home."

He twisted his lips up unhappily. "I see." If Elena had used that tone of voice, Joan would have prepared for a nuclear explosion. "That was your mother's wish?"

There were three little elf-creatures standing behind him. One of them was making a face, twisting its lips up like Fred's. Another one was dropping its trousers.

"Here, Fred, please help me get this thing lighted." Joan threw all compunction to the wind and gave him her best helpless-woman smile. "If there's a problem with the way Elena's inheritance was divided up, I'm sure we can work it out some time later."

"Ah. You're the accountant, right?" Fred's smile was sad and a little crooked. "I don't want to get math involved in this. I just worry sometimes about my Stephania's things and her wishes—"

"And what about her *house*—"

"Lena, my love," Joan interrupted, "could you make sure I got the right bedroom? This place is giant, and I was a bit rushed with our company arriving."

Elena glared at her for a solid five seconds before the word *company* clicked. "Sure, darling. Dad, don't let her burn her fingers. I might need those later. For fondue and spooning and things."

Fred and Joan sat there, staring at each other uncomfortably, until Elena left the room—stomped out of the room…flounced even.

"It's been hard—" they both began. Joan laughed first.

"It hasn't been an easy year," she offered, "for either of us. Trouble—trouble at work."

As much of an ass as Nathan had been, watching him die had been awful. And there'd been that mess with the Shtriga, and the living dolls had been pretty nerve-wracking.

"Her mother's death was hard on all of us," Fred offered in return. "Here, use the long matches. You want to get the flame right in the middle of the kindling." He demonstrated. "Then it's just letting the stove get hot."

"Like you and Laura?" While Joan was still trying to figure out if she should take it back, Fred blushed uncomfortably.

"Like Laura and I. The kindling was there, I suppose. Lots of fondue. And then Stephania was dead, and... Elena hates her, doesn't she?"

What could she say? Joan shrugged, keeping her eyes on the fire. "Elena has big opinions on every—"

"What in the seventeen names of Baal... I... Joan is that?"

Shit, shit, shit. Joan turned around slowly to find a small elfin creature just a few feet away. It reached up onto the counter and very deliberately knocked the bag of groceries onto the floor.

"Shit!" Pickles sausages, cheese, and a very long coil of hemp rope came spilling out, along with a pile of loose herbs. The pickle jar broke against the stone floor of the kitchen.

"Oh, lovely." The creature hurried off, only to be replaced by three more, each of them pulling drawers and doors open. "They're goblins with cat personalities." Joan wrinkled her nose in disgust.

All three creatures—no, now there were seven—looked at her. One had found the knife drawer. Another had found the weapons Joan and Elena had shoved into the kitchen cupboard. One was gnawing on the end of a stick of pepperoni. And now there were nine.

"Should I ask why you have rope in your groceries?"

"Hammock," Joan answered readily. The stove was behind them, but behind *that* was the back door. She took Fred's arm.

"Right. And the guns?"

"Those were here when we got here," she answered honestly. The door swung open behind them, just as one of the goblins leveled the ancient rifle with the modern scope at Fred. "Oh, no you don't." Training and instincts took over. Joan calculated route, grabbed the fireplace poker, and tightened her grip on Fred's arm. "Follow me."

"Now bring us some figgy pudding.
Now bring us some figgy pudding.
Now bring us some figgy pudding and
bring it right now."

The sudden song rang from the living room, where they'd left the stepmother. She had a lovely voice which, in the last notes, twisted upwards into something like a wail.

Joan, in a brief moment of hysteria, thought, *Banshee?* before all of the creatures started running into the living room. She grabbed the antique rifle from one of them as it passed her and followed, poker in one hand, rifle in the other, hoping she didn't have to shoot her stepmother-in-law.

Laura was standing on the hearth, the fireplace open, wielding a fireplace poker in one hand and a spray bottle in the other. She had started on the next verse.

"We won't go until we get some;
We won't go until we get some;
We won't go until we get some;
so bring some it right now."

The elves seemed mesmerized, jostling ever closer to her. And there were so many of them, dozens and dozens, one wielding a kitchen knife and another carrying a bag of flour. On the other side of the room, Elena was perched on the stairs, holding the viper's-head cane in one hand and the thick

Compendium in the other. It looked as if she had been fending off her own pile of the creatures until the singing began.

"Duck!" Laura sang out. Joan had excellent reflexes; she ducked, pulling Fred down with her, although he seemed to need far less help than she'd expected.

The spray gun went off in a series of hissing noises that were quickly echoed by the creatures. Every single elf-thing started running for the open stove door, and the smell of ginger quickly filled the air. Where the water hit the creatures, they melted, dissolving in a puddle of goo. Laura sprayed and sang, sprayed and sang, wielding "We Wish You a Merry Christmas" as a weapon.

When the last of the creatures had fled or melted, Laura dropped her arms and looked around at them.

"The one thing I never could stand about this cabin," she declared tiredly, "was the damn elves. Seriously, kids, you have to start baking cookies if you're going to live up here. The lore gets lost along the way, I know—but cookies. I'm sure even an accountant can handle that."

Elena flipped through the *Compendium*. "Elves," she read, her voice far too calm. "Variety: winter. Once fended off by ginger cookies left at the hearth and the front door. Extremely rare, thought to enjoy cold regions and mountains. It's in the *possibly apocryphal* section."

"Oh." Laura's head went up. "Is that *Tedwithle's Compendium?* Oh, good. You kids aren't completely helpless then. What?" She looked around the room again. "Do you think all we did up here was fondue and spoon? Yetis put a kibosh on skinny-dipping really fast, I can tell you that."

Joan looked between Laura, Fred, and Elena. "Merry Christmas to all," she murmured. At least they wouldn't have to spend the rest of the trip lying about it.

Fred met her gaze and smiled, perhaps sadly, perhaps only a little tiredly. "And to all a good night. Let's get dinner on the stove before the yetis attack, shall we?"

SADIE AND ROSA

by Alison Solomon

Sadie Green pulled her aging frame out of the blue velvet recliner in the living room of the well-appointed condo she shared with her lover, Rosa.

"I have something for you," she said as she walked over to the dining alcove, "a Hanukkah gift." The dining table was covered with a blue and white cotton tablecloth that they'd brought back from their most recent trip to Israel.

Rosa was in the process of picking candle wax off the brass menorah which sat in the center of the table. "I thought we agreed we wouldn't do gifts."

"I know, but this is something special." Sadie tried to take Rosa's hand, but Rosa pulled it back.

"You shouldn't have," she said. "But since you did, you can give it to me later, when we light the candles."

"Better yet, you could come with me to Johnny's, we'll all light candles together, and I'll give it to you there." Sadie couldn't hide the hopeful tone that crept into her voice.

Rosa huffed. "You know I won't."

"I'm tired of it, Ro," said Sadie, straightening the tablecloth. "We're seventy years old. These days everyone is out."

"Maybe they are in the schools your grandchildren attend, but people our age don't come out to their families."

"Yes, they do! Times have changed. We're not the only ones who watched *Grace and Frankie* and *Transparent*."

"That was television, not real life." Rosa hobbled slowly over to the maple credenza, bending to her right, her left hand holding the small of her back, which never seemed to stop bothering her. She pulled out a small packet of candles to place next to the menorah.

Watching her, Sadie thought back to the first time they'd lit Hanukkah candles together.

⁓

It had been the last night of Hanukkah. Sadie was sitting awkwardly by herself in the synagogue social hall, the first time she'd attended an event since Mark had died. Friends had come up to her to express their condolences, but no one had actually offered to sit with her or invited her to sit with them. She wondered whether they thought widowhood was contagious. An olive-skinned woman with large waves of undulating silver hair approached the table.

"May I sit here?"

Sadie didn't recall ever having seen the woman before. "Of course."

The two of them sat at the large trestle table that could easily accommodate another ten people and watched as couples settled in at the other tables. Sadie unwrapped one of the many chocolate gold coins scattered upon the table and popped it into her mouth.

"Looks like we'll have plenty of *sufganiot* to ourselves," the woman said, pointing at the plate in the center of the table piled with a dozen jelly donuts.

"Plenty of—?"

"*Sufganiot*—donuts. I'm Rosa Toledo, by the way." She held her hand out toward Sadie, who grasped it and noted what a good, firm grip Rosa had. She couldn't stand those women whose fingers floated toward her hand like jellyfish swaying in the ocean.

"Sadie Green. So are you a Hebrew expert?"

"No, the word was just in my mind because I was in Israel last year for Hanukkah."

"Me too! My daughter lives there, but I've never been able to get to grips with the language. I like celebrating Hanukkah in Israel because they don't make such a big deal of it."

"I think it only became a major holiday here because Jewish kids felt so left out of the Christmas gift-giving frenzy." Rosa ran her hand through her silver waves of hair and shook them out.

"Absolutely. And the politically correct folks thought they were being inclusive when they tacked Hanukkah and Kwanzaa onto everything to do with Christmas."

"Of course, if they really were PC, they'd know that it's much more important to wish us a happy New Year in September than to shower us with 'happy holidays' greetings at Christmastime."

Sadie smiled. "We sound like the crabby old people who have bumper stickers and yard signs exhorting the neighborhood to keep the Christ in Christmas."

"But I agree with them. At the university they used to call the big event in December a holiday party. But they wouldn't have been holding it if it weren't Christmas! They didn't do anything for Rosh Hashanah or Purim, did they?"

When the rabbi asked everyone to stand up and gather around the communal menorah so that they could light the candles, Sadie found herself disappointed. She'd been enjoying the animated conversation with this new woman so much that, surprising herself, she asked Rosa for her phone number.

They met for coffee the following Monday and decided to make it a regular occurrence. They learned about each other's histories: Rosa had grown up in Spain and immigrated to the USA when she was in her twenties. She'd taught Spanish at the local college and now enjoyed traveling in Europe and South America. She didn't have children, and she'd never felt the need to get married. Sadie told Rosa about her reasonably happy marriage, her daughter Hannah in Israel, and her son, who lived nearby in a Philadelphia suburb. After a few weeks, they started meeting for lunch on Wednesdays, which led to Sadie inviting Rosa for *Shabbat* dinner on the Friday night before Passover.

As she prepared the brisket, Sadie found herself humming a tune that had come into her mind unbidden, one she hadn't sung for so long it was almost forgotten. She tried to place it. A melody they used to sing on Friday nights. But where? When? Trees... sunshine... summer camp! Yes, Bnai Brith summer camp in the Catskills, that was it. All the kids singing and then Jenny Cohen grabbing her hand and pulling her into the empty parking lot behind the dining hall, asking her if she'd ever kissed a girl... Wow, she hadn't thought about that incident for fifty years.

When Rosa arrived, her silver hair was piled on top of her head, and sparkling stars dangled from her ears. Her long black caftan, embroidered with purple and blue threads, accentuated her height. In her arms, she carried three enormous bright yellow sunflowers, which she thrust toward Sadie.

"*Shabbat Shalom*," Rosa said and leaned forward to kiss her friend on the cheek.

Sadie felt a fluttering in her stomach as she accepted the flowers and the kiss. Her thoughts and heart both raced toward the same conclusion: Rosa was gorgeous.

❧

"You're sure you won't come with me?" Sadie picked up her purse and keys. "Not too late to change your mind."

Rosa handed Sadie her raincoat. "Don't start all that again. Your daughter-in-law says first night is only for family members. And as far as your family is concerned, I'm just your roommate and best friend; and that's the way I want it."

They'd been having the same argument on and off in different versions for the last five years they'd been together, ever since the first trip they took to Israel, when everything changed between them. On that trip, Ro had asked Sadie if she'd ever climbed Masada to see the sunrise, and when Sadie admitted she hadn't, they made a plan to start climbing Snake Path with all the teenagers and young people at four o'clock in the morning. As they stood on the top of the mountain, watching the sun begin to peek out from the dark horizon far below, Ro turned to Sadie.

"The year I've spent getting to know you has been one of the happiest of my life. I don't want to lose your friendship, but I have to tell you something."

Sadie kept her eyes on the horizon, watching the dark sky turn pink and the sliver of sun turn into a glowing ball. She had a feeling she knew what was coming. She'd been wanting to hear it and dreading it at the same time.

"You wouldn't be the first woman I've fallen in love with," Ro said, "but I'm hoping you'll be the last."

The Dead Sea became visible in the light, and Sadie's heart pulsed in rhythm with the sun.

"I… you… have you…?" She didn't know how to form her thoughts into words.

"I have. Not for a long time. I didn't think I'd ever find anyone I wanted to be with permanently, and then I met you," Rosa said. "I love being your friend, but I want to be more than that."

"I love being your friend too, Rosa. I can't say I haven't looked at women—I even kissed a girl once—but I've never been with anyone other than Mark."

"So you don't think you could—?" Rosa looked away, and in that moment Sadie imagined her life without Ro.

"Yes! Yes, I can. And I do. And I will. Yes!" She grabbed Rosa, and as the sun rose higher in the sky, they embraced and kissed, wrapping their arms around each other, just as the silk sheets would wrap around their legs later that night in the hotel.

When they returned home, Sadie announced to her family that her dear friend Rosa was moving in to keep her company and help with expenses. For the first couple of years, she hadn't been comfortable telling her kids the truth, and then when she was, Ro wouldn't hear of it. They'd argued back and forth, and even though Sadie knew Ro wouldn't change her mind about coming out, the day she stopped asking her to would be the day she put one foot in the grave. Five years later, this was still just as true.

"I don't think I'll ever understand why we can't speak up." Sadie sighed. "I love you so much, and I want everyone to know it." Impulsively, she pulled a small box from her purse.

"Here." She pushed it toward Rosa. "This is the gift I want to give you. It's a commitment ring. If I can't tell the world how much I love you, then let me at least tell you, Rosa Toledo, that the five years we have spent together have been the happiest of my life."

Rosa looked at her, head tilted slightly to one side, and the next thing Sadie knew, tears were starting to trickle down Rosa's cheek.

"I love you too," she said softly. "I guess it's time to tell you why I can't come out." She sat down at the dining room table and intimated to Sadie to do the same. "When we were first getting to know each other, I told you that I was born in Spain to a Sephardic Jewish family. That was true, but it wasn't the whole truth. When the war started, my family was living in Hungary, in a suburb of Budapest, where my father was from. Papa thought the family would be safe, and although there were some anti-Jewish laws, he thought we could wait out the war. Then, in early 1944, he heard that they were starting to round Jews up. Papa was able to connect with a wonderful man called Perlasca at the Spanish embassy who was smuggling Jews out of Hungary and into Spain."

"Perlasca? I've heard of him! He and Angel Sanz Briz saved thousands of Jews by telling the Nazis they were Spanish, even though almost all of them were Eastern European Ashkenazim. I never knew you were one of them!"

"Most people have only heard of Raoul Wallenberg, not Perlasca and Angel. But I'm not surprised you have, my little professor." Rosa squeezed Sadie's hand. "Perlasca told my father to come back the following day, and he would have papers for him, his wife, and his two daughters."

"Two?" Sadie asked. She thought Ro was an only child. Could she have forgotten this important piece of information?

"Yes. In 1944, I was just a baby, but my parents also had a seven-year-old daughter. The day my father went to the embassy to collect their papers, my mother sent my sister to Sarah Levy's house to play so she wouldn't be underfoot while my mother packed. Sarah was my mother's dear friend, and she had a daughter Hinda's age. Late that morning, soldiers came to Sarah's house and rounded up the family to take them on one of the dreaded transports. Sarah told them Hinda wasn't her daughter, that she was a Christian friend from kindergarten. They believed her—Hinda had our father's blond Hungarian features. One of the soldiers said he would take Hinda home. He took her hand in his.

'Is it true?' he asked my sister. 'Are you one of us?' All she had to do was say *yes*, and she and I would have grown up together; my father wouldn't have gone running and screaming to the train station, only to discover that the train had left and that no one knew where it was bound; my mother wouldn't have had to learn what had happened to her daughter years later when we were already in America, from a stranger who'd survived Auschwitz and had been there the same time as Sarah Levy."

"What did Hinda say to the soldier?" Sadie barely breathed the question, already knowing the answer.

"My brave, stupid, proud sister drew herself up and said to the soldier, 'I'm a Jew. I would never hide who I am or pretend to be someone I'm not. I'm proud to be a Jew.'"

Sadie got up and walked around to Rosa.

"Oh, my darling, why didn't you tell me?"

"It's a heavy story. I don't like to burden people with it. I myself didn't learn about it until I was much older, when a middle-aged Israeli tracked us down in Philadelphia. She had a number stamped on her arm—well, that wasn't unusual; so many of my parents' friends did. My mother gave her iced tea and sent me to bed. But I snuck out of my room and sat on the stairs listening while this woman told my parents about a woman she met in Auschwitz called Sarah, who'd been separated from her daughter and her daughter's friend the day they arrived. Sarah told as many people as she could the story of Hinda Toledo, so that if any of them ever found Miriam Toledo, they could tell her how brave her little girl was. I sat on the stairs and listened. And all I could think was, 'What a fool.'"

Sadie didn't know what to say. She stroked Rosa's hair and held her hand.

"I wish I'd known sooner. I can't believe the burden you've lived with."

"I learned a lot from that. I learned that you can get over almost any tragedy and move on; I learned that you make the most of every minute you have with the people you love. But I also learned that speaking up proudly for your identity isn't always the smart choice. I know it's easy for today's generation to think that everyone loves and accepts them, but I know better. You can call me paranoid if you want, but it's not a risk I'm willing to take."

"I understand," Sadie said softly. "I have to go over to Johnny's now." She pecked Rosa gently on the cheek.

"I'll see you later. *Hag sameach.*"

ഛ⁄◠

There were no less than five menorahs standing on the table, though only one of them looked like her own bronze candelabra. The others looked as if they belonged in either an art gallery or a toy shop: one was hand-painted wood that opened up like an accordion, its images depicting birds and flowers in vivid colors; another looked like little pieces of multicolored chewing gum stuck together; a third was a triangular shape in deep blue ceramic; and the fourth was composed of tiny golden cups interwoven with silver filigree. In her day, the candles were short, blue, and white. But these menorahs had a whole variety of candles in them: tall, slender, multicolored ones; thick, creamy, homemade beeswax ones; candles that seemed to change color depending on where you stood. There was also oil for the little gold cups.

"We promised the kids that this year, everyone would have their own menorah," Johnny said. "This way, the girls get to light candles from day one and sing the blessings too. Last year, Lily complained that Jason got to do all the lighting and reciting because he's the oldest. This year, everyone will be happy."

"Did you have your own menorah when you were a little girl, *Savta*?" asked dark-haired, brown-eyed Courtney.

"No, honey. In my day we just had one for the whole family. We children all had to be home in time for the lighting, even if it meant missing something at school. Then, as soon as my father was home from work, we all gathered around the menorah, and my father lit the candles and recited the blessings."

"How come he was the only one to light it?"

"That's how it was in those days. The men did all the rituals."

"Didn't you mind?" asked Lily.

"It didn't occur to me to mind. What you've never had, you never miss." It was true, but not entirely. In Sadie's day, women lit *Shabbat* candles and men lit Hanukkah candles, and that was fine with her. In fact, it still jolted her to see men lighting *Shabbat* candles. But as a thirteen-year-old, although she'd never wanted to wear a *tallit* or *kipa* or read *torah*, she *had* felt a little jealous of the *bar mitzvah* boys. Back then, girls didn't have a bat mitzvah, and even though bar mitzvahs weren't the elaborate affairs they were now, the boys got to show off their Hebrew talents and in return were showered with gifts.

"How's Rosa?" Johnny asked, "Her back doing any better?"

"Not really. I've begged her to go to the chiropractor you suggested, but she insists she won't go to 'a voodoo doctor.'" Sadie put the words into air quotes. "Her own doctor does nothing to help, but you know how stubborn she is: she won't take painkillers and won't go to an alternative practitioner."

Sadie lowered herself onto the white leather sofa. She could never get over the idea of having white leather in a house filled with children, but Johnny's wife was almost as stubborn as Ro, and she'd insisted on it, even though she spent most of the time eyeing everyone nervously any time they sat on it.

"How come Rosa didn't come with you to light candles with us? Doesn't she like Hanukkah? Doesn't she like us?"

"Now, now," Johnny cut in, "you know Mommy's rule in our house. Only family members for first night candle lighting. That's the way it was in her home, and that's the way it is here. Special family time. Your friends don't come over, and nor do *Savta*'s."

Sadie felt a lump in her chest. If only she could say something. But now, more than ever, she understood why she had to keep Rosa's silence.

"Let me help you in the kitchen," Johnny called through to his wife, then got up and joined her. Sadie suspected that it was the tantalizing scent of frying latkes that was drawing him in.

Sadie patted the seat of the sofa and beckoned Courtney and Lily to come and sit next to her. "Before we light candles, let's do the quiz," she said.

"Yes, yes!" Lily and Courtney jumped up and down.

"I'm gonna win!" shouted Courtney.

"No me, I'm gonna!"

"First question to Courtney: what are the four letters on the dreidel?"

"Oh, that's easy." Courtney stuck four fingers in the air, then counted them off, "*Nun, Gimmel, Hey*, and *Shin*!"

"That's not fair. Make it harder," Lily said.

"She's younger than you. Okay, for a bonus point: what do they stand for?"

"Um…" Courtney paused.

"I know, I know!" Lily's hand had shot up as if she were in class at school.

Sadie looked at Courtney, who clearly didn't know the answer.

"Okay, tell her, Lily."

"*Nes Gadol Haya Sham*—A Great Miracle Happened There."

"Excellent! Now here's your question. What are the four letters on the dreidel that your Aunty Hannah and her family use in Israel?"

"Is it a trick question? Surely they're the same?"

"No, one of them is different."

Lily's forehead scrunched up in thought.

"Do you want me to tell you?" Lily nodded her head.

"The fourth letter is different. It's a *Pey* instead of a *Shin*. Instead of saying *A Great Miracle Happened There*, in Israel, they say, *A Great Miracle Happened Here*—*po* is the word for *here*—because, after all, that's where the miracle took place."

Johnny's wife, Debbie, appeared in the doorway. "Jason texted and said he's running late. I think it was football practice. Said he'll be home within the hour. I told him we'll wait for him. After all, we don't want him to miss first night."

Sadie smiled, but the girls made faces. "The latkes will get cold! Do we have to wait for him to have them?"

"How about we have latkes before we light up, and we can keep the donuts till after the candles are lit?"

That seemed to satisfy everyone, and they all piled into the kitchen, where a plate of jelly donuts sat on the counter, and hot, fresh potato latkes sizzled in an enormous pan on the stove.

"So, what's the theme for tonight?" Sadie asked her son. In her day, there were no themes behind the eight days of the festival. On first and last day, her parents would give them each some *gelt*—usually a silver dollar each—and that would be that. Since then, Hanukkah had started to compete with Christmas in the gifts department, and for many children, it was just all about comparing their expensive presents. She was so appreciative of the fact that Debbie and Johnny not only kept to the spirit of the holiday but they added to it. Each night they created a theme that had to do with social justice, which the children discussed while the candles burned.

"I don't know. Jason said he wanted to take charge tonight, so we'll have to wait and see." Just then, the door opened and Jason himself appeared. He embraced his grandmother warmly.

"I know we always light candles before Dad gives us his *drash*, but I'd like to do my talk first. Would that be okay?"

Johnny and Debbie glanced at each other, then nodded their assent. Debbie brought in the donuts, and they settled in the living room to hear what Jason had to say.

"We all know that Hanukkah is about miracles. Co-co, can you tell us what the miracle of Hanukkah is?" He turned to his younger sister, and Sadie smiled, remembering how Jason used to be so protective of Hannah when she was that age.

"After the Maccabees had won the war against the Greeks, they went to rededicate the temple. They only had enough oil for one day, and they knew it would take a week before they could get more. But that one day of oil ended up lasting for eight days, and that's the miracle."

"Very good. But actually, there's a miracle behind that miracle, which happened before they even lit that lamp." Jason smiled indulgently at his little sister. "The Maccabees knew they needed eight days of sanctified oil but that they only had enough to last for one. They could have said, "There's no point lighting the oil, since we know it's only going to last for one day." Why didn't they say that, Li-li?" He looked at his middle sister.

"Um… well, I guess they figured they didn't know for sure, and that it was better to at least try to use what they had?"

"Right. But what lay beneath that logic—*Savta*, can you tell us?"

Sadie thought for a moment. "Even though they didn't know what would happen, they had faith." Sadie felt awkward using the word 'faith', because even though her Jewish identity was important to her, she didn't always feel as if she had a lot of faith, especially not on the spiritual side of things.

"Exactly, *Savta*. And faith is really just another word for trust. They trusted. That's the miracle. We get so caught up in thinking about the 'what ifs' that we can end up having no trust and living in fear. In Hebrew school, we learned that when the Red Sea parted, one man, Nachshon, had to be willing to walk into the water. He trusted, and because of that, everyone followed him, the seas parted, and the people were saved. Trust is the most important thing we can have. We have to trust outsiders, but first of all, we have to trust ourselves and our families. When we know our truth, we have to trust that we can share it with our families. Right, *Savta*?"

Sadie felt as if her cheeks were burning. Was he saying what she thought he was saying?

Just then, the doorbell rang. Debbie turned to her daughters.

"Did you invite your friends over? You know we don't—"

"No!" They both yelled in unison.

"I'll get rid of whoever it is, and then we'll light candles." Johnny got up and went to the front door. Sadie heard muffled voices. Then Johnny returned—with Rosa right behind him.

"Aunty Rosa!" The girls ran up to greet her. Jason stayed where he was, but the smile on his face was as broad as his football-playing shoulders.

Rosa turned to Debbie.

"Before you say anything, I have something to say. Jason stopped by our condo a little while ago, and he gave me a copy of the *drash* he was giving to you all this evening. At first, I thought he just didn't want me to miss out on his first sermon..."

Everyone laughed. It was well known in the family that they all thought Jason would end up being a rabbi, even though he was still convinced he was destined to be a first-round pick for the NFL draft.

"But then I realized what he was saying," Rosa said. "He asked me to come here with him, but I refused. After he left, I couldn't stop thinking. And the more I thought, the more I knew what I had to do." She stopped talking and went to stand next to Sadie. Sadie felt her hand being lifted and, with it, her heart.

"Sadie's wanted to tell you all for a long time, but I was the one who said 'no.' Well, I guess Jason is right. Sometimes we just have to trust, so I'm trusting that what I have to say will be well accepted." She looked at Sadie, then at each person in the room. "I'm not just your grandmother's roommate." She turned to the children. "Or your mom's best friend." She looked at Johnny. "Sadie and I are lovers and partners and have been for the last five years."

There was a moment of silence. Sadie froze. Had she read them all wrong? Had Rosa?

Then, all of a sudden, everyone was talking at once.

"We know, Mom; we figured it out a long time ago!"

"I told my friends at school I was sure my granny was gay!"

"What's a lover?" This last one came from young Courtney.

"It means," Sadie turned to her youngest grandchild, "that Rosa and I love each other the same way your Mom and Dad love each other."

"Oh." Courtney looked puzzled. "Well, I knew *that*. It's kinda obvious."

And with that, everyone laughed and picked up their matches and lighters to light candles and say blessings.

"What were those four words on the dreidel again?" Courtney asked.

"*Nes Gadol Haya Sham*—A Great Miracle Happened There." Lily punched her little sister lightly on the arm.

"That's right," said Sadie. And under her breath she added, "But more importantly, *Nes Gadol Haya Po*—A Great Miracle Happened Here."

GLOSSARY:

Drash: A talk about any topic

Gelt: Money/coins

Hag Sameach: Happy Holidays

Kipa: Yarmulke/head-covering

Latkes: Potato Pancakes

Savta: Grandma/Granny

Shabbat Shalom: Greeting made on the Sabbath to wish someone well

Sufganiot: Donuts

Tallit: Prayer shawl

Torah: Scripture

KICKER'S CHRISTMAS

by Lois Cloarec Hart

Christmas Eve, 1917

KICKER PAUSED IN FRONT OF the door to stomp her boots. It had snowed much of the afternoon, but by the time she'd sent her employees home, the storm had tapered off to a few persistent flakes. She pushed open the door and entered the log cabin.

Madelyn looked up from the stack of papers on her desk and smiled. "Welcome home, dearest. How was work? Is everyone excited about being off for the holidays?"

Kicker hung up her coat and kicked off her boots before crossing the room to kiss Maddie. "All but Pudge."

"What's wrong with Pudge?"

"He was still madder than a wet hen about yesterday. Din't I tell you 'bout that?"

Madelyn shook her head. "No. What happened?"

"I sent Pudge and Clarence into Calgary with the las' of the deliveries and to talk to our suppliers. Some damn fool woman saw them walking down the street, came up behind 'em, and stuck a white feather in the collar of Clarence's coat."

"Oh no, not again."

"Aye. Pudge was so mad, he near took the woman's head off. If Clarence hadn't pulled him away, Seamus pro'ly would've had to make his brother's bail."

"Oh, poor Clarence. That's so terribly unfair."

"Aye. Clarence says Pudge swore a blue streak and tol' the woman plain that Clarence was no coward. Said the lad was first in line to join the 10th Battalion, and the only reason he wasn't in some trench in France was 'cause of his heart condition."

"I hope the woman had the good grace to slink away."

"Ran like a weasel caught in a chicken coop, according to Clarence."

Madelyn took her glasses off and rubbed her eyes. "I worry so, dearest."

"'Bout Clarence?"

"Not really, though I do hope this war doesn't go on so long that they take even men with medical conditions. I'm thinking more about all the boys I've taught who are over there, particularly Laird. He's been in battle for so long now. Since Billy's death, Laird's letters to Wynne have been terribly despondent, though I know it is not his wish to worry his mother."

Kicker snorted. "Like he stood any chance of that, eh? Wynne worried sum'pin fierce from the moment the king declared war and the firs' Canadian contingent sailed for Britain with Laird and Billy on board."

"It's so sad to think of our local lads shedding their blood on foreign soil."

"E'en Archie Mason?"

Madelyn smiled. "Can you believe he's a decorated officer? He was such a bully as a boy. I find it quite amazing that he turned into a leader of men."

"Guess he jus' had to fin' his station."

"You're right. As we have done. But I so wish this war would end and they'd come home."

Kicker wrapped her arms around Madelyn and pressed a kiss into her hair. "I know, love. May the good Lord bring 'em all home safe and soun'."

Billy won' e'er come home.

The thought made Kicker's breath catch. Her memory drifted back eighteen years to when she and Madelyn had first stepped off the train in Galbraith's Crossing. Young Billy Donnelly had been sent to wait for their arrival. He'd been small of stature, all bright blue eyes, messy, straw-coloured hair, and bubbling with eagerness to earn enough money for a new wagon. But when he left for war in 1914, he'd been a married man with a pregnant wife. His son was born while Billy survived the first use of poison gas at Ypres.

Laird and Billy had grown up together on the Steeple Seven Ranch; Laird, the son of the owner, and Billy, the son of the foreman. One was rarely seen without the other, and when the Canadian Expeditionary Force was raised in the fall of 1914, they'd gone together to enlist.

Madelyn had been Laird and Billy's teacher for many years, and they worshipped her. She, in turn, loved them, and Kicker felt the same. They had become like family. When word arrived in Galbraith's Crossing of the death of Corporal Billy Donnelly on Vimy Ridge, Easter Sunday, 1917, they had joined the entire town in mourning alongside the Donnelly family.

Madelyn squeezed Kicker's arms. "I miss him too, dearest."

"Aye."

As always, Kicker was amazed by her partner's uncanny ability to read her thoughts. It hadn't always been thus. They'd mucked about and misread each other often in their early years together, to the point of a disastrous miscommunication that had split them apart for many weeks. But in the years since, they had committed utterly to one another, even as the townsfolk, with few exceptions, regarded them as the widowed schoolteacher and her oddball blacksmith cousin.

Kicker's rise to prosperity through her ornamental ironworks factory had quieted gossip about her unconventional lifestyle. The factory had converted to wartime production in 1915 and, given the shortage of available manpower, provided employment for fifty local women and older men.

Kicker smiled. Wealth had a way of stilling criticism and smoothing one's path in society. It worked similar magic for their equally unorthodox friend, Wynne. Despite her gender, she was the most powerful rancher in southwestern Alberta.

"Is Seamus joining us for dinner tonight?"

"Aye. He said he'll be out after the six-twenty train."

Madelyn stood and stacked her papers. "And Pudge? Will he be joining us as well?"

"No. B'lieve it or not, Pudge has a date."

Madelyn spun and stared at Kicker. "Our Pudge? A date?"

"I know. It shocked me, too. Apparently the Widow Boyle invited Pudge to dinner and Mass t'night. At leas' should lift his mood after the white feather smear."

"I know he's gotten much better about socializing, but this positively stuns me."

Kicker grinned and went to wash her hands in the basin. "Seamus always says that e'er since Turtle Mountain tried to kill Pudge and failed, Pudge has been working his way back to his ol' self."

"Coming to work for you was certainly a huge step."

"Aye. Bes' foreman I e'er had, and having e'ryone accept him, ruined face and all, has bin good for him."

"I'm pleased about the date, but I'm still stunned."

Kicker dried her hands as Madelyn slipped her arms around Kicker's waist. Kicker leaned back and enjoyed her partner's familiar warmth. "I still remember the Pudge we met on the *S.S. Assiniboine.* He was such a ladies' man, I thought sure some father would be after him with a shotgun to get him to the altar. It was only after the fire that he drew away from e'ryone."

"Everyone but you and Seamus."

"Aye." Kicker turned in Madelyn's arms and drew her head down for a lingering kiss.

When they parted, Kicker nodded at the kitchen end of the great room, where the table was set and the scent of roasting chicken filled the air. "Anything I can do to help?"

Madelyn stole one more kiss. "Would you make your biscuits, dearest? They're always a treat."

"Aye." Kicker bustled about and, as always, blessed the memory of the cook in Madelyn's London family home who had taught her culinary basics.

"Did you stop to check the mail?"

"Aye, but t'was none for us, nor the Steeple Seven."

Madelyn resumed her seat at the desk and put her glasses on. "Hardly surprising, with mail being so slow these days. I had hoped there might be something for Wynne, though. It's been so long since Laird's last letter."

Kicker measured out the flour. "But there's been no telegram, and that's good news. Laird ain't dead or missing, or Wynne would know."

"Then why hasn't he written? Wynne looks more drawn every time I see her, and I'm terribly worried about her."

Kicker's heart clenched. Wynne had aged a decade in the three years since her son had boarded the troop train leaving town. "As am I, love. But all we can do is be there for her, bes' we can."

"I wish I could keep all the newspapers from her. The news is so grim, and I know she obsesses over every article about the Western Front."

"Aye. I thought sure when we won provincial suffrage last year t'would be a distraction, since she fought for it so long. But she barely celebrated. She don' e'en care that having a soldier-son means she can vote federally now, an' her so ad'mant about women's rights. These days all she talks about is the debate over conscription."

"That's because she fears greatly that conscription will mean her young nephews will be the next to join their brothers and cousins. You know Samuel has been begging his father to let him go."

"Aye, and him only sixteen. Tis far too young." Kicker shook her head as she cut the lard into the flour.

"The last time we were at Wynne's, I overheard the two of them arguing. Albert forbade Samuel to even consider enlisting, but Sam raged that his father was preventing him from doing his patriotic duty. I believe, conscription or not, Samuel will be on the first train out after his seventeenth birthday next spring."

"I fear you're right, love, but tis naught to be done. Samuel has been hard-headed since the day he was born."

Kicker turned the conversation to lighter matters. By the time the rattle of Seamus' beloved 1912 McLaughlin motorcar sounded in their lane, dinner was nearly ready.

Madelyn swung the door open. "Merry Christmas, Seamus."

Seamus greeted her and Kicker with his usual hugs, but their smiles faded at his serious demeanour.

Kicker tensed. Their gentle friend emanated distress. "Seamus? What's wrong?"

Madelyn's hands flew to her mouth. "Has news come? Is it Laird?"

Seamus nodded. "It's Laird, but not news."

"What d'you mean, not news? Ha' you heard sum'pin?" Kicker rested her hands on Madelyn's shoulders as she eyed Seamus. "Out with it, man."

Seamus shrugged out of his coat. "Could I trouble you for a drink? It was a cold drive from town."

"Of course." Madelyn took his coat and hung it up.

Kicker hastened to pour him a whiskey. She handed it to him as he took his customary seat, and watched with concern as he drained it in two gulps.

Seamus rolled the empty glass in his hands but shook his head at Kicker's offer of a refill. "I was shutting down after the six-twenty. It was pure happenstance that I glanced out at the platform before leaving. I didn't think any passengers had gotten off, but someone was sitting outside on the bench. It was a soldier. I waited to see what he'd do, and then thought perhaps he needed a ride somewhere, so I went out to make the offer. It was Laird."

Madelyn clapped her hands. "Oh, thank God, he's home!"

But Kicker studied Seamus' grim face. They didn't have the whole story yet. "What's wrong?"

Seamus took a deep breath. "He had crutches resting beside him. He's missing a leg."

Madelyn gasped.

Kicker closed her eyes. "Bless'd Jesus." Then she opened them. "Matters not. He's home from the war. So many will not return."

Seamus nodded. "As I thought, too, but... I don't know how to describe this. When I greeted him, he stared at me blankly, like he knew not who I was, and me knowing him since he was a young lad. I offered him a ride home, and he looked through me as if my words made no sense. I tried to coax him into the warmth of the station, but he paid me no heed. He just sat there, staring off into the dark. I got a blanket and put it around his shoulders. He didn't throw it off, so I left and came right here. I thought with you being as close to Wynne as family, you might know what's best to do. Do you think I should go straight on to Wynne?"

Madelyn started to nod, but Kicker laid a hand on her arm. "I think we should talk to him firs', love. I'll go ready the sleigh. Seamus, can you go to Wynne and bring her here? Don' tell her why, jus' yet. We need to suss out the lay of the land. Could be we'll keep Laird in the station for the night if it seems bes'. Per'aps he's jus' tired and needs to rest before he sees his ma. Seamus, you kin stay with us t'night if tis necess'ry."

Seamus nodded and rose to put his coat back on.

Madelyn took the chicken and biscuits out of the oven and moved the soup to the counter. The celebratory dinner was forgotten as all three were out the door within moments.

The silence of the winter night was broken only by the creaking of the sleigh's runners over the fresh snow and the jingle of the horse's harness as Kicker drove swiftly to town.

When she pulled to a stop in front of the train station, Madelyn turned to her. "Would you allow me to speak to him first, dearest?"

"Aye. Without hes'tation." Kicker had a great deal more confidence in Madelyn's ability to communicate than in her own. Give her a horse or a forge, and none were better, but stress still returned her speech to the patterns of her youth.

They pushed the thick lap blanket aside and clambered out of the sleigh. Kicker offered Madelyn an arm as they negotiated the platform around to trackside.

Laird sat hunched on a bench in front of the station. It appeared that he'd gone no further than he had to when he had disembarked from the train. His empty left pant leg was rolled up and pinned at the thigh. A duffel bag lay next to his right foot, and crutches rested against the bench. The blanket Seamus had placed around him had fallen in a heap on the bench. He didn't raise his head as Kicker and Madelyn approached.

Kicker knelt in front of him.

Madelyn sat beside him and took his hand.

Laird flinched and shuddered.

Kicker stood and pulled the blanket up around his thin shoulders.

He looked at her, and she understood what Seamus had told them. The boy who had left in high spirits, determined to bring honour to King and Country was nowhere to be found in this gaunt man's bleak stare.

Madelyn raised Laird's hand to her lips, and his head slowly swivelled to her.

"Laird, do you remember me?"

"Mrs. Bristow. You were my teacher."

"Yes. I'm so pleased to see you again. I—"

"You were our favourite teacher, me and Billy's. You went away for a while. We didn't like the new teacher."

Madelyn shot a glance at Kicker. "I did go away for a little while, but I came home, didn't I?"

Laird nodded.

"And now you've come home, too. We're so glad to see you again, aren't we, Kicker?"

"Aye, that we are."

"Billy won't be coming home." Laird's voice was as arid as the prairie in a rainless summer.

Madelyn slipped her arm around Laird's shoulders. "No, he won't. We were all so sorry to learn what happened to him."

Laird shook his head. "You think you know what happened? Did you know he saved my life from a potato masher? That it took half my best friend's face off and blew out his guts? Did you know that I held him while he tried to speak his last words, but he had no mouth to say them? Did you know that I had to leave him behind as some sodding half-wit ordered us over the top for a useless charge across no-man's land? I ran between the trenches with Billy's blood soaking me as much as the rain. Once the shooting stopped, it took me half the night to find him again. Did you know the rats had already been at him, and the only way I could recognize him was his wedding ring? I took that off him. I've worn it on a chain every goddamned day since, and I brought it home for the son he will never see, the son who will never know his father."

Kicker softly blew out her breath and glanced at her partner. "Maddie, would you wait for us inside the station?"

For a moment, Madelyn studied Kicker's face in the dim haze of the platform's gaslight, then she rose and patted Laird's shoulder before she walked away.

Kicker took her place beside Laird. They silently stared into the darkness until the station door opened and closed.

"D'you remember Pudge Kelly, Laird?"

"Yes."

"Twas a long time ago and you a wee lad, so you might not recall this. Pudge saved my life from an evil man who was seconds away from blowin' me to bits."

"I remember."

"You pro'ly don' remember Pudge before he was burned so bad in the fire at our Shadow Creek home."

"Not really, no."

"He was a handsome man, full of fun and music and life."

"Billy was like that too."

"I know. Well, Pudge, he was ne'er in battle with people shooting at him, but his heart and soul warred for many years."

Laird shot Kicker a shame-faced glance. "We called him the melting man."

"B'cause of his face run together?"

"Yes. I'm sorry about that. I hope he never heard us."

Warmth rose within Kicker. The sweet young man she'd known was still there inside. "If he did, he ne'er said anything to me nor Seamus. I wouldn't worry about it. 'Sides, worse things happened to him. D'you know a mountain fell on his head?"

Laird blinked at her. "And he lived?"

"Aye. He was working a shift the night half of Turtle Mountain slid down on the town of Frank. He and the other miners had to tunnel their way to the surface, but they survived. He tol' me that when he poked his head out into the morning light, he made himself a promise."

"What was it?"

"To live."

"He had two good legs left."

"Aye, he did. But he come out of that mine and he's still the meltin' man, ain't he?"

Laird hung his head.

"Kids still taunted him; women still looked away in horror, but he figured God saved his life twice and was waiting on him to appreciate that. So he paid no more heed to the stares and the whispers. He lives, every day. He works. He makes music. He laughs and tells the worst jokes, and he loves his brother and his frien's."

The church bells rang out from the far end of town, and Kicker smiled. "And t'night, he's got a date with the Widow Boyle. D'you understan' what I'm telling you, lad?"

"Some people have it far worse than me."

"Nope, that ain't it. What you seen, where you been—it was hell. Ain't nothing those of us back here on the home front can e'er understan', and that's the truth. But that don' mean your life is over, unless you will it so."

Laird cocked his head as the bells of the Catholic church rang on.

Kicker waited until they were done. "I can't tell you life is going to be easy with only one leg. I can't promise that children won' stare or whisper. But I can tell you some special woman won' care that you wear only one boot."

"Ghislaine."

"Clarence's sister?"

A ghost of a smile flickered on Laird's lips. "She's been writing to me since I left. I got almost every letter in here." He tapped his foot on his duffel bag. "I lost a couple when..."

Laird stared off into the darkness. "It wouldn't be fair to court her, though. She deserves more than half a man."

Kicker shook her head. "Don' be silly, lad. The mark of a man ain't two good legs. The bastard who tried to blow me to bits had two good legs and a heart blacker 'n coal. Ghislaine is a fine young woman. I b'lieve she'll be nineteen on her nex' birthday. If she's bin writing all these years, I expect she's waiting for you to come home to her. She won' care about your leg. She cares about your heart. An' e'ryone aroun' here knows your heart to be good an' true. We've known that since you were a wee lad. War din't change that, and tis all that matters."

Laird turned to her. "Do you really think so?"

"Aye, I do. Let me tell you a story. A long time ago, I went through hell myself. Someone I loved let me down sum'pin fierce, and I mourned so deep that I turned away from e'ryone I knew."

"He's why you never married? The fellow who let you down?"

Kicker hesitated for only a second. "Aye. I had gi'en away my heart, and what was left was torn to pieces. My bes' frien' worried I wouldn't live through it."

"Mrs. Bristow? Your cousin is your best friend?"

"Aye, that she is. But them that loves you, don' give up on you. They make you eat when food is like dust in your mouth. They keep you company when all you can do is cry. They offer comfort and love when you don' think you warrant either. Tis what your family and friends stan' ready to do too, Laird. You jus' gotta give them a chance. Can you do that? Because I can tell you that your ma wants nothing more than to see your face and hug the stuffing out of you."

"I won't be of much use to her or the ranch."

"Pah! D'you think she cares about that? Wynne has suffered every moment you been gone. All she wants is her boy home. If she can see you across the Christmas dinner table, t'will be the grandest gift she's e'er gotten. Don' you know that?"

Laird stared at the emptiness below his left thigh. "I...I... Some of the men I was in the military hospital with said they couldn't go home again. They couldn't bear the thought of seeing pity in their family's eyes. Said they couldn't stand to be a burden the rest of their lives. I didn't know what to think. I tried to write Ma many times, but I couldn't make the words come. I've been sitting here tonight, not knowing what to do. I made Billy a promise, and that's what held me here on this bench. But I've been thinking maybe I should get back on the morning train and go east, all the way to the Atlantic."

"Damn fool idea, lad. Firs' off, you don' need to be anything to your family but who you already are. And if you're worried about being a burden, I'll make you a leg."

Laird's head swivelled, and he blinked at Kicker. "Make me a leg?"

"Aye. I got a factory and a lot of skilled workers. I've never made a leg b'fore, but I 'spect there's not much I can't make if I put my mind to it. Jus' gotta research the right materials and way to do it. I'll get Clarence right on it. Man has a mind sharper than a quill. We'll have you back up on a horse b'fore you know it. Or if you'd a min', Seamus can teach you to drive one of those damn fool motorcars that are ruining our countryside. There's always ways to get aroun', Laird. You want to work the land? You want a wife and family? Tis up to you. You're ne'er going to forget the hell you bin through for three years, but you don' have to stay stuck in that trench fore'er. Honour the brothers who fought and fell b'side, but do it by livin' a full life. Don' dishonour their sacrifice by leaving all you know to become a stranger on some strange coast. This is your home. Claim it. We're all waiting, an' you know tis what Billy would wan' for you."

"He would, wouldn't he?"

"Damn right. He was your brother in all but blood, and if you live on, so does he. Now…are you ready to go see your ma?"

Laird didn't say anything for a long moment, and Kicker held her breath.

Then Laird sighed and nodded. "Yes. And thank you."

"Seeing the joy on Wynne's face tis all the thanks I need."

Kicker picked up Laird's duffel bag and Seamus' blanket as Laird tucked the crutches under his arms and began his slow trek across the platform.

To Kicker's surprise, Madelyn was already seated in the cargo area of the sleigh.

Laird's eyes widened. "Oh, no, Mrs. Bristow. Please, I'll ride back there. Ma would have my hide for denying a lady a seat."

Madelyn tucked the warm travel robe more tightly around her legs. "I'm perfectly comfortable, thank you. You climb on up there with Kicker."

He did so, but cast several mortified glances back at Madelyn, who affected an expression of perfect serenity.

Kicker grinned and winked at her partner as she tucked the duffel bag and crutches next to Maddie. She got an impertinent smile in return and swung up on the driver's seat.

The church bells began to ring again as the horse cantered away from the station.

At the edge of town, where they turned north into the woods, Kicker wordlessly offered the reins to Laird.

He took them and guided the horse over the familiar back road that led to Kicker and Madelyn's Shadow Creek cabin, and to the Steeple Seven Ranch—Laird's home.

Confident that the sleigh was in steady hands, Kicker leaned back and studied the night sky. It was black and brilliant with stars, the earlier clouds having long since vanished. The cold air curled between her toque and the sheepskin collar of her jacket, making her shiver and long for her forgotten wool scarf, but the frigid night was no match for the warmth within.

Laird had come home from the war, and they got to deliver him to his mother. Of all the gifts they'd exchanged with Wynne over the years, none came close to equalling what they were bringing her this night.

Joy and sorrow filled Kicker's soul. Tonight Wynne's heart and arms would be filled, but Mrs. Donnelly would never again hold her son. Still, Billy's son was growing like a prairie weed under his grandmother's roof and his mother's care. Kicker hoped he would prove consolation enough for Billy's family.

As they neared Shadow Creek, Kicker pointed ahead to the lane that led to their cabin. "Your ma will be waiting at our place, 'less Seamus o'erturned his motorcar again. But the snow's not so deep tonight, so I'm sure he made it back fine."

"Does Ma know I'm home?"

Kicker shook her head. "No. The best gifts are unexpected ones, don' you think?"

Laird snapped the reins, and they took the turn into Shadow Creek far too fast for Kicker's comfort, but she understood Laird's eagerness.

They pulled up in front of the cabin in one piece. Warm lantern light spilled out of the windows and created bright patches on the snow.

Laird almost fell in his haste to dismount from the sleigh, but Kicker caught him as Madelyn hurried around with the crutches. They flanked him as he struggled through the snow.

Kicker stepped forward and threw open the door.

Wynne looked up from her seat beside Seamus. "Kicker, what's going on? Seamus won't tell me a thing. He only insisted that I come with him. Are you all right? Is Maddie?"

"Aye, we're fine. Bett'r than fine. Tis sorry I am to pull you from your family's hearth on such a col' night, but I s'pect you'll forgive us. We brought you a gift, Wynne." Kicker stepped out of the doorway and Laird entered.

Tears streamed down his face. "Ma, I'm home."

Wynne hurtled across the room. She laughed and cried as she swept Laird into her arms.

Laird wobbled and almost fell from the onslaught of his mother's embrace, but Madelyn grabbed his coat and steadied him from behind.

For several long moments, the only sound in the cabin was of mother and son sobbing together.

Kicker dashed her sleeve across her eyes and noticed Seamus doing the same. Madelyn dabbed at her eyes with a lace handkerchief.

Finally Wynne pulled back and cupped Laird's face. "You're so thin."

He smoothed the hair back from her brow. "And you're so white. Did I do that?"

Wynne smiled through her tears. "You sure did. Every last hair on my head. But I don't care one whit. You're home, and that's all that matters. Come, get in out of the cold, son."

Wynne helped Laird off with his greatcoat and made room for him to hobble across to the divan. She sat next to him and clasped his hand. She patted it, stroked his cheek, and pushed his long hair back behind his ears, securing the tactile reassurance that he was really, finally, beside her again.

Seamus cleared his throat. "I thought perhaps, unless Wynne is in a hurry to get Laird back to the ranch, we might cobble together some supper. The chicken and biscuits will be fine cold."

Wynne's gaze never left Laird's face. "I'm in no hurry, unless you are, son. Let me keep you to myself for just a little while longer. We'll be swamped with family by the morning."

Laird smiled. "Suits me, Ma."

Kicker tore her gaze from mother and son, and nodded. "Then dinner it is. Chicken and biscuits are ready. Tis pumpkin cream soup and rum sauce to be heated, and hardboiled eggs and plum pudding in the icebox. Maddie made carrot loaf a few days ago, and we can have that with jam."

Laird rested his head on Wynne's shoulder for a moment. "It sounds like a feast. Last Christmas we had giblet pie and red cabbage that Billy found somewhere. He was the best forager in the battalion. He'd go off in the night and come back with everything from wild turkeys to Fritz' rifles. He could find things in places that had been scavenged to the bare bones by both sides. We ate a lot more bully beef after he died. I even saw some Tommies roasting trench rabbits."

Kicker cocked her head. "Trench rabbits?"

"Rats." Laird shrugged. "We weren't brass hats. We ate what we had."

Wynne shuddered and put her arm around Laird. "Wait until you meet Billy's son, Ford. He's the spitting image of Billy when he was a boy."

Laird tugged a chain with a ring from beneath his uniform jacket. "I brought this for him. His papa never took it off, and

I want to give it to Ford, though maybe Mary will want to hold on to it until he's a little older."

"I'm sure she will, son."

"I want to be there for her and Ford, Ma. I can't take Billy's place, but I promised him—I swore I'd look out for them, always."

Wynne kissed Laird's head. "I'm glad. Mary will be so pleased to see you again."

"I know I look pretty worthless right now—"

"You stop right there, Laird Angus Glenn. I don't care if you left a leg over there. I wouldn't care if you left both legs in those damned trenches. The only thing I care about is that you're here now. It's all I've prayed for since the day you left."

"I know, Ma. But this is important to me. I swear I'm going to make myself useful again. You just wait and see. Kicker promised to make me a new leg, and as soon as I get it, I'll be back to work. I'm never going to be a burden to you or to the ranch."

Wynne glanced at Kicker with glistening eyes. "You could never be a burden to your family. I hope you know that, and if you don't, I'll spend the rest of my life telling you so. But if Kicker says she's going to make you a leg, you can bank on it. One way or another, you and me will be out together checking the herds by springtime."

Laird nodded, determination in his eyes. "Yes, we will, Ma."

Epilogue

Kicker and Madelyn waved from the doorway as Seamus drove their guests away. Dinner hadn't been lavish, but Kicker couldn't remember a meal she'd enjoyed more.

Laird had spoken little of his experiences, except to say he'd taken his war-ending wound in the late October mud and rain of Passchendaele, when the Canadian Corps was sent to relieve the ANZAC's. Instead, Laird was hungry to hear the smallest details of life on the home front, particularly life inside Madelyn's schoolhouse and on the Steeple Seven. The only time he returned to the topic of war was when he heard that Kicker's nephew, Jeremiah, a Royal Flying Corps pilot, had perished in 1915.

"Those aerial reconnaissance spotters saved our asses a few times—Oh, sorry, Ma. I'll try to watch my language."

Wynne shrugged. "I don't care. I've been waiting three years to hear the sound of your voice, and every word is as sweet as an angel song to me."

The whole dinner had been like that. One moment they'd be laughing over Laird's attempts to convince his mother how handy a biplane could be at the ranch, and the next, Laird or Wynne would rip their hearts out with a few words that alluded to the pain both had suffered. Even the Christmas concert Seamus had played after dinner with the fiddle he always left at their home had ricocheted between rollick and melancholy.

Kicker was exhausted by the time she closed the front door.

Madelyn went to their Christmas tree and snuffed out the candles, then turned to Kicker and opened her arms. Kicker walked into them and laid her head on Maddie's shoulder.

"Tired, dearest?"

"You have no idea."

"I listened, you know."

Kicker tilted her head back to look into Maddie's eyes. "Sorry?"

"To you and Laird talking. I opened one of the station house windows so I could hear you."

"Ah, tis how you made it to the sleigh b'fore us."

"Yes. I'm so proud of you. You knew just what to say to reach Laird. I couldn't have done half as well."

"Aye, you could've."

"No, dearest. I really couldn't. But it shames me still that the reason you were able to reach him was the pain I put you through so long ago."

Kicker brushed a tear from Madelyn's cheek. "Tis many years and much water under the bridge since then. It matters not."

"I think that I will go to my grave some day with that regret above all others—that I hurt you so terribly."

"You came back. Twas all that mattered. I hold no grudge, Maddie. I ne'er did."

"I know."

Madelyn took Kicker's hand and led her to their bedroom. Though they kept two bedrooms for the sake of propriety, the second bedroom had only ever been occupied by Seamus, on the odd occasion. Since the day Madelyn had returned, they had never spent another night apart, and if Kicker had her way, they never would.

At the doorway to their room, Madelyn stopped and drew Kicker into an embrace. "Merry Christmas, dearest. You are the greatest gift I've ever or will ever receive. I hope you know that."

"Aye, and you as well to me, though t'night tis a toss-up, is it not? Wynne may have gone home with the greatest Christmas gift e'er."

"She did. I cannot begin to comprehend the agony she endured, not knowing from day to day if Laird was even alive."

Madelyn's shudder rippled against Kicker's body, and she tightened her embrace. "I'm here, love. I'll ne'er be away from you again. I swear."

Madelyn drew away slightly and cupped Kicker's face. "You cannot make that promise, dearest. None can. But it reminds me to cherish every day I have with you—and every day we've had together since I so foolishly threw our love away."

"You ne'er threw it away. You only put it aside for a bit. Let us set this sadness aside and cel'brate proper."

"Laird's return?"

"Aye, that. But also Wynne's joy, Pudge's date, Seamus' music, and mos' of all, the love that guides my e'ry step."

Madelyn smiled and caressed Kicker's face. "And you think I'm the poet."

"Aye, you are. But as you always say, tis more to life than jus' words." Kicker drew Madelyn with her as she backed into the room and kicked the door closed behind them.

This night they would rejoice.

Love had brought the lost home once again.

If you enjoyed this short story, you might want to read Lois Cloarec Hart's ***Kicker's Journey***, the novel in which Kicker and Madelyn met and fell in love.

JUST A NORMAL CHRISTMAS

by Caren J. Werlinger

JULES DROPPED HER SUITCASE ON the foyer floor. She closed the front door and leaned against it, her eyes closed. "I love our home. I never want to leave it, ever again."

Holly and Mistletoe came running to greet them, meowing nonstop as they wound around their legs.

Kelli smiled and set her own suitcase down. She leaned down to pet the cats for a moment and then stepped nearer so she could wrap her arms around Jules. "Well, I don't know about that, but we'll only have it to ourselves for a few weeks before they're here."

Jules peered at Kelli through one partially opened eye. "We really invited them for Christmas?"

"You really invited them for Christmas," Kelli corrected. "They were supposed to come for Thanksgiving, remember?"

Jules made a face. "I know, but somehow it seemed easier for us to go there. I forgot how bad holiday traffic is. And then Mae had to start dropping all kinds of hints about how long it's been since she's been anywhere, and it just came out. Damn. Why didn't you stop me?"

Kelli chuckled. She kissed Jules's cheek and released her. "At least we're already decorated for Christmas, so that part's done. It'll be fine. Ronnie will share the driving, and Bertha will pack enough food to feed them for three weeks in case they get stranded somewhere."

Holly stretched up on her hind legs, pawing at Jules. She picked the cat up, holding her as she purred, and carried her into the kitchen. "Let's get the girls fed, and then we can carry everything upstairs."

A few minutes later, they were up in their room, tossing clothes from their suitcases into the laundry hamper.

"I can't believe we have to go back to work tomorrow," Kelli said with a yawn. "Why didn't we come home yesterday so we could have had a day to rest?"

"We're getting old," Jules said, smothering a yawn of her own. "I used to do that drive to Ohio and back like it was nothing."

She looked longingly at the bed. "Just a short nap?"

Kelli dropped onto the mattress. "I'm so glad you said that. Just a short one."

∞⟲

"Shit!"

Jules sat up, looking around dazedly. "What?"

"We slept all night and forgot to set the alarm." Kelli exploded up from the bed and ran into the bathroom to brush her teeth. She came back into the bedroom and looked at the rumpled clothes she'd fallen asleep in. "Crap. I've got to go. I'll be in scrubs anyway. I'll see you tonight."

She gave Jules a quick kiss on the cheek and ran down the stairs. Jules heard the garage door open and close as Kelli's Tahoe rumbled up the street. She undressed and showered.

Feeling slightly more awake by the time she was dressed for work, Jules went down for breakfast and found a hastily scribbled note from Kelli.

Remember to talk to Donna about next weekend.

"Yeah, yeah," Jules muttered. She turned to the cereal cupboard and pulled down a box of Wheaties.

On the way back from Ohio, Kelli had been talking about having a small holiday party, and she really wanted Donna to be there. It wasn't exactly awkward seeing Donna these days—in fact, Jules was scheduled to have a meeting with her later this afternoon about one of her students—but it wasn't like the old days. *And that's probably a good thing.* Jules wasn't really in the mood for a party, but, as the entire holiday season the previous year had been overshadowed by Kelli's mother's cancer, she couldn't say no to Kelli wanting a bit more of a celebration this year.

She sat, eating her Wheaties as she stared out the window at the backyard, all leafless trees and naked bushes now except for the nandina glowing red against the fence. She smiled a little, picturing Mae and Bertha in the kitchen at Thanksgiving, arguing over the best way to make the gravy. Mae was still Mae, but there was something about her grandmother now that Jules couldn't remember ever being there, a softening of the hard edges. And Bertha seemed to finally be emerging from twenty-four years of mourning, sporting a new hairdo and probably the first new dress she'd had since Hobie's death.

"I took her shopping," Ronnie had whispered. "Me, shopping for dresses. It was totally embarrassing, but she wouldn't have gone by herself."

"You got new clothes, too," Kelli said.

Ronnie blushed furiously, smoothing the creases in her new khakis. "I needed some nicer clothes for school."

"You look great," Jules had said, wrapping an arm around her shoulders and giving her a squeeze.

"Speaking of different," Ronnie had said, looking at Jules. "Your hair."

"Oh, yeah." Jules ran a hand over her short hair, mussing it. "Gone is the tail."

"It looks good on you. Softer."

Softer. *Mae is softer, I'm softer,* Jules thought now, spooning the last of her cereal from the milk. Soft was good. It was so much easier than keeping armor up all the time, making sure no chinks showed to let things in that might hurt her. True, soft made her more vulnerable, and that wasn't always comfortable, but Kelli was always there. She choked up, as she often did now, thinking about how loyal Kelli had been, even after everything Jules had put her through. She blotted her eyes with a napkin and carried her bowl to the sink.

❧

Jules made sure she got to the high school early. The parents wanted to attend, so the meeting had been scheduled for after school. She poked her head around the door of Donna's classroom.

"Hey."

Donna looked up from her desk where she was grading papers. "Hey, yourself."

"Good Thanksgiving?" Jules set her briefcase down and took a seat at one of the desks.

"Yeah." Donna nodded. "Mom said to give you her best."

"Mae, too. We ended up going out there. They're all coming here for Christmas."

"Really?" Donna couldn't hide a smirk. "That should make for an interesting Christmas."

"Tell me about it." Jules snorted. "It'll be okay. We're all still getting used to… everything."

Her eyes locked with Donna's for a moment, and she knew there was still some getting used to going on here as well. She cleared her throat.

"New place working out well?"

"Yeah," Donna said, looking back down at her papers. "Elaine finally re-financed with Carrie, so I got my share from the house. Cut my last tie to her. It's a lot better now."

"Took her long enough."

Donna shrugged. "It's over and done with."

"Hey, we're having a little holiday get-together this Saturday evening. We'd like you to come."

Donna glanced up. "Who's coming?"

"Not Elaine and Carrie, if that's what you were wondering. I think Kelli said something to Marianne and a few people she works with. Barbara and Chris are coming. You. We're keeping it small, but last year was so…"

"Yeah," Donna said, understanding the unspoken. "It was. Okay, I'll come. What can I bring?"

"Your mom's potato salad?"

Donna grinned. "Done."

Just then, the principal knocked on the door and came in with the parents. Donna gave Jules a last nod before they all moved to the table at the back of the room.

Saturday evening found Donna driving slowly down Jules and Kelli's street. It felt weird. When they invited her to move in after her breakup with Elaine, this house had become home—for a little while. More like home than living with Elaine ever had. She could never have admitted it to them, but she'd thought about what it might have been like for the three of them to live together permanently. Until the night Jules came to her. She knew why Jules had done it, and it worked. *Finally, after twelve years apart, I can say I'm not in love with her anymore.*

But after that, it was just not possible for Donna and Jules to live under the same roof.

It had been weeks after she moved out before she'd seen either of them. It was Kelli who called, suggesting she join them for dinner with Barbara and Chris. She knew Kelli was trying to ease her back into being comfortable around them, and she was grateful. It had been awkward at first, but good friends—old friends—were too hard to come by. She didn't want Jules and Kelli to disappear from her life.

She pulled into the driveway with five other cars, most of which she didn't recognize. She rang the front bell. Kelli answered, pulling her in for a hug.

"It's so good to see you."

"Thanks for inviting me." Donna held up her bowl. "Want me to take the potato salad to the kitchen?"

"I'll take your coat," Jules said, appearing behind Kelli.

No hug.

Donna nodded and allowed Jules to help her take her coat off. The kitchen table and island were crowded with bowls and platters of food. Kelli joined her and re-arranged some things to make room.

"How have you been?"

"Good." Donna took the plastic wrap off the bowl and inserted a large serving spoon. "Settled in at the townhouse now. Busy at work."

"Come on," Kelli said, taking Donna by the hand. "I think you know almost everyone."

She introduced Donna to a couple of other nurses she worked with who were there with their husbands and boyfriends. Donna wandered over to Kelli's sister, Marianne.

"How are you?"

Marianne swallowed a sip of her wine and said, "I'm good. Got an early Christmas present. Finally lost that last two hundred pounds."

At Donna's puzzled glance, Marianne added, "The divorce is final."

"Oh. Mine, too. I only had to get her to pay me for the house."

They clinked their glasses together.

"Good riddance," Marianne said.

At that moment, someone bumped into Marianne, tossing the contents of her drink all down Donna's sweater.

"Oh, my gosh! Oh, my gosh. I am so, so sorry."

A woman stepped around Marianne and started to reach out with a napkin, but stopped, her hand hovering over the red stain spreading across Donna's chest.

"Perfect," Donna muttered, blotting the spilled drink with her own napkin. "Just perfect."

"I'm so sorry."

"So you said."

Marianne squatted down to mop up what had spilled to the floor. Donna stepped into the kitchen to get a damp towel. To her irritation, the woman who had bumped into Marianne followed her, still stammering apologies. Donna dampened a corner of a kitchen towel and used it to blot at the wine stain.

"Look," Donna turned and froze as she found herself looking into a pair of large gray eyes framed by long, dark lashes.

"I'll pay to have it dry-cleaned."

"Um…sorry, what?"

"The sweater," the woman said. "I'll pay to have it dry-cleaned."

"No." Donna blinked and looked down. "It's okay. It was kind of an ugly sweater anyhow."

The woman held her hand out. "I'm Toni, by the way. Toni Marsell. Not T-O-N-Y like Tony Soprano. T-O-N-I, like Toni Collette, the actress. I mean, not that I look like Toni Collette. You know, she's just so gorgeous. I mean, when you go back and look at her in, like, *Emma*, and then how different she looked in *The Sixth Sense*, it's like, wow, what a difference. And I'm not named for her, you know. She's not that old, and I'm not that young. I mean, we're probably close to the same age, but…"

She paused to take a breath while Donna just stared, still holding Toni's hand.

"Um, yeah." She withdrew her hand with a twinge of regret. "I'm Donna."

"I work with Kelli. At the hospital." Toni nodded. "I'm a nurse. I'm new to Charlottesville, and Kelli thought it would be nice for me to meet some other people, and it was really nice of her and Jules to have me. Jules is great. I was so nervous about meeting her, I mean, Kelli talks about her all the time, and she's great. Kind of intimidating, you know? But really great. You know them both?"

Donna nodded. "Yes. I've known Jules since college, and Kelli since she and Jules met."

"Sorry, I know I'm talking a lot, but I'm just really nervous, meeting new people." Toni stood there, her hands wringing the stem of her wine glass. "And spilling things on people. That makes me nervous, too. Not a good way to meet someone, you know? I really am sorry."

For a long moment, Toni actually shut up, and she and Donna stared into each other's eyes.

"Hey."

Jules came unexpectedly into the kitchen. Donna backed away.

"Everything okay? I heard there was a little accident."

"It's fine." Donna managed a small smile. "It really is okay."

Jules's gaze moved back and forth between them. "I take it introductions aren't necessary?"

"No," Toni said with a nervous laugh. "I think I made an impression she won't forget. I mean, you always hope you'll make a memorable impression on someone, but it doesn't usually involve a permanent stain on her clothing."

Donna dipped her head to one side. "You are indelible."

∽

Kelli turned off the bathroom light and crawled gently into bed. "You asleep?"

"Not yet."

Kelli turned on her side, her head resting on Jules's shoulder. "It was a nice party. Thanks for going along with it."

Jules kissed Kelli's forehead. "No need to thank me. Donna made a new friend tonight."

"Who?"

"Toni."

Kelli lifted her head. "Really? I haven't been able to tell if she's family. I just invited her because she's new here and seems really nice."

"Well, she spilled wine all over Donna's sweater. If that's not a good beginning, I don't know what is."

"Poor Toni. She does seem a little accident-prone." Kelli paused, her hand resting against Jules's neck where the artery pulsed. "Last year is kind of a blur. Just Mom being sick and doctors and traveling every other day."

"I know." Jules yawned. "We'll have a normal Christmas this year."

∽✺∼

Kelli hummed "We Three Kings" as she packed a few boxes full of her pottery. She held the pots up, choosing the ones she wanted to take to Elaine's studio and padding them with towels for protection. She reached for another one and paused. There, unfinished, was the special pot she'd been making last year for her mother. It was modeled after one her mom had admired in a museum once, and Kelli had spent hours on it, starting over six times before she got the shape right. She had intended it as a Christmas present…before her mother's cancer was diagnosed. She touched a gentle finger to it now. She'd never been able to bring herself to finish it. She cleared her throat and packed one last box. The cats looked up sleepily as she carried the boxes out to the garage and placed them in the cargo area of her Tahoe.

The air was cold, and the sky was filled with low, leaden clouds that threatened snow. The studio, as expected, was decorated to the hilt, with enormous wreaths on the doors and festive bows in all of the windows. Christmas music played through the speakers and the air smelled of cinnamon and cloves when Kelli opened the door to carry the first box in.

"Kelli!"

Elaine rushed over to greet her with an air kiss on each cheek.

"How have you been, Elaine?"

They went back outside to gather more boxes.

"Wonderful. Just wonderful." Elaine looked askance at Kelli. "When I called, I wasn't sure you were still okay having contact with me."

Kelli laughed. "Just because things didn't work out between you and Donna doesn't mean we can't stay friends. Besides, you're my best customer. I was worried you wouldn't want any more of my pottery."

"My customers love your work. And I'm glad you feel that way."

They carried the boxes inside and Elaine pulled a few out. "Oh, Kelli, you are getting better and better. These are exquisite."

"Thanks." Kelli reached into one of the boxes. "Here's a list of what I brought. Anything you don't need just set aside, and I can come back to get them."

"Do you have time for a cup of tea?"

"Sure."

Kelli took her coat off and followed Elaine back to an antique sideboard set up with coffee maker and delicate china cups and saucers.

"Most of my customers prefer coffee, but this will make tea also." Elaine held out a basket with a selection of teas.

They sat while the machine churned out hot water.

"So how have you and Carrie been?"

Elaine positively glowed. "She's wonderful." A frown creased her brow. "I imagine you're still seeing Donna, so I feel a little guilty talking to you about Carrie, but we fit together so much better than Donna and I ever did."

Kelli stirred some sugar into her tea. "I can see that," she said evenly, trying to hide her dislike of Carrie.

Elaine must have sensed something. "I mean, I know Carrie tried to make a play for Jules, but I hope you can let that go."

Kelli forced a smile. "Of course."

Elaine leaned forward and laid a hand on Kelli's knee. "We'll have you and Jules over after the holidays. You need to see what we've done with the house."

Fat chance of getting Jules over there, but Kelli kept that thought to herself.

◦●◦

Kelli got up to join Jules for breakfast, though she had the day off.

"I'm going to drive up and see Dad today," she said as she scooped coffee into the coffeemaker. "He called and asked if I would. I feel bad. I haven't been up to see him for a few weeks."

Jules scrambled eggs for both of them. "You shouldn't feel bad. You and Marianne were going up there two or three times a week for months. You've eased off gradually. He has to figure out how to rebuild his life on his own."

"I know." Kelli came up behind Jules, wrapping her arms around her and burying her face in her hair. "I know he's been lonely, though."

"Marianne going with you?"

Kelli shook her head, making Jules's head move, too. "He asked me to come by myself."

Jules turned to her. "What do you think that's about?"

"No idea."

Jules scraped the eggs onto the waiting plates. "Will you stay there for dinner?"

"Not sure yet. I'll call you."

They ate breakfast, filled travel mugs with coffee, and left at the same time. Two and a half hours later, Kelli pulled into her dad's driveway in Hagerstown. Before she could knock, Jerry opened the door and pulled her into a hug.

"Hi, Kelli. It's good to see you."

She accompanied him inside. "Dad, the house looks good." She looked around more carefully. "Some of these decorations are new."

"Come on to the kitchen. I've got some gingerbread and tea waiting for you."

Kelli frowned. "Gingerbread? Since when do you bake?"

He chuckled. "I still don't. Someone...someone made it and gave it to me."

Puzzled, Kelli sat while her father cut thick slices of gingerbread and set a mug of tea in front of her. He kept clearing his throat, something he did when he was nervous or didn't want to talk about something. Kelli spread some butter on her gingerbread, waiting for her father to sit. He joined her with another mug.

For long seconds, he didn't say anything, just looked at her. "You look so like your mother."

Kelli set the gingerbread aside and leaned her elbows on the table. "Dad, what's up?"

"Always straight to the point." He ran his hand through his hair and cleared his throat again. "I'm not sure how to tell you this."

Kelli grabbed his arm. "You're not sick?"

"No, no." He placed a hand over hers. "Nothing like that. I've... I've met someone. A really nice lady. Actually, I've known her for years. She was married to Walt, down at the hardware store. You remember him."

Kelli nodded. "He had a heart attack and died a couple of years ago."

"Yeah." Jerry stared hard at his tea. "Anyway, Evelyn has been alone since then. And after your mom...well, she started looking in on me, bringing me a homemade meal or a cake every now and again."

Kelli heard the quaver in his voice and felt the pounding of her own heart as she listened.

"We started going out, you know, to dinner or movies." Jerry met her eyes. "It was just so lonely, Kelli, coming back to this empty house every evening, walking around, looking for... I don't know what."

"Dad, I'm sorry—"

Jerry waved his hand. "It's not your fault. You and Marianne have your lives and families. I had to find a way to start over without Carol. But I really do like Evelyn. I'd like you and your sister to meet her."

Kelli sat back. "That's why you wanted to talk to me alone."

Jerry shrugged. "You're the reasonable one. You know what your sister is like."

Kelli snorted, remembering only too well the hysteria when Marianne found out her husband was cheating on her. "Yeah. I know."

She frowned. "But isn't it kind of soon?"

"It's been ten months, Kelli," Jerry said quietly. "I know it doesn't feel like it's been that long, and in some ways it hasn't, but it's been ten months of being alone here."

They sat in silence for a bit, Kelli picking at her gingerbread. She pointed at it. "She made this?"

Jerry nodded.

"It's good."

"Kelli, I'd like you to invite Evelyn for Christmas."

"What?"

"Her kids are scattered and won't be home. She'll be alone. I know you're going to have a full house that day—and we'll only come for the day."

Kelli had her mouth open, ready to argue that Christmas was different, a day for family, when Jerry added, "Remember when you asked us to invite Jules?"

Kelli closed her mouth.

"You like her this much?"

Jerry nodded. "I do."

"Do you…do you love her?"

"I think I might." His hands tightened around his mug— strong hands that Kelli remembered could fix anything, hands she had watched clench in despair at hearing Carol's diagnosis of pancreatic cancer and knowing he couldn't fix that.

Kelli reached out to him again, squeezed his hand. "I'll talk to Marianne, and we'll invite her for Christmas."

Jerry blinked away sudden tears. "Thank you."

ॐ

Jules was just leaving the elementary school when her cell phone rang. She looked at the screen. "Hey, Donna. What's up? Is everything okay?"

"Everything's fine. I, uh, I just wanted to thank you and Kelli for having me over the other week. It was really nice."

Jules pulled the phone away from her ear and stared at it as she got into her car and tossed her briefcase to the passenger seat. This wasn't like Donna. She put the phone back to her ear. "You're welcome. I'm glad you came."

"Really?"

"Yes, really." Jules closed her eyes and pressed her fingers to her forehead. "I know it hasn't been the easiest thing for us to stay friends, but... I've missed you. I hope we can figure out how to be around each other again and have it be okay."

There was a long silence.

"I'd like that, too," Donna said at last.

"So was there a reason you called?"

"Well," Donna began and then paused. "I was wondering if you or Kelli could get me Toni's phone number."

Jules chuckled. "Gonna give her your dry cleaning bill?"

Donna laughed a little. "Something like that."

"I don't have it, but I'll have Kelli give you a call."

"Thanks. Didn't mean to interrupt. Catch you later."

"Bye, Donna."

Jules hung up and sat staring at the phone, wondering why it felt weird to see Donna interested in someone else. They'd both been involved with other people since their breakup, and Jules had cheered Donna's split with Elaine—*she was never good enough for Donna, but then, neither was I.*

She turned the ignition and drove home to find Kelli's Tahoe in the garage. She deposited her briefcase in the foyer and found Kelli in her studio.

"Hi. I didn't expect you home so early."

Kelli didn't answer immediately, her head bowed over a pot she was painstakingly glazing with a fine brush.

"I had lunch with Dad and came on home."

Jules sat and waited with both cats pushing for space on her lap.

Kelli finally sat up and swiped her forearm across her nose, her eyes red and swollen. Jules went to kneel beside her.

"What is it? What happened?"

"Nothing really. I'm just being silly." Kelli looked at Jules. "Dad has found someone. Evelyn. She's the widow of a man Dad worked with at the hardware store. He really likes her, maybe loves her, and wants us to invite her for Christmas."

Jules fell onto her butt. "Holy shit."

"That is exactly what I was thinking, but I didn't say it."

"Marianne."

Kelli scoffed. "Yeah. That's why he wanted to talk to me alone. I get to tell my sister."

"Holy shit." Jules shook her head. "Christmas is two weeks from tomorrow."

"I know."

They both sat in silence for a moment.

"Are you going to invite her?"

Kelli gave a tight smile. "He reminded me of when I asked them to invite you."

Jules dropped her forehead onto her hand. "He had you there."

"Yup."

Jules released a long breath. "This Christmas just keeps getting better and better."

∞

Jules refolded Kelli's new sweater three times before she was satisfied it looked right. She reached for the box to find Holly tucked up inside it.

"Get out of there."

She shook the box free of cat hair and carefully laid a sheet of tissue paper printed with Christmas trees inside, only to turn and find Mistletoe curled up on the sweater.

"You two are so much help."

She gathered both cats in her arms and dumped them unceremoniously in the hall, shutting the office door before they could shoot back inside. She got a sticky roller and rolled the cat hair off the sweater as two cat paws reached under the door, trying to rattle it open.

"It's not going to work."

It was probably stupid to worry about cat hair. As soon as Kelli wore the sweater and picked up one of the cats, it would be flocked anyhow, but at least it could look new when she opened it.

She taped the box shut and pulled out a length of wrapping paper printed in holly leaves. Try as she might to get the ends neatly folded and taped, her packages always looked as if a ten-year-old had wrapped them. She held the package up, inspecting it.

"Whatever. A bow makes everything better."

She stuck a large red bow on the box and set it with the others. She had so little time alone in the house that she had to take advantage of the evenings Kelli worked to get her shopping and wrapping done.

The cats had finally given up on the door. She heard the thunder of cat paws running down the hall as they chased each other downstairs. She was reaching for the next thing to be wrapped—an Ohio State University sweatshirt for Ronnie—when the phone rang.

"Hello?"

"Is this a good time?"

Jules smiled. So like her grandmother. No *hello* or *how are you*. Just get down to business. "This is a good time. What's up?"

Mae sighed. "It's the girl."

"Ronnie? What's going on?"

"We're not sure. She's acting up a bit."

Jules frowned. "Acting up how?"

"Bertha says she's been snippy and rude lately."

"That's not like Ronnie."

"I know," Mae said. "She even said something about not coming with us."

"What?"

"I reminded her she promised to help me with all the driving, so she said she'd come, but she didn't sound happy about it."

"She's probably missing her mother," Jules said. "She was already thinking about this last summer, what it would be like to spend Christmas away from her mom."

"Girl's been through a lot."

"I know." Jules fingered the sweatshirt. "When are you coming?"

"We're planning on leaving here the morning of the twenty-first. Is that okay with you and Kelli? You can put us up for that long?"

Jules smiled. "We both took the whole week off and we have plenty of room. No problems. But we may have more people here on Christmas Day than we had planned on. Just to let you know, it'll be a houseful."

Mae was quiet for a moment. "Been a while since I've had a houseful. Might be nice."

"We'll see you soon."

"Bye."

Jules hung the phone up. She knew Ronnie was much better off living next door to Mae with Bertha Fahnestock and getting away from her mom and stepfather, but better off didn't always equal easy. With a stab of guilt, she realized she hadn't sent Ronnie an e-mail for a couple of weeks. She flipped open her laptop and dashed off a quick message saying she and Kelli were looking forward to seeing them and wishing her luck with end-of-term exams.

She got back to wrapping and was placing all the wrapped packages under the tree by the time Kelli got home from the hospital.

"Hey."

Kelli gave her a hug and kiss. "You've been busy, I see."

"Yup. And no shaking or poking."

Kelli held her hand up. "I promise." But she peeked over Jules's shoulder toward the tree. "What's that big one over there?"

"Never you mind. Go shower. I've got the oven heating up for some fresh biscuits with our soup."

"Wow. Soup and biscuits? I love it when you're all domestic. Be down in a minute."

Kelli ran upstairs for her shower—"got to wash the ICU off me," she always said—and was back downstairs by the time the biscuits were done baking.

Jules ladled soup into two bowls and carried them to the table while Kelli filled two glasses with water.

"Mae called," Jules said as they sat.

Kelli glanced up as she buttered a biscuit. "Everything okay?"

"Something's bothering Ronnie, but she won't talk about it to Bertha."

"Holidays without her mom?"

Jules nodded. "That's my guess."

Kelli reached for Jules's hand. "We haven't really talked about this, but how are you this Christmas? It's the first one since…"

Jules looked down at their intertwined fingers. "A little bittersweet. In some ways, it's the happiest I can remember being since before Hobie died, but it feels as if he just died this summer, not twenty-four years ago. Now that I can let myself remember him more, it's been kind of hard."

Her jaw worked back and forth as she swallowed hard. "Your first without your mom, too."

Kelli nodded, her eyes bright with tears. "Will it always be like this?"

"Maybe not like this, but it'll never be the same as it was."

∽◯

Jules's phone pinged.

Pick up a bottle of wine. White.

Why? she texted back to Kelli.

You'll see.

Oh, that sounded ominous. Surely, Kelli hadn't invited Elaine and Carrie to the house?

She swung by the grocery store on her way home and picked up a bottle of Pinot Grigio, and then on impulse, another of Riesling. She knew nothing about wine other than color, but knew she preferred the sweet ones. And she had a feeling she might need a whole bottle herself.

When she got home, there was an unfamiliar car in the driveway. When she entered the house, she heard Kelli talking to someone. She dropped her coat on a chair in the foyer.

"Hi, Jules!"

"Toni," Jules said as she set the bag on the island. "Nice to see you."

"Thanks. I hope you don't mind me barging in on you guys for dinner tonight," Toni said as she peeled an avocado. "But Kelli invited me, and it sounded way better than another night of a microwave dinner for one."

"So, should I open a bottle?" Jules asked.

Kelli turned from the stove and looked at the two bottles of wine Jules held. "I'll have Pinot. Toni?"

"Sure. Whatever you're having."

The avocado pit popped loose and shot at Jules.

"Sorry. Gosh. I am so sorry." Toni scrambled to pick up the slippery pit.

Jules looked at Kelli. "White. Not red tonight."

Kelli grinned. "No stains."

Toni, who hadn't heard that little exchange, stood up with the pit in her hand. "Got it. Sorry."

She tossed the pit in the garbage and turned back to the avocado as Jules poured three glasses of wine—Riesling for herself.

The doorbell rang.

"Get that, will you?" Kelli asked as she flipped the chicken tenderloins sautéing in the pan.

With a puzzled glance back at her, Jules went to the front door.

"Donna."

"Hi." Donna stepped inside holding a baking pan and then abruptly stopped at Jules's expression. "Kelli didn't tell you I was coming."

"Um…no, but I just got home. Come on in."

Jules stepped back and took Donna's jacket. "They're in the kitchen."

Jules hung Donna's jacket up and followed her into the kitchen in time to see Toni turn to greet Donna, brushing her knife off the cutting board. It landed on its point in the vinyl flooring, the handle quivering.

"Oh, my gosh! I am so sorry, you guys."

"It's okay," Jules said, pulling the knife out of the floor. "Look, not even a mark." She turned to Kelli with a look. Kelli gave a small smile and an apologetic shrug.

"I brought brownies," Donna said into the ensuing emptiness.

"I love your brownies," Kelli said, pouring some kind of sauce over the tenderloins.

Jules did a double take at the flush coloring Donna's cheeks as she and Toni stared at each other. She handed Donna a glass of wine. "Come on," she said. "We can set the table."

A few minutes later, they were all seated.

"So, Toni," Jules said, "where in the hospital do you work?" *No place with sharp instruments, I hope.*

"Peds." Toni glanced up while she spooned some rice onto her plate. "I work with kids."

"Isn't it hard, working with sick kids?" Donna asked.

Toni shrugged, but before she could reply, Kelli said, "She's wonderful with the kids. She sings songs and plays games with them to calm them down before needles and scary stuff."

Toni blushed. "I always wanted playmates. Now, I have tons of them."

"You're an only child?" Jules asked as she passed a basket of rolls.

"Yeah. My dad works for the State Department, so he and my mom have been posted all over the world. I've lived in eight different countries. We never really had a home for very long. Just when I was making friends, he'd get posted to a new location and off we'd go."

Donna snorted. "My mom couldn't get my dad to go anywhere. She always wanted to travel, but he always had livestock to tend to or a new dog he was training. My poor mom never got to go anywhere. I've spent every Christmas of my life in the same house with three brothers and now their families."

Toni looked up, her expression wistful. "That sounds wonderful. We were hardly ever in the same place for two Christmases together. And we never had family around. Only the other diplomats. And they always had us kids sequestered off by ourselves while they socialized. Always work."

Kelli paused her fork. "Where are your parents now?"

"Brazil."

Jules glanced over as she swallowed. "Brazil? You're not traveling there for Christmas, are you?"

"No." Toni smiled. "No. I volunteered to work Christmas. Everyone else has family they want to be with."

Kelli caught Jules's eye. Jules tipped her head a bit in answer to Kelli's unspoken question. "You need to come here when you get off," Jules said.

Toni opened her mouth to protest, but Kelli cut her off. "We're having a boatload here for Christmas Day. One more won't be a hardship for us, and there's no reason for you to go home alone when you get off."

Toni glanced from Kelli to Jules. "You're sure?"

"We're sure," Jules said. "If you can stand a crowd."

Toni's face lit up. "I love crowds."

"Well, our crowd is getting more interesting by the minute," Jules said as she took a big gulp of wine.

⌗

The morning of the twenty-first found Jules and Kelli busy putting fresh sheets on the bed in the guest room and the futon in the office. Off to one side sat an uninflated air mattress.

"The young spine gets the floor," Kelli said, standing up to stretch her own sore back. She made a fist and rubbed her knuckles into her muscles. "How did we ever do stuff like camp and sleep on the ground in sleeping bags?"

"I never did," Jules said, tucking the bedspread into the foot of the bed. "Mae figured I had a bed and needed to be in it every night. Bertha wouldn't have let Hobie sleep outside anyhow."

Kelli glanced at her watch. "Where do you think they are by now?"

"Should be almost in Virginia by now."

"Time to get the bathrooms scrubbed then."

"Thank goodness you're here," Jules said two hours later. "If you'd been any longer, Kelli would have had me cleaning out the garage next."

She opened the back door of Mae's Oldsmobile for Bertha while Mae gave Kelli a hug. Ronnie, Jules noticed, got out from behind the wheel without saying anything and went to the trunk.

"I'll help with those," Jules said, taking a suitcase in each hand.

Upstairs, she set Mae's bag down in the guestroom and Bertha's in the office.

"Sorry, Ronnie. We'll blow the air mattress up at night, but for now, you'll have to be a vagabond."

Ronnie dropped her backpack on the office floor. "Nothing new."

Jules looked at her, but Ronnie was already walking back out into the hall and down the stairs. Jules followed to find Mae and Bertha busy in the kitchen, helping Kelli with dinner preparations. Ronnie accepted a Coke and went to the living room.

"We've got this," Kelli said in an undertone to Jules.

Jules nodded and went to the living room to find Ronnie sitting on the floor with Holly curling up on her lap. Mistletoe eyed them from under the Christmas tree where she lay with her front feet tucked under her.

"So how are things going?"

Ronnie shrugged. "They're going."

Jules sipped her Coke. "Exams went well?"

"I guess. Don't have my grades yet."

They sat in silence while Ronnie stroked Holly's silky coat as she purred contentedly.

"Anything else going on?"

Ronnie frowned. "I wish everyone would stop asking me that. I'm fine. Things are fine. My grades are fine. Work is fine. Okay?"

Jules bit her lip to keep from smiling. "Okay."

She got up and went back to the kitchen.

"Everything okay?" Kelli asked.

"Nope. But she's not ready to talk. Let's just leave her be."

Mae overheard and said, "She doesn't have to talk to help set the table. Ronnie!"

Jules grinned and went to get the dishes from the cupboard.

Over dinner, Bertha chatted more than Jules could remember since she was a kid. Mae had talked her into helping out with the church soup kitchen twice a week, and it seemed having a purpose had been just what Bertha needed. Her hair was clean and cut to shoulder length, her eyes were bright, and there was some color in her cheeks. *Hobie looked so much like her,* Jules thought as she watched her talking to Kelli.

"And how's your family, Kelli?" Mae asked.

"Fine," Kelli lied. Her talk with her sister had not gone well. Jules waited to see if Kelli would go into any of that, but she just said, "My dad has been seeing a woman. We'll all get to meet her at Christmas."

Mae's sharp gaze probed Kelli's face. "I'm sure it's nice for him to have company."

Kelli nodded. "I think you're right. We all have to move on."

"Moving on doesn't mean forgetting," Bertha said.

Jules squeezed Kelli's hand under the table.

Through dinner, Ronnie poked at her food, eating very little and saying nothing. As soon as she could, she cleared her dishes and excused herself to go upstairs.

"So this is what she's been like?" Jules asked Bertha, who nodded.

"She comes home from work and stays in her room almost all the time," Bertha said. "I've tried to get her to talk, but she won't."

"Has there been any trouble at the high school? Anything like last year when they were writing stuff on her locker?"

Bertha shook her head. "Not that I've heard. And I don't think she's had any contact with her mother. It started after she got a letter from Ohio State. I think maybe they turned her down, but I've been afraid to ask."

"You're kidding," Kelli said. "She's a good student."

"That's not all they base admissions on, though," Jules said.

"Well, this is getting tiresome," Mae said. "She needs to stop making everyone else miserable."

"She's seventeen," Kelli said. "It's her job to make everyone else miserable."

"I'll give her a little time and try again," Jules said. "In the meantime, let's just leave her as alone as she wants to be."

∾◠◡

"Well, I guess we didn't need to worry about what we were going to do with Mae and Bertha for three days, did we?" Kelli said as she handed two grocery bags to Jules.

"What in the world did they buy?" Jules peered into the bags.

That question was soon answered as the house was filled with the smell of baking cookies—dozens and dozens of cookies.

"We'll be eating Christmas cookies until Memorial Day," Jules said, looking around at the cooling racks and Tupperware containers covering every inch of counter and tabletop.

"They freeze," Bertha said happily, her cheeks pink with the heat of the oven as she placed another baking sheet inside.

On the second day of the baking marathon, Mae looked over at Jules and said, "Don't you think this has gone on long enough?"

Jules glanced upward to where Ronnie had ensconced herself in the office as soon as Bertha woke and vacated the futon. She'd spent the entire previous day up there with her laptop, emerging only for meals.

"I think you're right."

Jules packed a large plastic bag full of a variety of cookies. "For the energy it's going to take to pry the truth out of her."

She went upstairs and gave the door one sharp rap before opening it. "Come on."

Ronnie looked up. "What?"

"We're going for a drive."

Ronnie's expression darkened. "Where?"

"Just for a drive. You've been in this room too long. Come on."

Ronnie just stared at her.

"It's not really a request." Jules stepped out into the hall and waited.

Scowling, Ronnie closed her laptop and got to her feet.

"Not sure when we'll be back," Jules announced cheerfully as she led the way out the front door.

Jules got into her Subaru while Ronnie buckled herself into the passenger seat. She backed out and drove without speaking, letting Ronnie sulk.

Finally, Ronnie said, "Where are we going?"

"Thought you might like to see UVA's campus." Jules wove her way toward downtown Charlottesville.

Ronnie didn't reply, just turned to stare out the window.

With the campus nearly deserted for the holidays, Jules easily found parking near the central grounds.

She snugged her scarf around her neck and grabbed a messenger bag containing the baggie of cookies, slinging it over her chest. Without waiting, she headed off, leaving Ronnie no choice but to follow. They skirted the McIntire Amphitheatre and walked toward the Lawn and the Rotunda.

Jules stopped and looked around. From the corner of her eye, she saw Ronnie's mouth gape at the sight. Jefferson's image for the campus never failed to impress.

"Ohio State's campus isn't as old or as grand," she said. "But it has some beaut—"

"I'm not going."

Jules turned to face Ronnie. "What?"

Ronnie's hands were jammed into her jacket pockets and her chin was tucked into her scarf as she repeated, "I am not going to college."

Jules led the way to the steps of a building and sat. Ronnie sat beside her as Jules dug into her bag and then held it out. "Have a cookie."

Wordlessly, Ronnie reached into the baggie. They munched in silence for a few minutes.

"Did OSU turn you down?"

Ronnie didn't answer. She got up and walked along the path. Jules followed.

"Ronnie, you gotta talk to someone."

Ronnie stopped. "I got accepted, okay? But I'm not going."

Jules opened her mouth to question further, when she suddenly recalled the day she got her acceptance letter.

"I was terrified."

Ronnie half-glanced in her direction. "What do you mean?"

Jules squinted at the dome of the Rotunda, remembering. "I'd waited and waited for that acceptance letter, and then, when it came... I kind of panicked. OSU was too big and too far away. I told Pappy I wasn't going."

Ronnie shifted to look at her fully. "What did he say?"

Jules smiled and nibbled on an oatmeal cookie for a moment. "I told him I'd be lost there. He told me I'd find myself."

Ronnie broke a piece off a chocolate chip cookie and put it in her mouth. She chewed for a moment. "One lecture hall is bigger than my whole high school."

"Yup."

"The campus is bigger than the town of Aldie."

"Yes, it is." Jules leaned over and bumped Ronnie's shoulder. "And you'll meet all kinds of people you'd never meet in Aldie. You won't be judged by them because they don't know you. You get to start completely fresh, invent yourself as the person you want to be."

Ronnie seemed to think about this as she ate the rest of her cookie.

Jules laid her arm across Ronnie's shoulders. "I know it's intimidating, but I promise you, it'll be okay. Your whole world will change. You wanted change, right?"

Ronnie hiccupped with laughter and swiped her sleeve across her face. "Be careful what you ask for?"

Jules smiled and gave Ronnie a shake. "Yeah. Something like that."

ഐ

"What did you say to her?" Kelli whispered Christmas Eve as Ronnie peeled potatoes for dinner and chatted with Bertha.

"Not much." Jules smiled. "Mostly just remembered. By the way, you and I are going to be taking a trip to Columbus this summer to help her learn her way around."

Kelli gave Jules a kiss on the cheek and went to check the ham.

There was a knock on the front door, and Marianne called out from the foyer. She came into the kitchen a moment later.

"Hey," Jules said. "Wine?"

"Sure." Marianne got a glass and poured for herself, topping off Jules's glass also.

"The kids with Brian tonight?"

"Yes. Not that he's cooking. He took them to his parents', so they'll do their Christmas tonight, and I won't have to cut our day short tomorrow." Marianne's expression darkened as she took a huge gulp. "Of course, I may want to skip out of here tomorrow."

Jules glanced over sympathetically. "Give her a chance. She might be really nice."

"Doesn't matter if she is. It's the whole idea. Mom hasn't even been gone a year. It's like he just locked her memory away in a trunk and got himself a new model."

"I don't think that's true," Jules said, stepping gingerly around this prickly topic. "Kelli said there are still pictures of Carol all around the house. I think Evelyn is smart enough not to try and replace her. No more than she wants to replace her first husband. They just want to share each other's company."

Marianne snorted. "Share each other's bed more likely."

Jules thought it best not to reply. She folded the freshly laundered napkins Kelli had laid out while Marianne wandered off to see if she could help Mae with anything.

Jules went to set the dining table and paused, looking back into the kitchen. Never would she have expected to have her grandmother and Hobie's mom working in her kitchen, chatting with her partner as they prepared Christmas Eve dinner. She hadn't spent Christmas with Mae for years. It had just gotten too hard to go home for the holidays. *Too many memories.* She finished setting the table.

"Jules? What time is church tonight?"

Jules turned to find Mae looking at her. "Excuse me?"

"It's Christmas Eve. We are going to church, young lady."

Kelli bit her lip, but Ronnie didn't bother to hide her glee at hearing this exchange.

"I'll have to call and see," Jules mumbled.

∞∕◯

Kelli rolled over and wrapped an arm around Jules. "I think the kids are awake."

Sleepily, Jules groaned. "We don't have any kids."

"We do this Christmas." She kissed Jules and got out of bed. "And she's sleeping on an air mattress right next to all the presents."

Jules sat up and ran a hand through her hair, which was sticking up in all directions. Times like this, she missed her ponytail. Still half-asleep, she pulled on a sweatshirt and flannel pants printed with Christmas lights. She went to brush her teeth when Kelli left the bathroom. By the time she finished, Kelli was downstairs. She sniffed as she descended the stairs.

"Do I smell—"

"Cinnamon rolls!"

Bertha beamed from where she was kneeling, peering through the oven window. "Merry Christmas. I thought I'd make something special for breakfast this morning."

Kelli handed Jules a cup of coffee. "What time did you get up? We didn't get home until after midnight."

Bertha shrugged. "I don't mind. I like having people to cook for."

262

Ronnie bounced into the kitchen. "Mattress is back upstairs. When do we open presents?"

Jules scowled over her coffee.

"You'd better let her get at least one cup into her system first," Kelli said, chuckling.

Mae came downstairs. "About time you got up. Santa left stockings for everyone."

Jules choked. "Stockings?" She coughed, pounding her chest with her fist. "You told me stockings were silly when I was a kid."

Mae's cheeks flushed a bit. "Well, I was wrong there."

The oven timer beeped, cutting off further discussion. Bertha pulled a cake pan out of the oven and drizzled icing over the rolls. In a minute, everyone was seated at the table with a couple of cinnamon rolls each.

"Oh, Bertha," said Kelli. "These are heavenly."

Jules closed her eyes and moaned, nodding. Ronnie wolfed down a third roll while everyone else was finishing a second.

"Presents now?"

Kelli laughed. "All right. Presents. Come on."

She led the way into the living room where the Christmas tree lights provided the only illumination. She clicked on a couple of lamps as everyone took a seat.

Ronnie dove under the tree, distributing the wrapped gifts there. There was a lot of ripping of paper followed by exclamations of delight from everyone except Jules.

Kelli glanced over and saw her sitting cross-legged on the couch, staring at a thick book in her lap.

"Jules?"

Ronnie nudged Bertha, and Mae glanced over.

"What is it?" Kelli asked.

Jules turned it to reveal a photo of two smiling kids—a skinny girl and a chubby boy—standing with their arms around each other, wearing army helmets and canteens belted around their waists.

"We scanned all of Bertha's and Mae's old pictures," Ronnie said.

"We thought you might not have any photos of Hobie," Mae said. "Thought it might be time for you to have some."

Jules blinked rapidly, turning the photo album back around and flipping through the pages. Kelli came to sit beside her, leaning over to see. Jules pressed her fist to her mouth.

"Do you like it?" Bertha asked tremulously.

"I love it," Jules said, though her voice cracked. "Thank you all."

An awkward silence filled the room for a moment.

"Thanks for my sweatshirt," Ronnie said, slipping it over her head and staring down at the scarlet letters emblazoned across her chest.

Conversation resumed as the others all continued opening presents, but Jules just sat with her photo album, smiling at the images staring up at her.

They all helped clean up the torn wrapping paper and boxes, stuffing everything into a bag to take out to the recycling bin, and then it was time to get back to work in the kitchen.

"It's like an assembly line in here," Ronnie said to Jules as Mae prepared the turkey and Bertha made the stuffing.

"Yeah, and I think we better not get in the way."

Kelli stood at the refrigerator. "I don't think we have enough rolls. How could we not have enough rolls?"

"We'll go," Jules said quickly.

Ronnie caught her look and ran upstairs to change into jeans, still wearing her new sweatshirt.

A few minutes later, they were in the car.

"We escaped." Ronnie let her head sag against the headrest.

Jules smirked. "I know. But it's later I'm going to want to escape. What were we thinking, inviting all these people for dinner?"

Ronnie glanced over. "Kelli seems tense. Is she gonna be okay, seeing her dad with another woman?"

Jules didn't answer immediately. "I'm not sure how that's going to go. For Kelli or Marianne."

She parked in the lot of the grocery store and turned to Ronnie. "This might be a good time to call your mom."

Ronnie blanched. "I can't. What if he answers?"

"I can't believe Steve would keep you from talking to your mom on Christmas Day. You have to try. I'll bet she's waiting, hoping you'll call. She doesn't have a number for you, so it's all on you to take that step."

Ronnie pulled out her cell phone and stared at it.

"Take as long as you need. Come find me inside," Jules said as she got out of the car.

Jules took her time wandering the aisles. She picked up more eggnog and Christmas candy, wishing the employees working there a Merry Christmas and thanking them for working. Ronnie found her in the frozen food aisle.

"She answered. We talked. I can't believe it's been so long. Thanks for pushing me to call. It was good to hear her voice."

By the time they got back to the house, they could already smell the turkey roasting. Kelli put them to work setting up an extra table and chairs. The cats wandered around the kitchen meowing hopefully for scraps of anything.

When the doorbell rang, Kelli jumped. Jules opened it to find Marianne and the kids, who had brought their new electronics. She made the introductions, and then Ronnie and the kids disappeared upstairs to the office to play computer games.

Marianne poured herself a large glass of wine. "Hope we have plenty of this today."

When the bell rang again, Kelli and Marianne stared at each other.

"I'll get it," Jules said.

"Jerry," she said when she opened the door to find Kelli's father standing there. She gave him a hug and stepped back as he held the storm door for the woman with him.

"Jules, this is Evelyn. This is Kelli's partner, Jules."

Jules shook hands with a woman in her sixties who handed Jules two Tupperware containers.

"I know you probably have a mountain of food, but here's a spice cake and a pumpkin pie," Evelyn said.

"You didn't have to do that, but thank you."

Jerry took Evelyn's coat.

"Jerry, can you take the coats up to our room? The kids are in the office with our friend, Ronnie. I'll take care of Evelyn."

Jerry gave her one worried glance before heading upstairs.

Jules led the way into the kitchen and made another round of introductions. Kelli came over to shake Evelyn's hand.

"I've heard so much about you and your sister from your father," Evelyn said, glancing toward Marianne, who was busily laying cheese and crackers on a platter without acknowledging Evelyn at all. "Your home is lovely."

"Let me show you around," Kelli said, turning to glare at her sister.

"She's not much to look at," Marianne muttered as Kelli led Evelyn away to the pottery studio.

"And if she was all made-up and pretty, you'd say all your dad saw was her looks," Mae said. "You had your mind made up not to like her, no matter what."

Jules covered a smile.

"What I see is a nice, down-to-earth lady who probably makes your father happy," Mae continued. "And a spoiled daughter who is too busy with her own life to keep him company, but doesn't want him to move on."

Marianne's cheeks colored at this brutal assessment of the situation, but when Kelli returned to the kitchen and Evelyn asked if she could help with anything, she said, "You can help me with the appetizers if you don't mind."

Kelli turned to Jules with a questioning look.

"Mae strikes again," Jules said in an undertone.

By the time Toni got to the house, there was barely room to move in the kitchen with all the women swarming about. Jerry and Jules wisely stood out of the way, munching on slices of Evelyn's spice cake.

"Oh, my gosh, everything smells heavenly," Toni said when Jules answered the door. She held out a bag. "I don't really cook, and now it seems like a good thing I didn't try to. Here's some wine. White, not red, so no stains." Jules took her jacket. "It's so nice of you and Kelli to invite me. I thought I was going to have a quiet Christmas by myself, but this is so much nicer. Do you always have such a houseful?"

"No," said Jules. "This is the first year. But something tells me it won't be the last."

She was just leading Toni toward the kitchen when the doorbell rang again. "We're not expect—"

She opened the door to find Donna there, holding a bag.

"Sorry to barge in," Donna said. "I spent Christmas morning with my family and then thought I might join you guys." Her face lit up as she saw Toni standing behind Jules.

Jules stepped aside—*as it should be*. "Come on in. You make us an even twelve. A much better number."

Donna followed Toni into the kitchen where Jules heard Kelli's exclamation of welcome. She went upstairs to the office where Ronnie and Marianne's kids were sprawled on the floor.

"Donna's here," she said as she picked up the office chair. "Need an extra seat."

"Really?" Ronnie closed her laptop and followed Jules downstairs to greet Donna.

Jules found Kelli setting another place at the table. They listened to the voices and laughter coming from the kitchen.

"So much for a normal Christmas," Jules said.

"Maybe this is our normal from now on." Kelli's eyes shone with tears when she looked at Jules. "Our family looks a little different now, doesn't it?"

"It does." Jules wrapped her arms around Kelli. "You okay?"

Kelli held Jules tightly. "As long as I have you, I'm okay."

"Then you'll always be okay."

If you enjoyed this short story, you might want to read Caren Werlinger's **Turning for Home**, the novel which introduced Jules, Kelli, and their family and friends.

CHATTING WITH CHARLIE

by Catherine Lane

SWEAT DRIPPED DOWN MY BACK, and my sweatpants stuck to me in all sorts of unpleasant places. What was it, a thousand degrees? I glanced at the school's temperature gauge at the edge of the softball field. It was only pushing ninety, but still, way too hot for this time of year, even for Los Angeles.

I could already hear the whining, loud and clear, that would come at my off-season practice after school.

"Coach, can we have a water break?"

"I think I'm getting heat stroke."

"Run laps? You're kidding. Do you really want a call from my dad's attorney?"

No, seriously, I got a call from a lawyer once after a particularly tough conditioning day. If I were smart, I would race to the storage shed right now, fill the ice buckets and hope that a water fight would cut the complaining by half.

When had it come to this? When had I turned into a glorified babysitter?

Eighteen years ago, I took a team all the way to the Division Championships. Our banner hung in the gym to prove it: a gigantic softball and our 24-0 record stitched in royal blue against the white background. But that was then. Now, I was surrounded by girls who barely cared. Joining the softball team was just a way to fill in another line on their college applications or get out of regular P.E. I loved the game, but often felt like the only one.

"Hey, Alyx. You going to the thing?"

I looked up to see Julie James, the adorable sculpture teacher, bouncing toward me as she cut across the field from her studio at the far end of our campus. Her curly brown hair swung around her shoulders, and her sundress hugged her in all the right places. She looked impossibly fresh in this unseasonable heat. A Santa Claus pin, a jolly nod to the holiday season, sat right at her breastbone.

"What thing?" I hadn't read the school bulletin this morning and had no idea what she was talking about.

"You know, Chatting With Charlie. That thing in the Black Box Theater where the kids get up and speak about whatever is meaningful to them for five minutes."

"Shoot. That's today?"

Julie glanced at her watch. "Yeah, in ten minutes. You coming?"

The right answer was no. I had a dozen scheduling calls on my to-do list, and those pesky ice buckets wouldn't fill themselves. But why not? I needed a break from my funk, and walking to the Black Box with Julie would be just what the doctor ordered. Truth be told, I had a little work crush on Julie. It would never go anywhere, of course. She was straight, and I was very happily married to my wife, Demi, for over seven years now. But I looked forward to chatting with Julie; her enthusiasm for life was infectious. I always came away from our moments with a big smile on my face.

Except today.

"I'm so excited," Julie said as we started down the concrete path that led to the Black Box Theater. "Next week this time, we'll be on winter break, and William and I will be in Germany on our river cruise. He said he booked it for the Christmas markets and just to get away, but I think—at least I hope—he's going to pop the question."

"Really?"

"Yeah, I think so. He and my dad went out to lunch last weekend. He said they were discussing an investment opportunity, which could be true. I mean, William is an investment banker, after all. But the timing seems a little coincidental, don't you think?"

She seemed to need confirmation, so I nodded.

"William's an old-fashioned guy, and my mom keeps looking at me with these big doe eyes. So I'm kind of thinking... I can't imagine anything more romantic. Getting down on his knee with the river and the twinkling lights of the shore at his back. Can you?"

"I can't really say. I don't have much experience with marriage proposals."

"But you and Demi are married, right?"

"Yeah, we are. But we kind of rushed into it."

"You don't have a proposal story?"

"No. We did it quickly because of that craziness with Prop 8 a couple of summers ago."

Julie tilted her head.

"We were worried that Prop 8 would take away the right for us to marry here in California. Which it did, of course. So we just got married before it was too late. Looking back, honestly, it was more a political statement." I didn't want to meet her gaze, which was suddenly flooded with sympathy, so I trotted up the stairs to the Black Box a step ahead of Julie.

"But surely one of you must have asked the other?" Julie scampered after me. "Getting married doesn't just spontaneously happen."

"No, of course not. But you're not going to believe me—I don't remember the exact moment we decided to get married. We had already been together for over thirteen years before the wedding. There was just a before and an after. It's not a big deal."

"Huh." Julie clearly wasn't convinced.

Neither was I. Frankly, I always wished we had navigated that part better. I wrenched open the door to the Black Box and thankfully stepped inside, away from the conversation. True to its name, the room was square and dark. I could easily avoid Julie's concerned gaze here.

The room was organized for the event. At the far end, a podium with a microphone and a large white screen sat in front of a thick, black curtain. Folding chairs in neat, symmetrical rows backed up almost to the door. Students and other teachers sat in groups of their own kind, chatting quietly and waiting for the show to begin.

We squeezed by two administrators who stood at the door, trying to look important and only pulling off slightly uncomfortable. I quickly found two seats at the edge of a back row, and as soon as we slid into them, the lights dimmed. The annoying tap, tap, tap of someone hitting the microphone jumped out of the speakers. We had just made it, and I settled back in my chair, hoping that whatever the kids' topics were, they would take me out of my sour mood.

"Good afternoon, and welcome to Chatting With Charlie. Today, as we ring in the holiday season, we have something very special for you." The debate teacher, Mark "Charlie" Charles, wore red and green and danced with excitement at the podium like a Christmas elf. His deep voice rang throughout the room as he waved his hand at three people sitting in the front row. "Not the students and friends you see every day in our classrooms and hallways, but alumni who have come back to speak about ideas and events which have moved them after high school. A holiday gift, shall we say, as these young men and women from the past hope to inform all of our futures with their recollections. I am so proud to present our first speaker: Sara Banks, class of 2000, who has just won the prestigious Animal Veterinarian of the Year Award. She will speak on why we all need to..." He froze dramatically. "Stop, and Listen to the Birds."

Charlie threw out his hand in an affected flourish, and a tall, thin woman with loose, dark hair glided to the podium. I tried to rearrange her adult features back into the face of a child I might have known, but had no luck.

My back tensed against the thin cushion in the seat as Sara smiled out into audience and began. Apparently being a vet was unbelievably rewarding. That was a shocker. Had she come back just to tell us how fulfilled she was since she left high school? Lucky her.

I watched Sara's lips open and close, but all I heard was the go-to joke of the P.E. office: "If you can't do, teach. And if you can't teach, coach." I had always laughed, along with the rest of my colleagues. The joke was that coaching was hard work—managing hormonal adolescents with subjective standards that no parent really understood. And all wrapped up in long, long hours. But now the punch line was a full-blown commentary on my life. I certainly hadn't won any awards lately. What exactly was I doing with my life? I rolled this and other negative thoughts around in my head until a bird's melodic trill echoed through the room, jolting me back into the moment.

"And that's why we all need to stop and listen to the birds." Sara bowed her head as the crowd burst into applause. Lost in my own mind, I had missed the whole point. This funk was now officially a depression.

"That was great!" Julie whispered. "Who knew she had that kind of insight in her?"

"You remember her?"

"Not well. She took pottery."

Julie didn't even teach her, and she still knew who Sara Banks was.

I had to get out of there and scanned the room looking for a way out. The administrators stood by the doors like prison guards. It was a no-go. I wasn't getting sprung until the next two *special gifts* had spoken.

The second student, a man now in his late thirties, spoke in a quiet, uninspired voice about paying it forward. I tried to listen to every word. Maybe he would say the one thing that would change my world.

Nope. He was a big fat dud.

Julie leaned over again when the man had finished, her shoulder brushing against mine. "That was nice. But we've all heard it all before."

Finally, the third speaker stood up and faced the audience on her way to the podium. My heart pounded in my chest. No introduction was needed; I would have recognized her anywhere even though she looked nothing like she did in high school.

It was Jenny Marsh, perhaps my biggest failure as a coach.

Jenny had been a great player, a terrific catcher and a steadying influence on a temperamental team. We had been making a real run for the play-offs and a second championship when she edged up to me at lunchtime the day before our biggest game.

"I can't play," she said, shrugging her shoulders.

"You mean tomorrow?" My heart and all hope sank, and full irritation rose quickly in its place. We had no backup catcher.

"No, I mean anymore. I have to quit."

"What? You can't quit!" My surprise sounded harsh and judgmental even to me.

"Coach, I can't do it anymore." Real emotion cracked in her voice as she took a step back from me. "It's too hard."

I took a deep breath. Then another. This was far more than a teenage girl flaking out. "What's too hard?"

"The whole competition thing. I mean, I get it's a sport and all, and there has to be a winner and a loser by definition. But I don't understand why we cheer for our great plays and not for the other team's. Shouldn't we be celebrating the great plays on both sides? Isn't it about coming together as a whole sporting community rather than separating into two different teams that want to destroy each other?" Her plea rang out with passion and eloquence, and even though I had spent my whole life on one softball field or another chasing the win, I nodded.

"Yeah, Jenny. You make a good point."

Her whole body sagged in relief, and I saw what it had taken for her to speak with me. Even so, I gritted my teeth as I spoke next.

"Okay. I can see how hard this was for you. And I want you to know that I respect you for your beliefs. And if you don't feel that you can play anymore, I can appreciate that. But do me a favor: take a day to really think about it, and if this is what you truly want, I will drop you from the team."

We ended up losing the game 14-6. The center fielder who had come in to play catcher had let ten girls steal home.

And this is the part I am still ashamed of to this day. After that loss, I cornered Jenny in the senior hallway and begged her to come back. I laid it on pretty thick. Even when I saw her shoulders tense up, I still talked about what another championship would mean for the team and the school. I only stopped when the tears swelled in her eyes.

"God, Jenny, I'm sorry." I dropped my hand on her shoulder before walking away from her for good.

As I said, Jenny Marsh was my biggest failure as a coach.

That tearful girl in the hallway was long gone. Before me at the podium stood a confident woman in a dark pantsuit with short, cropped hair, black-rimmed glasses, and a broad, charismatic smile.

"Hi, I'm Jen Marsh," she said. "And I love my job, too. I am a staff attorney for the National Center for LGBTQ Youth."

Another one who had made something of her life. But it made sense that Jenny Marsh, who had wanted to cheer for everyone, had grown up to root for the people who had no one. And I had been the one who tried to talk her out of her convictions.

"But I'm not here to talk about me. I am here to talk about Erin Levy. A high school freshman, a girl just like many of you." She waved a hand out to the audience and smiled again. A few of the girls nodded in response. "Except that she is not like you. She started out as Aaron—A-a-r-o-n—Levy. A boy who felt trapped in his body, imprisoned by his maleness. You're not going to believe this, but she was one of the lucky ones. Her parents did not place her in conversion therapy. They didn't pay a doctor or a charlatan hard cash to convince their daughter that she was really their son."

The face of a pretty, slight girl popped onto the screen behind her. Erin, I gathered. The kids murmured their disbelief as a series of pictures flashed of Erin at the beach, playing tennis, running around with a large collie—she looked so innocent and happy, and above all, so feminine.

"Unbelievably, courageously, her parents went with it. They got her a state I.D. card and a passport which recognized her as female. They let her grow her hair long, put on a skirt, and moved to another school district where they enrolled their daughter as a freshman in the local high school. They hoped and prayed that Erin would find respect, and more importantly, a new, safe home."

Jenny took a breath as her audience, children and adults alike, shifted in their seats. We were in the hands of a master. She knew exactly when we needed a minute to grapple with this story of a pretty young girl and where it was going.

"Her parents did everything right. They informed the new school of Erin's history and fought for their daughter every step of the way. I'm sure I don't have to tell you what high school is like. Within a month, everyone knew. Erin was banned from the girls' restroom and had to use the teachers' restroom instead. Imagine if you had to go to the front office and ask permission every single time you needed to go?"

Nervous laughter filled the room. Jenny rocked back on her feet a little and settled deeper into the story. I leaned forward in my chair, almost as if to get closer to her words. She was that good.

"That wasn't the half of it. I'm sure you can imagine the teasing and bullying that she endured. And ladies, I hate to break it to you, but the girls at that school were so much meaner than the boys. Finally, everything exploded when the freshmen went on a bonding retreat, and all the girls refused to room with her. The school had to request an extra cabin, and when no faculty member stepped up to be a chaperone, her mother had to do it."

She actually got a few gasps at this point—a freshman's worst nightmare was a parent chaperoning anything.

"That's when they came to us. We filed a suit under the state's anti-discrimination act, since clearly the school's actions created a hostile, intimidating, and unsafe environment. People mistake gender identity with sexual orientation all the time. Sexual orientation is all about who you love and might want to marry someday, but gender identity is who you are deep in your core. It may seem silly, but denying Erin the right to use the girls' restroom at her school denies her soul. All she wanted was the same dignity, respect, and opportunities afforded to other girls everywhere. That's what she deserved. And that's what we got. The court ruled in our favor."

The audience let out a collective breath. A boy right in front of me pumped his fist and gave a soft hoot.

"That's right, a high point for transgender rights, but it's not over. There is still so much to do, there and here, too. Maybe you don't have an Erin at this school, but I'm sure you still have a lot of people like I used to be. Someone who knew she identified as a lesbian way before high school. Someone who was so scared she wouldn't be accepted that she actually had a few suicidal thoughts. I made it, obviously, but there are lots of kids who don't. It doesn't take much to help those kids who might be in this room right now."

The kids—and the teachers, too—all glanced at their neighbors. Julie reached over to give my leg a friendly squeeze.

"Create a space on campus that is safe and openly welcoming to all LGBTQ kids. By the way, the Q is for questioning, so these safe spaces are for just about everyone. A counselor's office maybe, or a certain classroom, or a Gay-Straight Alliance. Everyone needs the opportunity to live an authentic life. And you can be part of that change." She smiled broadly. "Thank you very much."

Swept up in the fairy tale ending of her story, the audience clapped loudly. Charlie swung his hands up toward the roof, and the crowd got to its feet. Jenny blushed at the standing ovation and shrugged as if to say *what else can we do?* I jumped to my feet as well, driven as much by shame as by inspiration.

"Alyx, I gotta go. I have a class next block." Julie pulled me into a brief hug. "If I don't see you before break, have a great vacation. Merry Christmas."

"You too." We smiled at each other.

"Wish me luck," she said.

"I'm sure you don't need it." With that smile, William would be a fool many times over if he didn't get down on bended knee in Germany.

Julie slid out the back and most of the kids followed her, eager to grab the last precious minutes before afternoon classes began. Others headed to the podium. Most sidled up to Charlie, whose affectations made him a perennial favorite with the students, but a few nervously approached Jenny. A boy in shorts a little too short asked her how to make a GSA club meaningful and not just a place where kids could get free pizza, and a tough girl in cowboy boots talked to her about volunteer opportunities with her organization. I stood off to the side, listening to her answer their questions patiently and thoughtfully, and for the umpteenth time that day wondered what I was doing with my life. What made it worse was that Jenny had given a vocabulary to my funk. Was there anything about my life that was *authentic?*

The kids finally cleared out, and Jenny looked at me. Heat flooded my face almost instantly. The last time we had been together, I was trying to convince her to give up all her principles.

"Hi, Coach," she said.

"Hi." An awkward silence fell between us, and I struggled for something to say. "Thank you, Jenny, for representing all of us so well. You're truly amazing. I don't know how you do it."

"Are you kidding? I couldn't have done it without you."

"What?" Surely I had heard wrong. "What are you talking about?"

"Coach, you were and still are my role model."

"For what?" I laughed nervously. "For trying to get you to play a game that was obviously way beneath you? Look, I am so sorry about that. You quit and I should have respected your feelings—"

"Coach, stop. You wanted to win, I get that. It's your job, after all. But that's not what I'm talking about."

"What, then?"

"There was this game, right before I quit, when your girlfriend showed up to support us. I watched you as you went over to say hello. You hugged her, and then you kissed her on the lips. Right in front of everyone. I'm sure you don't remember it."

She was dead wrong. I remembered that moment well. When Demi had said she wanted to come to that game, I had gone back and forth on whether to officially invite her. I was out to the faculty, and with my cropped hair and androgynous clothes, I wasn't trying to hide anything from the kids. But that was a far cry from parading my girlfriend in front of the whole school. When Demi showed up, I went over to her intending just to say hi, but she looked so cute in our school colors and team visor that I threw all caution to the wind and kissed her.

"It looked so loving and natural." Jenny broke into my thoughts. "And that was the exact moment when I knew I'd be okay."

"Really?"

"Yeah, I mean, I knew you were gay, we all did, but I couldn't believe the earth didn't open and swallow you up. You looked like you had a nice, normal life, and that's when I thought that maybe I could, too."

"Oh, Jenny, I had no idea." Another round of embarrassment whipped through me. Apparently, I couldn't recognize authenticity even when it bit me on the ass.

"You were all I needed, Coach. I was grappling with my sexuality and there was no place that I felt safe. Not here and not at home, but seeing you with your girlfriend—that gave me the courage to be who I needed to be. Even if it meant quitting softball and coming out to my parents after graduation."

We just looked at each other. I didn't know what to say, but finally managed, "She's my wife now."

Jenny's eyes sparkled with real happiness. "Congratulations. I'm married, too. Her name's Kristen. We're expecting our first child next month."

"Oh, my goodness. That's wonderful!" Joy flooded through me, its warmth spreading all the way to my toes. Jenny reached out with both arms, and I stepped into a big bear hug. Her words came in a whisper, her mouth right at my ear.

"You saved me, Coach."

"And you've saved me right back."

Sometimes, you don't have to struggle to find meaning in things. It's right there all along.

❧

I couldn't stop grinning. Everything had turned out so much better than I hoped. How often does that happen?

Twinkling lights sparkled from every tree in our backyard. A huge bouquet of white and red roses laced with holiday touches of pine cones, evergreen boughs, and holly sat on the picnic table. Delicate mist from dry ice poured out of the fountain in the back corner. I had spent the whole day slaving like a madwoman, and now I stood in a magical winter wonderland.

Demi's favorite songs played softly on a loop in the background, and the scent of a freshly baked cake wafted through the air. Even Clayton and Wesley, our normally crazy golden labs, hadn't scratched off the big bows attached to their collars. In fact, they sat quietly on either side of me, ears up, as if they knew exactly what was going on.

Clayton's tail flapped against the ground, and I heard the front door open and close.

"Babe? Where are you?" Demi's voice was low and melodic, as always.

"Out here." The nervous catch in my voice surprised me. It wasn't like I didn't already know the answer.

A small *thud* sounded as her briefcase hit the dining room table. "Where?"

"In back."

Demi's jaw dropped as she opened the sliding glass door. "Oh, my God. What's all this?" She spun around to take it all in and laughed softly. "Seriously, what's going on?"

"Well..." I took her hand and led her back to the spot between the dogs, then dropped to one knee and looked up at her expectant face. "It has come to my attention that while I love you dearly and I believe that we have a very happy marriage, it didn't quite start out precisely how it should have."

"No?" Demi's eyes softened. "And how do you propose to remedy that?"

"See, you already know."

"Know what?"

"This." I took her hand with both of mine and squeezed gently. "Demi Balsan, I've loved you since the moment I first saw you. I'm not sure I knew it then, but I know it now. In fact, I didn't even know how much love was in the world until I met you. You give my life significance and joy and laughter and a thousand other things that I can't even put words to. You would make me the happiest woman alive if you became my wife."

Tears filled Demi's eyes as she pulled me up. "We're already married, silly."

"Yes, I know. But I don't remember asking you, or you asking me." I slid my arms around her waist and pulled her close. Her eyes were clear and bright, the reflections from the fairy lights dancing in their deep brown. "Do you?"

"No." A smile tugged at her lips. "Come to think of it, I don't."

"So will you? Demi, my sweet love, will you marry me?"

"I will." Her smile broadened into a grin, and we laughed together.

"Then all is right with my world."

I leaned in to kiss Demi and seal the deal. Our lips met the way they had a million times before, but this kiss felt fresh and new, and dare I say it, authentic.

The dogs raced around the yard, barking their joy, as if released by invisible hands. The mist bubbled up from the fountain and enclosed us all in a magical world of our own making.

And there it was: the moment that would create our proposal story, and for us, even better than a romantic cruise.

If any of the other teachers at school asked what I did over winter break, I would tell them quite simply that I asked my wife to marry me.

And she said yes.

ABOUT THE AUTHORS

JOVE BELLE

Jove Belle lives in Vancouver, Washington with her family. Her books include *The Job*, *Uncommon Romance*, *Love and Devotion*, *Indelible*, *Chaps*, *Split the Aces*, and *Edge of Darkness*.

Connect with this author:
Website: jovebelle.com

B.A. CALDWELL

A native Oregonian, B.A. Caldwell worked in book publishing, corporate communications, and healthcare before returning to school for a library science degree. With graduate school out of the way, she found she finally had the time to do something she had been thinking about for many years: fiction writing. By day she works in a medical library, and by night she tries to get some writing done. She enjoys writing and reading (of course) as well as photography, crafting, and spending time with her family. She lives in a 100-year-old house in Portland, Oregon, with her son and too many cats.

Connect with this author:
Website: bacaldwell.com
E-mail: thebroadnib@gmail.com

EVE FRANCIS

Eve Francis's short stories have appeared in *Wilde Magazine*, *The Fieldstone Review*, *Iris New Fiction*, *MicroHorror*, and *The Human Echoes Podcast*. Romance and horror are her favourite genres to write in because everyone has felt love or fear in some form or another. She lives in Canada, where she often sleeps late, spends too much time online, and repeatedly watches old horror movies and *Orange Is The New Black*.

Connect with this author:
Website: evefrancis.wordpress.com
Tumblr: paintitback.tumblr.com

LOIS CLOAREC HART

Born and raised in British Columbia, Canada, Lois Cloarec Hart grew up as an avid reader but didn't begin writing until much later in life. Several years after joining the Canadian Armed Forces, she received a degree in Honours History from Royal Military College and on graduation switched occupations from air traffic control to military intelligence. Having married a CAF fighter pilot while in college, Lois went on to spend another five years as an Intelligence Officer before leaving the military to care for her husband, who was ill with chronic progressive Multiple Sclerosis and passed away in 2001. She began writing while caring for her husband in his final years and had her first book, *Coming Home*, published in 2001. It was through that initial publishing process that Lois met the woman she would marry in April 2007. She now commutes annually between her northern home in Calgary and her wife's southern home in Atlanta.

Connect with this author:
Website: loiscloarechart.com
E-mail: eljae1@shaw.ca

CATHERINE LANE

Catherine Lane started to write fiction on a dare from her wife. She's thrilled to be a published author, even though she had to admit her wife was right. They live happily in Southern California with their son and a very mischievous pound puppy.

Catherine spends most of her time these days working, mothering, or writing. But when she finds herself at loose ends, she enjoys experimenting with recipes in the kitchen, paddling on long stretches of flat water, and browsing the stacks at libraries and bookstores. Oh, and trying unsuccessfully to outwit her dog.

She has published a novel, *The Set Piece*, and several short stories and is currently working on a second novel.

Connect with this author:
Website: catherinelanefiction.wordpress.com/
Facebook: facebook.com/profile.php?id=100004577749399
E-mail: claneauthor01@gmail.com

PATRICIA PENN

When Patricia was a teen, her school's job qualification test said that she should be a surgeon since she has a big ego, and she doesn't like other people. Later, she read a theory about how all authors secretly are social outcasts anyway, and decided that the pen suited her even better than the scalpel. She currently also sells her soul to a day job in marketing in Frankfurt, Germany. She lives with her dog in a small town near Frankfurt, and has given long-distance relationships a new meaning with her girlfriend, who lives in Massachusetts.

BLYTHE RIPPON

Blythe Rippon holds a PhD in the humanities and currently teaches writing to undergraduates. Until now, her publishing has been of the academic variety. When not grading papers or imagining plots for future novels, she is usually holding forth about the political injustice of the day, hiking, or experimenting in the kitchen. She has lived all over the United States and at present can be found in the San Francisco Bay Area, where she lives with her wife and children.

Connect with this author:
Website: sites.google.com/site/blytherippon/
Facebook: facebook.com/blythe.rippon
E-mail: blythe.rippon@gmail.com

RUTH F. SIMON

Originally from a small town in southern Arizona, Ruth F. Simon escaped the desert to spend twelve years in the Seattle metro area. She and her wife transplanted to Brooklyn in 2006 so Ruth could study medieval British literature at New York University.

A fountain pen and hat fanatic, Ruth is a member of the Golden Crown Literary Society, Sisters in Crime, the Mystery Writers of America, the Romance Writers of America, and the National Writers Union. She is a proud graduate of the first-ever GLCS Writing Academy program.

Connect with this author:
Website: ruthfsimon.com
E-mail: ruth@ruthfsimon.com
Facebook: facebook.com/RuthFSimonAuthor
Twitter: twitter.com/rfsimon

ALISON RUTH SOLOMON

Alison Solomon might be defined as the archetypal "Wandering Jew": she grew up in England, lived for many years in Israel, moved to the USA, where she has lived on the East and West Coast, and also spent a number of years in Mexico. She is happily married to Carol. They live in Gulfport, Florida, with two rescue dogs, who very kindly allow the couple to take care of them.

Alison has published numerous articles and chapters on feminism, mental health, and diversity in academic textbooks, anthologies, journals, and newspapers. She authored *Witch Hazel*, a humorous, lesbian-feminist column that ran in the *Philadelphia Weekly* in the 1990s and an advice column in the *Sacramento Jewish Voice*.

Connect with this author:
Website: AlisonRuthSolomon.weebly.com
E-mail: AlisonSol@gmail.com

LYN THORNE-ALDER

Lyn Thorne-Alder was born in rural New York State and grew up in a log cabin (not a barn, as she often claims). She lives in the Finger Lakes region with her husband and three cats. Her garden occasionally threatens to take over the world.

Connect with this author:
Website: lynthornealder.com/
E-mail: thornealder@gmail.com

CAREN J. WERLINGER

Caren was raised in Ohio, the oldest of four children. Much of her childhood was spent reading every book she could get her hands on and crafting her own stories. She completed a degree in foreign languages and later another degree in physical therapy. For many years, her only writing was research-based, including a therapeutic exercise textbook. She has lived in Virginia for over twenty years, where she practices physical therapy, teaches anatomy, and lives with her partner and their canine fur-children. She began writing creatively again several years ago. Her first novel, *Looking Through Windows*, won a Debut Author award from the Golden Crown Literary Society in 2009. In 2013, *Miserere*, *In This Small Spot*, and *Neither Present Time* all won or placed in the 2013 Rainbow Awards. *In This Small Spot* won Best Dramatic Fiction in the 2014 Golden Crown Literary Awards.

Connect with this author:
Website: cjwerlinger.wordpress.com
E-mail: cjwerlingerbooks@yahoo.com

CHRIS ZETT

Chris Zett lives in Berlin, Germany, with her partner. TV inspired her to study medicine, but she found out soon enough that real life in a hospital consists more of working long hours than performing heroic rescues. The part about finding a workplace romance turned out to be true, though.

She uses any opportunity to escape the routine by reading, writing, or traveling. Her favorite destinations include penguin colonies in Patagonia and stone circles in Scotland.

Connect with this author:
E-mail: chris-zett@web.de

OTHER BOOKS FROM YLVA PUBLISHING

www.ylva-publishing.com

UNWRAP THESE PRESENTS

Astrid Ohletz & R.G. Emanuelle

ISBN: 978-3-95533-277-8
Length: 130,000 words (443 pages)

Twenty-three authors of lesbian fiction contributed holiday stories that give you snow, presents, plenty of food, Holiday cheer and nicely wrapped curvy women under the tree.

This anthology won the 2015 Golden Crown Literary Society Award in the category anthology/collection (fiction).

LOVE BENEATH THE CHRISTMAS TREE

Jae

ISBN: 978-3-95533-135-1 (mobi),
978-3-95533-136-8 (epub)
Length: 15,000 words

Three short stories that follow the lives of Rachel Lewis, self-confessed Christmas Grump, and Lillian Coleman, the woman who makes her believe in the magic of Christmas again.

CAST ME GENTLY

Caren J. Werlinger

ISBN: 978-3-95533-391-1
Length: 100,000 words (353 pages)

Teresa and Ellie couldn't be more different. Teresa still lives at home with her Italian family, while Ellie has been on her own for years. When they meet and fall in love, their worlds clash. Ellie would love to be part of Teresa's family, but they both know that will never happen. Sooner or later, Teresa will have to choose between the two halves of her heart—Ellie or her family.

ALL THE LITTLE MOMENTS

G Benson

ISBN: 978-3-95533-341-6
Length: 132,000 words (350 pages)

Anna is focused on her career as an anaesthetist. When a tragic accident leaves her responsible for her young niece and nephew, her life changes abruptly. Completely overwhelmed, Anna barely has time to brush her teeth in the morning let alone date a woman. But then she collides with a long-legged stranger...

POPCORN LOVE

KL Hughes

ISBN: 978-3-95533-265-5

Length: 113,000 words (347 pages)

Her love-life lacking, wealthy fashion exec Elena Vega agrees to a string of blind dates set up by her best friend Vivian in exchange for Vivian finding a suitable babysitter for her son, Lucas.

Free-spirited college student Allison Sawyer fits the bill perfectly.

TALES OF THE GRIMOIRE - BOOK 1

Edited by Astrid Ohletz & Gill McKnight

ISBN: 978-3-95533-428-4

Length: 93,000 words

On a dark and stormy night a coven of writers gathers to spellcheck under a hallowed moon. The result is a bubbling cauldron of fear, suspense, and absolute sexiness.

From the ghostly seduction of a Victorian governess, to vampires in the substance abuse clinic, with witchery in the coffee house, and cannibalism in the kitchen, this selection of stories is dark, damning, and terrifyingly erotic.

To be read by candlelight, and never alone!

COMING FROM YLVA PUBLISHING IN WINTER 2015/2016

www.ylva-publishing.com

THE BUREAU OF HOLIDAY AFFAIRS

Andi Marquette

Corporate executive Robin Preston didn't get where she is by being nice. That's why the Bureau of Holiday Affairs has scheduled an intervention for her that'll take her to her past, present, and future in hopes she'll be able to change her ways and open her heart to the one woman Robin thought she'd left in her past. Will the Bureau's agents succeed in their mission? Or is Robin a lost cause?

JUST PHYSICAL

Jae

After being diagnosed with MS, actress Jill takes herself off the romantic market. On the set of a disaster movie, she meets stunt woman Crash, whose easy smile makes her wish things were different.

Despite their growing feelings, Jill is determined to let Crash into her bed, but not her heart. As they start to play with fire on and off camera, will they be able to keep things just physical?

Do You Feel What I Feel. A Holiday Anthology
© by Jae & Fletcher DeLancey

ISBN: 978-3-95533-545-8

Also available as e-book.

Published by Ylva Publishing, legal entity of Ylva Verlag, e.Kfr.

Ylva Verlag, e.Kfr.
Owner: Astrid Ohletz
Am Kirschgarten 2
65830 Kriftel
Germany

http://www.ylva-publishing.com

First edition: October 2015

No part of this book may be reproduced, scanned, or distributed in any printed or electronic form without permission. Please do not participate in or encourage piracy of copyrighted materials in violation of the author's rights. Thank you for respecting the hard work of this author.

This is a work of fiction. Names, characters, places, and incidents either are a product of the author's imagination or are used fictitiously, and any resemblance to locales, events, business establishments, or actual persons—living or dead—is entirely coincidental.

Credits
Edited by Sandra Gerth, Fletcher DeLancey, Sheri Milburn, and Michelle Aguilar
Cover Design by Streetlight Graphics

"S. Claus" © Blythe Rippon 2015
"This Thing" © Jove Belle 2015
"Red Suits and Second Chances" © Eve Francis 2015
"A Gift of Words" © Patricia Penn 2015
"Snow, With a Chance of Love" © B.A. Caldwell 2015
"Crossroads" © Ruth F. Simon 2015
"More Than a Holiday Romance" © Chris Zett 2015
"We Wish You a Merry Christmas" © Lyn Thorne-Alder 2015
"Sadie and Rosa" © Alison Ruth Solomon 2015
"Kicker's Christmas" © Lois Cloarec Hart 2015
"Just a Normal Christmas" © Caren J. Werlinger 2015
"Chatting With Charlie" © Catherine Lane 2015

www.ingramcontent.com/pod-product-compliance
Lightning Source LLC
Chambersburg PA
CBHW031553240626
47153CB00002B/484